COWBOY'S
LEGACY

Also available from
B.J. Daniels
and HQN Books

B.J. DANIELS

COWBOY'S LEGACY

ISBN-13: 978-0-373-80420-7

Cowboy's Legacy

www.HQNBooks.com

Printed in U.S.A.

This book is dedicated to Debbie Hammond and Margaret Hanson, sisters extraordinaire and amazing quilters. You two brighten even the gloomiest Montana winter days!

CHAPTER ONE

She was in so fast that she didn't have a chance to scream. The icy cold water stole her breath away. Her eyes flew open as she hit. Because of the way she fell, she had no sense of up or down for a few moments.

Panicked, she flailed in the water until a light flickered above her. She tried to swim toward it, but something was holding her down. The harder she fought, the more it seemed to push her deeper and deeper, the light fading.

Her lungs burned. She had to breathe. The dim light wavered above her through the rippling water. She clawed at it as her breath gave out. She could see the surface just inches above her. Air! She needed oxygen. Now!

The rippling water distorted the face that suddenly appeared above her. The mouth twisted in a grotesque smile. She screamed, only to have her throat fill with the putrid dark water. She choked, sucking in even more water. She was drowning, and the person who'd done this to her was watching her die and smiling.

Maggie Thompson shot upright in bed, gasping for air and

swinging her arms frantically toward the faint light coming through the window. Panic had her perspiration-soaked nightgown sticking to her skin. Trembling, she clutched the bedcovers as she gasped for breath.

The nightmare had been so real this time that she thought she was going to drown before she could come out of it. Her chest ached, her throat feeling raw as tears burned her eyes. It had been too real. She couldn't shake the feeling that she'd almost died this time. Next time...

She snapped on the bedside lamp to chase away the dark shadows hunkered in the corners of the room. If only Flint had been here instead of on an all-night stakeout. She needed Sheriff Flint Cahill's strong arms around her. Not that he stayed most nights. They hadn't been intimate that long.

Often, he had to work or was called out in the middle of the night. He'd asked her to move in with him months ago, but she'd declined. He'd asked her after one of his ex-wife's nasty tricks. Maggie hadn't wanted to make a decision like that based on Flint's ex.

While his ex hadn't done anything in months to keep them apart, Maggie couldn't rest easy. Flint was hoping Celeste had grown tired of her tricks. Maggie wasn't that naive. Celeste Duma was one of those women who played on every man's weakness to get what she wanted—and she wanted not just the rich, powerful man she'd left Flint for. She wanted to keep her ex on the string, as well.

Maggie's breathing slowed a little. She pulled the covers up to her chin, still shivering, but she didn't turn off the light. Sleep was out of the question for a while. She told herself that she wasn't going to let Celeste scare her. She wasn't going to give the woman the satisfaction.

Unfortunately, it was just bravado. Flint's ex was obsessed with him. Obsessed with keeping them apart. And since the woman had nothing else to do...

As the images of the nightmare faded, she reminded herself that the dream made no sense. It never had. She was a good swimmer. Loved water. Had never nearly drowned. Nor had anyone ever tried to drown her.

Shuddering, she thought of the face she'd seen through the rippling water. Not Celeste's. More like a Halloween mask. A distorted smiling face, neither male or female. Just the memory sent her heart racing again.

What bothered her most was that dream kept reoccurring. After the first time, she'd mentioned it to her friend Belle Delaney.

"A drowning dream?" Belle had asked with the arch of her eyebrow. "Do you feel that in waking life you're being 'sucked into' something you'd rather not be a part of?"

Maggie had groaned inwardly. Belle had never kept it a secret that she thought Maggie was making a mistake when it came to Flint. Too much baggage, she always said of the sheriff. His "baggage" came in the shape of his spoiled, probably psychopathic, petite, green-eyed blonde ex.

"I have my own skeletons," Maggie had laughed, although she'd never shared her past—even with Belle—before moving to Gilt Edge, Montana, and opening her beauty shop, Just Hair. She feared it was her own baggage that scared her the most.

"If you're holding anything back," Belle had said, eyeing her closely, "you need to let it out. Men hate surprises after they tie the knot."

"Guess I don't have to worry about that because Flint hasn't said anything about marriage." But she knew Belle was right. She'd even come close to telling him several times about her past. Something had always stopped her. The truth was, she feared if he found out her reasons for coming to Gilt Edge he wouldn't want her anymore.

"The dream isn't about Flint," she'd argued that day with Belle, but she couldn't shake the feeling that it was a warning.

"Well, from what I know about dreams," Belle had said, "if in the dream you survive the drowning, it means that a waking relationship will ultimately survive the turmoil. At least that is one interpretation. But I'd say the nightmare definitely indicates that you are going into unknown waters and something is making you leery of where you're headed." She'd cocked an eyebrow at her. "If you have the dream again, I'd suggest that you ask yourself what it is you're so afraid of."

"I'm sure it's just about his ex, Celeste," she'd lied. Or was she afraid that she wasn't good enough for Flint—just as his ex had warned her. Just as she feared in her heart.

The wind lay over the tall dried grass and kicked up dust as Sheriff Flint Cahill stood on the hillside. He shoved his Stetson down on his head of thick dark hair, squinting in the distance at the clouds to the west. Sure as the devil, it was going to snow before the day was out.

In the distance, he could see a large star made out of red and green lights on the side of a barn, a reminder that Christmas was coming. Flint thought he might even get a tree this year, go up in the mountains and cut it himself. He hadn't had a tree at Christmas in years. Not since…

At the sound of a pickup horn, he turned, shielding his eyes from the low winter sun. He could smell snow in the air, feel it deep in his bones. This storm was going to dump a good foot on them, according to the latest news. They were going to have a white Christmas.

Most years he wasn't ready for the holiday season any more than he was ready for a snow that wouldn't melt until spring. But this year was different. He felt energized. This was the year his life would change. He thought of the small velvet box in his jacket pocket. He'd been carrying it around for months. Just the thought of it made him smile to himself. He was in love and he was finally going to do something about it.

The pickup rumbled to a stop a few yards from him. He took a deep breath of the mountain air, and telling himself he was ready for whatever Mother Nature wanted to throw at him, he headed for the truck.

"Are you all right?" his sister asked as he slid into the passenger seat. In the cab out of the wind, it was nice and warm. He rubbed his bare hands together, wishing he hadn't forgotten his gloves earlier. But when he'd headed out, he'd had too much on his mind. He still did.

Lillie looked out at the dull brown of the landscape and the chain-link fence that surrounded the missile silo. "What were you doing out here?"

He chuckled. "Looking for aliens. What else?" This was the spot that their father swore aliens hadn't just landed on one night back in 1967. Nope, according to Ely Cahill, the aliens had abducted him, taken him aboard their spaceship and done experiments on him. Not that anyone believed it in the county. Everyone just assumed that Ely had a screw loose. Or two.

It didn't help that their father spent most of the year up in the mountains as a recluse trapping and panning for gold.

"Aliens. Funny," Lillie said, making a face at him.

He smiled over at her. "Actually, I was on an all-night stakeout. The cattle rustlers didn't show up." He shrugged.

She glanced around. "Where's your patrol SUV?"

"Axle deep in a muddy creek back toward Grass Range. I'll have to get it pulled out. After I called you, I started walking and I ended up here. Wish I'd grabbed my gloves, though."

"You're scaring me," she said, studying him openly. "You're starting to act like Dad."

He laughed at that, wondering how far from the truth it was. "At least I didn't see any aliens near the missile silo."

She groaned. Being the butt of jokes in the county because of their father got old for all of them.

Flint glanced at the fenced-in area. There was nothing visible behind the chain link but tumbleweeds. He turned back to her. "I didn't pull you away from anything important, I hope? Since you were close by, I thought you wouldn't mind giving me a ride. I've had enough walking for one day. Or thinking, for that matter."

She shook her head. "What's going on, Flint?"

He looked out at the country that ran to the mountains. Cahill Ranch. His grandfather had started it, his father had worked it and now two of his brothers ran the cattle part of it to keep the place going while he and his sister, Lillie, and brother Darby had taken other paths. Not to mention their oldest brother, Tucker, who'd struck out at seventeen and hadn't been seen or heard from since.

Flint had been scared after his marriage and divorce. But Maggie was nothing like Celeste, who was small, blonde, green-eyed and crazy. Maggie was tall with big brown eyes and long auburn hair. His heart beat faster at the thought of her smile, at her laugh.

"I'm going to ask Maggie to marry me," Flint said and nodded as if reassuring himself.

When Lillie didn't reply, he glanced over at her. It wasn't like her not to have something to say. "Well?"

"What has taken you so long?"

He sighed. "Well, you know after Celeste..."

"Say no more," his sister said, raising a hand to stop him. "Anyone would be gun-shy after being married to her."

"I'm hoping she won't be a problem."

Lillie laughed. "Short of killing your ex-wife, she is always going to be a problem. You just have to decide if you're going to let her run your life. Or if you're going to live it— in spite of her."

So easy for her to say. He smiled, though. "You're right. Anyway, Maggie and I have been dating for a while now and there haven't been any...incidents in months."

Lillie shook her head. "You know Celeste was the one who vandalized Maggie's beauty shop—just as you know she started that fire at Maggie's house."

"Too bad there wasn't any proof so I could have arrested her. But since there wasn't and no one was hurt and it was months ago..."

"I'd love to see Celeste behind bars, though I think prison is too good for her. She belongs in the loony bin. I can understand why you would be worried about what she will do next. She's psychopathic."

He feared that that maybe was close to the case. "Do you want to see the ring?" He knew she did, so he fished it out of his pocket. He'd been carrying it around for quite a while now. Getting up his courage? He knew what was holding him back. Celeste. He couldn't be sure how she would take it—or what she might do. His ex-wife seemed determined that he and Maggie shouldn't be together, even though she was apparently happily married to local wealthy businessman Wayne Duma.

Handing his sister the small black velvet box, he waited as she slowly opened it.

A small gasp escaped her lips. "It's beautiful. *Really* beautiful." She shot him a look. "I thought sheriffs didn't make much money?"

"I've been saving for a long while now. Unlike my sister, I live pretty simply."

She laughed. "Simply? Prisoners have more in their cells than you do. You aren't thinking of living in that small house of yours after you're married, are you?"

"For a while. It's not that bad. Not all of us have huge new houses like you and Trask."

"We need the room for all the kids we're going to have," she said. "But it is wonderful, isn't it? Trask is determined that I have everything I ever wanted." Her gaze softened as the newlywed thought of her husband.

"I keep thinking of your wedding." There'd been a double wedding with both Lillie and her twin, Darby, getting married to the loves of their lives only months ago. "It's great to see you and Trask so happy. And Darby and Mariah... I don't think Darby is ever going to come off that cloud he's on."

Lillie smiled. "I'm so happy for him. And I'm happy for you. You know I really like Maggie. So do it. Don't worry about Celeste. Once you're married, there's nothing she can do."

He told himself she was right, and yet in the back of his mind, he feared that his ex-wife would do something to ruin it—just as she had done to some of his dates with Maggie.

"I don't understand Celeste," Lillie was saying as she shifted into Drive and started toward the small western town of Gilt Edge. "She's the one who dumped you for Wayne Duma. So what is her problem?"

"I'm worried that she is having second thoughts about her marriage to Duma. Or maybe she's bored and has nothing better to do than concern herself with my life. Maybe she just doesn't want me to be happy."

"Or she is just plain malicious," Lillie said. "If she isn't happy, she doesn't want you to be, either."

A shaft of sunlight came through the cab window, warming him against the chill that came with even talking about Celeste. He leaned back, content as Lillie drove.

He was going to ask Maggie to marry him. He was going to do it this weekend. He'd already made a dinner reservation at the local steak house. He had the ring in his pocket. Now it was just a matter of popping the question and hoping she said yes. If she did... Well, then, this was going to be the best Christmas ever, he thought and smiled.

CHAPTER TWO

Every day that Maggie didn't run into Flint's ex in the small town where they both lived was a great day. In fact, it had been so long since she'd seen the woman that Maggie was beginning to think that either Celeste had left town or become a housebound recluse.

So it was no surprise when her luck gave out. She was starting down the produce aisle at the only grocery store in town when she smelled the woman's perfume and made the mistake of looking up.

Celeste made a beeline for her. Dressed in a navy-and-white suit with matching spectator shoes and bag, the blonde looked like something out of an old movie. This was Gilt Edge, where no one dressed up except for weddings and funerals.

Maggie, of course, was dressed in jeans, a T-shirt and sneakers since it was her day off. Her long curly auburn hair was pulled up in a ponytail. Nor was she wearing any makeup. She hadn't even put in her favorite earrings, a pair of silver hoops Flint had given her on her birthday.

"I was just picking up a few things on my way home from

the park planning committee meeting," Celeste said, as if Maggie had asked.

Her blond hair was cut in a perfect bob that was short enough it didn't hide the large diamonds at her ears. She blinked her big green eyes, clearly waiting for Maggie to respond.

Taken by surprise and feeling as if she'd been ambushed, Maggie had no comment. She put the cantaloupe she'd been holding into her cart and simply smiled at Celeste. She'd been raised to not be rude, so it was hard for her, even with Flint's ex.

"Well," Celeste said in that bubbly way of hers—at least around Maggie. "I thought for sure I'd be hearing you and Flint were getting married." She cocked her head a little as she stared at Maggie's left hand resting on the edge of the grocery cart. "But I don't see an engagement ring on your finger." She lifted a brow as if to ask, "What's up with that?"

"Sorry to disappoint you," Maggie said and told herself to leave it at that. But, of course, she couldn't. "We're taking things slow, for obvious reasons."

All the bubble left Celeste's face. "His first marriage wasn't that bad, no matter what he says."

"I was actually referring to your inability to let him go so he can be happy."

The woman looked taken aback. "Is that what he thinks?"

"It's what we both think. Why else would you have vandalized my beauty shop or tried to burn down my house?"

Celeste shook her head. "If that were true, wouldn't I be behind bars? Anyway, your house didn't burn down."

"No thanks to you. Lucky you didn't leave any evidence or you'd be in jail right now."

Celeste shook her head as if sad. "As I told Flint, I haven't done anything to keep the two of you apart. Maybe one of you is using it as an excuse. If you wanted to be together, I couldn't keep you apart no matter what I did. Flint sure didn't have any trouble asking *me* to marry him."

The woman always had to remind Maggie that she'd had Flint first. She bit her tongue, afraid of what might come out, and willed Celeste to walk away before it was too late. But, of course, she didn't.

One of the woman's finely honed brows lifted. "So if Flint is dragging his feet, it isn't because of me. Maybe he's realized what I've been telling him, that the two of you are wrong for each other, nothing personal. Then again, Flint has never listened to any advice I ever gave him. Why would he now?" With that, Celeste let out a light laugh and said, "Merry Christmas!" and turned and left, her high heels tapping briskly as she rounded the corner of the aisle.

Maggie stood, shaking violently with rage. Why did she let the woman get to her like that? Because Celeste was determined to keep her and Flint apart, no matter what she said. It wasn't that long ago that Celeste had stopped by the beauty shop as she was closing and warned her to leave Flint alone. She might act innocent, but she was far from it.

Feeling sick to her stomach, Maggie leaned against her grocery cart and tapped in Flint's number. For weeks, *she'd* been the one dragging her feet.

"I want to move in with you," she said into the phone when he answered now.

He laughed. "Just like that?"

"Just like that."

"Well, whatever made you change your mind, I couldn't be happier. When?"

"I think I'll bring a few things over today." She knew if she put it off, she might change her mind again.

"Great. We're still on for our date Friday night, though, right?"

"Absolutely," she said, feeling herself calm down a little. Flint had that effect on her. She loved this man and had for

some time. If it wasn't for Celeste they would have been together long before this.

As she disconnected, she reminded herself that when Flint
had suggested they move in together it was right after an incident at her beauty shop. Maggie had said she wasn't going
to let Celeste run her life and be the impetus that had them
living together. Had she just let Celeste force her into this?

She sighed and looked into her nearly empty grocery cart.
Her refrigerator was almost as empty. She really needed to
shop, but her heart wasn't in it. She was moving in with Flint.
As much as she'd tried, she couldn't work up any enthusi-
asm about it because...*she'd let Celeste goad her into it*. This
was definitely not the way she wanted her relationship with
Flint to go.

Maggie almost called him back, but stopped herself when
she saw Celeste at the end of the aisle. Had the woman overheard her phone call to Flint? She groaned at the thought. Now
if she called Flint back, Celeste would still think they were
moving in together, so the damage was already done. And
Flint would think she'd lost her mind for changing it again.

Maybe she had lost her mind, she thought, because she
should be happy. She realized a part of her was happy. She
wanted to be with Flint. She had let Celeste keep them apart
too many times. Moving in was the right thing to do. She
took her time shopping, hoping if she dragged it out long
enough, Celeste would have left the store. She wasn't up for
another run-in.

It had been months since Celeste had done something to in-
terfere in her relationship with Flint. If Celeste had overheard
the call, then now she knew. Better to hear it from Maggie
than from the local gossips. Maybe this would all turn out
fine, Maggie told herself as she took her full cart and headed
for the checkout. She'd bought something special for dinner
tonight—at Flint's.

★ ★ ★

"I'm a little worried about Flint," Lillie said when she found her brother Darby behind the bar at the Stagecoach Saloon, the bar and café they owned together.

"This is something new? What did he do? Arrest Dad again?" her handsome brother asked, not sounding worried.

"No, but only because Dad has been up in the mountains since our joint wedding," she said. "Which reminds me—where is Mariah?"

"She went into town. She thinks we need more than one set of sheets."

Lillie laughed. "She is going to domesticate you yet."

He grumbled under his breath. "So what is up with Flint?"

"He's going to ask Maggie to marry him." She climbed up on a stool and he poured her a cola. Having shared the womb together, she and Darby often communicated without a word. Lillie loved how close they were, so close that they'd had a double wedding.

"So he's finally going to do it," Darby said. "Good luck with that."

She took a sip of her cola and frowned. "What?"

"Just that word will get around. Isn't he worried about Celeste, given her former reactions to him and Maggie? The woman always did seem...unhinged."

"I know. Flint's worried, considering what Celeste has done to keep them apart. But he isn't going to let her stop him. Why does she have to be like that? It makes me want to go over to her house and—"

"Punching her in the mouth probably wouldn't be helpful, but please be my guest. I suspect she just can't let go of him. She certainly took him on a wild ride when she was married to him. She always has to get her way. I often wondered if she wouldn't go over the edge if Flint ever found someone else. Maggie is perfect for Flint. I'm just glad he realizes it."

"They deserve a happy-ever-after."

"You're such a romantic," Darby said with a shake of his head, but he was smiling. "Maybe we're all worrying for nothing. As far as I know, Celeste hasn't done anything crazy for a while."

"No, but Maggie and Flint haven't moved in together, either. Once he pops the question and puts that big diamond on her finger…" Lillie shrugged and finished her cola. "I have a doctor's appointment." She slid off her stool and patted her tummy, grinning. "How is Mariah feeling? When I talked to her she hadn't had any morning sickness yet." Lillie mugged a face. "I wish I could say that. Too bad it isn't only in the mornings."

"So far so good," he said, tapping the top of the wooden bar. "I can't believe you two might give birth just days apart."

"Days, ha," Lillie said. "I'm going into labor when she does. I want our kids to be close. We couldn't have planned this better."

He shook his head. "Knowing you, you probably *will* go into labor when Mariah does. Once you make up your mind on something…"

"I hope Maggie lets me help with the wedding," Lillie was saying, having already shifted gears. "Where do you think she'd want to have it?"

Her brother threw up his hands. "I'm not talking wedding with you. Go find Mariah. Or better yet, go see what Hawk and Cyrus would suggest for the wedding." He laughed. Their brothers were rancher bachelors who hardly dated. They'd had a hard enough time getting through the recent double wedding and reception since they spent more time with their cows than people.

"Maybe I *will* go visit Hawk and Cyrus. Did you see Hawk talking to that old girlfriend of his at our reception? I think there is still something there."

The front door opened and two couples came in. Darby looked relieved to get out of that conversation as he headed down the bar to serve them.

Maggie didn't spend any more time worrying about her decision. Moving in with Flint had been impulsive, but now that she'd said she would, darned if she wasn't going to do it. She hurried home and began to pack.

She would haul over just a few things to begin with. She'd taken Flint by surprise on the phone. She hoped he was happy about this. The more she thought about it, the more she thought it really was a good idea. She'd never let herself think about the future with Flint. It seemed too good to be true.

Now, though, she let herself consider it. She had one desire that she'd never shared with anyone, maybe especially Flint. She wanted children before her biological clock ran out. She and Flint had never discussed it, but maybe they would now. He would make such a great father.

Once inside the house she rented, she loaded a few things into an overnight bag and took them out to her car. She slowed as she started to go back inside for more, feeling as if someone was watching her. Looking around, she didn't see anyone. It was a quiet street, the houses on large lots with pine trees providing privacy. She'd always liked that about the neighborhoods in Gilt Edge.

But right now, the hairs on the back of her neck prickled. Someone *was* watching her. The thought made her feel foolish. She blamed it on running into Celeste at the grocery store earlier. The woman gave her chills. To the rest of the townspeople, Celeste might seem normal, but Maggie and the Cahills all suspected she could be more than vindictive. She could be dangerous.

Back inside the house, she threw a few more things into a bag, excited about the special meal she'd make for Flint tonight. It would be their first night together in his home. *Their* home. It would be a surprise—just like her moving in had been.

Getting excited about the idea of them being together all the time, she went to the freezer for the shrimp she'd picked up at the market. It didn't take her long to put all the ingredients she would need into a small cooler. As she did, she was mentally making lists in her head.

She had to let her landlord know that she was moving. She'd have to see about getting some time off from work so she could move in properly. She didn't want to have a bunch of boxes sitting around Flint's house. It would be an adjustment for them both, but maybe especially for Flint.

Celeste seemed to think that Flint had talked to her about his first marriage. But it had been just the opposite. He'd made a point of avoiding the subject. Whatever problems they'd had, Maggie knew nothing about them. Which was good because she hadn't wanted to talk about her past, either. She just hoped that she would be a better wife to him.

The fact that she was even thinking about the woman made her grit her teeth. But unfortunately, Celeste had been a factor since the beginning. Maybe now, though, all that was behind them. She had to believe that. She loved Flint. Didn't love conquer all?

As she took the rest out to the car, she still found herself looking around. She tried to shake the feeling that someone was watching her, but it was too strong. Sliding behind the wheel, she started the car and pulled out. As she did, she glanced in her rearview mirror.

Maggie knew she was looking for Celeste's huge dark SUV. There was one like it parked way down the block, but she couldn't be sure that was hers. Closer, she spotted a brown van parked on the street a couple of houses back. It was hard to tell with the sun glinting off the windshield, but it appeared someone was sitting behind the wheel.

Probably just a repairman waiting for one of her neighbors, she told herself. She had to quit this. For so long, she'd been running scared. She liked to blame Celeste, but Maggie suspected her real fear was of losing Flint. She loved him so much. What if she moved in with him and he realized he didn't feel as strongly about her? Maybe Celeste was right. Maybe there was a reason Flint hadn't asked her to marry him. Maybe he never would.

With a curse, she shifted her car into gear, angry that she'd let Celeste back in her head. She had to stop always thinking something terrible was going to happen when she and Flint were together. She had to believe in the two of them. She also had to believe that she could overcome her past.

Sometimes their future seemed like a brass ring suspended in front of her. All she had to do was grab it—and not look back. But her life hadn't been easy, far from it. A part of her wondered if she deserved to be happy.

As she drove down the street, she noticed all the Christmas decorations in the yards. Red, green and white lights twinkled in the afternoon light. From one yard, a huge snowman waved to her in the breeze. She smiled and tried to relax. It was almost Christmas. She needed to be thinking about what she was going to get Flint. It would be their first Christmas together. They should get a tree and decorate it together, she thought as she drove, her mood lifting.

At the stop sign, she couldn't help herself. She glanced back in her rearview mirror. The brown van was two vehicles back.

The moment the light changed, she peeled out, burning rubber as she took off. She thought about calling Flint. And telling him what? *I saw a van on my street and now it's behind me?*

In a town this size, that wasn't unusual. But as she neared Flint's street, she noticed the time. Maybe he'd get off work early knowing she was going to be there. Maybe he'd be at the house waiting for her. It would ruin her dinner surprise, but she didn't care. Sometimes she just needed his arms around her and right now was one of them.

The van was still behind her. Only one car back now. She still couldn't see the driver for the glare of the setting sun. She turned onto Flint's street and glanced in the mirror, afraid she would see the van turning in behind her. Instead, it sped on past and disappeared around the next corner.

She pulled into Flint's drive and slumped against the wheel. What was wrong with her? She couldn't keep going like this, making trouble where there wasn't any. She thought about her past relationships and the mistakes that she'd made. She wasn't going to do that with Flint. She'd learned her lesson. Wasn't that why she'd moved to Gilt Edge? She'd wanted to be someone else. Anyone but the Margaret Ann Thompson she'd been born.

She shut off the car engine and looked toward Flint's house in the pines. The place fit him. It was secluded with the nearest neighbor back up the street and hidden in the trees. The house sat on a slight hill, the empty lot behind it falling to the next street in a thick grove of pine trees.

Maggie was sure that the seclusion had been part of the charm. The house itself was small and neat, nice inside, though basic. She thought of ways she could make it more homey. Make it more theirs, since he'd lived in this house with Celeste. But that had been a long time ago, so she wasn't going to let that bother her.

Excitement filled her as she grabbed a couple of her bags and headed for Flint's back door. As she did, she saw one of the neighbors down the street out at her mailbox. The neighbor waved. Maggie waved back, feeling as if she'd finally come home.

Flint had given her a key last time they talked about moving in together. She'd never used it. But she doubted she would have to now. He always left the back door unlocked. Just like a sheriff, she thought with a smile. He wasn't worried about anyone breaking in.

She'd been worried when he'd told her. "What about Celeste?"

"She took everything she wanted when she left," he'd said with a laugh. "Trust me, she has no reason to return."

But Maggie thought once she was moved in, they would definitely get the locks changed and start locking the doors.

The afternoon sun was casting long shadows. It had been a mild fall. But the weatherman was forecasting a white Christmas. She glanced toward the dark pines and felt a shiver. That feeling that someone was watching her made her turn to look back up the road. She saw no one, but still couldn't shake off the feeling that she wasn't alone.

As the door swung open, she started to step in, but stopped to look down into the pines again. The breeze stirred the trees. The boughs moaned softly and cast dark shadows on the ground.

Hurrying now, she stepped inside. She started to lock and bolt the door behind her, but she had more things to get from the car. She knew she was being silly. If Flint could see her now, he'd have second thoughts about her moving in. Tossing her purse on the table by the back door, she pulled out her phone and smiled, anxious to hear Flint's voice.

The call went straight to voice mail. Disappointed, she almost hung up, but at the last minute, she decided to leave a message. "Hi, it's me. I'm at your house. I should warn you. I ran into Celeste earlier. I'm pretty sure she overheard me telling you that I'd changed my mind and I was going to move in with you. Oh, and I got something for our..." She realized that she'd run out of time on the message. Not that it mattered. She'd been babbling anyway.

She disconnected and realized she'd almost told him about the dinner she had planned as a surprise for him later. But then it wouldn't have been a surprise, huh.

Maggie pocketed her phone. She was still smiling at the thought of their first night together there when she heard a sound behind her and spun around. Her smile vanished as her heart began to pound. She took a step back as she fumbled for her cell phone with trembling fingers. "What are *you* doing here?"

CHAPTER THREE

"Maggie?" Flint called as he opened the back door to his house. He'd been thrilled when he'd gotten her message. But just seeing her car parked in the drive made it seem all the more real. He couldn't wait to see her. He had no idea why she'd changed her mind; he was just glad that she had, especially since he would be giving her the ring this weekend.

Her deciding to move in only made him all the more sure about asking her to marry him. It was time. They'd come through the worst of it, he told himself, remembering the message she'd left him about running into his ex.

Flint could imagine how unpleasant it was for Maggie. Every time he crossed paths with Celeste, it ruined his day.

He noticed that the passenger-side door of her car was open as if she was still in the process of moving a few things in. He thought about checking to see what else needed to come in, but he was too anxious to take her in his arms. After her call, he'd decided to come home early. He'd had to make one stop after hearing that his father had been seen coming out of the mountains. Not that he'd found him at his cabin. He told himself he'd deal with Ely later. He was too anxious to see Maggie.

He had big plans for tonight, he thought with a smile. Maybe he wouldn't be able to wait until this weekend to ask her.

"Maggie?" He started to step deeper into his house when he saw the overturned bookcase. Books were strewn across the floor. The lamp that had been next to it lay on the floor, the globe shattered. *"Maggie?"* Goose bumps rippled over his skin as the hair on the back of his neck quilled. *"Maggie!"*

He rushed toward the kitchen even though the lawman in him told him not to. This looked like a crime scene and if it was… She wasn't in the kitchen or the dining room. He headed for the stairs at a run, all the time telling himself he might be destroying important evidence.

Taking the stairs three at a time, he reached the landing. "Maggie!" No answer. The silence of the house had an ominous feel to it. "Maggie!"

She wasn't in any of the bedrooms or the bathrooms. She wasn't there, and yet all the way he'd been praying that, yes, there'd been an accident, but she was all right. They could buy another lamp. He could clean up the mess. Everything was fine.

But in his heart he'd known the moment he saw the overturned bookcase and the broken lamp. There'd been a struggle—and Maggie had lost.

Trying not to panic, he stopped on the landing and called her cell phone. As he waited for it to ring, he told himself there was an explanation, one completely different from the scenario playing in his head right then.

The sound of a phone ringing drew him back down the stairs and into the living room again. He stepped closer to the fallen bookcase, his pulse in overdrive. There, poking out from under one of the books, was her phone. He bent down and instinctively reached for it, but stopped himself. The screen was smeared with blood.

Half-blind with fear, he stepped back and keyed in 9-1-1. "I need Mark over at my house right away," he said to the dispatcher. His undersheriff, Mark Ramirez, had a cool head in emergencies and right now he needed that. He hung up, desperately wanting to put out a BOLO on Maggie right away. Just as he wanted to call in the experts from the Division of Criminal Investigation out of Billings. All his instincts told him that he had to find Maggie and fast.

But even as a law-enforcement officer, he couldn't call in the cavalry until he knew for certain that she was even missing. He also had to stop thinking like Maggie's boyfriend. He needed to be the lawman he was.

From where he stood, he could see drops of blood on the wood floor. They were still wet. He looked at his watch. Whatever had happened here hadn't happened very long ago.

Telling himself not to jump to conclusions, he called the hospital. It was possible there had been an altercation and the other person involved had taken Maggie to the emergency room. It took everything in him to remain calm and wait for the phone to be answered.

"Hello, yes, this is Sheriff Cahill. I need to know if Maggie Thompson was admitted to the emergency room. Yes, I'll wait," he said even though he wanted to beg her to hurry. He knew that if his instincts were right, every minute counted.

"I'm sorry, Sheriff. We have no record of her being in the ER. No one here has seen her." The hospital was small. Gilt Edge had only a couple of doctors. "Her family doctor is here doing rounds. He said he hasn't seen her, either."

"Thank you." He quickly dialed Just Hair, the salon that Maggie owned. Daisy, the only other stylist, hadn't seen or heard from her. Neither had her best friend, Belle. He was just disconnecting when he heard a vehicle pull in.

All his fears rushed back. His first instinct was right—just as he'd known in his gut. He hurried to the front door rather than the back and stopped, the lawman in him kicking in again. The lock didn't appear to have been jimmied. He hadn't checked the back door, hadn't taken the time to do anything but search the house for Maggie.

Using his shirtsleeve, he carefully opened the front door. The last thing he wanted to do was destroy any fingerprints that might have gotten left behind. The action felt foolish. Whoever had taken her had used the back door, the one he was sure he'd left unlocked.

Not that he didn't already know who had done this. He knew who had Maggie. That was why he was so terrified.

"Come in this way," he called to Mark as the undersheriff got out of his patrol SUV.

The moment Mark saw his face, his eyes widened in alarm. "What's wrong?"

"There appears to have been a struggle. Maggie's missing." His voice broke. He waved Mark in and pointed toward the scene near the back door. "She was moving in today. Her car door is still open. Her purse is on the table by the door. She must have been surprised by someone."

Mark pulled out his phone and began shooting photos of the room as he moved cautiously toward the fallen bookcase. "I saw Maggie's car by the back door. You're sure no one stopped by, maybe took her to the emergency room for stitches? Maybe she called to a neighbor?"

"She hasn't been admitted to the hospital. I called while I was waiting for you. Nor has her doctor seen her."

His undersheriff nodded as he knelt down to get a closer shot at something on the floor. Even from where Flint was standing, he could see that Mark was shooting the blood splattered on the floor and on the spilled books. Too much blood and yet not enough to indicate that she was mortally wounded. He tried to find hope in that.

"Maggie's friends and associate?" Mark asked calmly.

"No one has seen her." Flint was surprised how calm he sounded. His heart pounded so hard he could barely hear himself think. He felt as if he was shaking all over. He knew better than to jump to conclusions, but all his instincts told him Maggie had been taken. It made no sense and yet...

"I know who has her," Flint said. "Maggie left me a message earlier. She ran into my ex. She thought that Celeste overheard her on the phone telling me she was moving in with me. I don't have to tell you that Celeste has done everything possible to keep us apart. If she is as determined as I think she is..."

The undersheriff nodded. "I can see why you would suspect Celeste, but let's wait until we have all the facts, okay?"

At least Mark hadn't said, "Try not to panic." The words would have been wasted on him. He was panicking and with good reason. The scene in his living room showed a struggle. Maggie had been injured. Her cell phone smeared with blood indicated that she had possibly tried to call for help.

"I'm going to run over to the neighbors and see if they saw anything," Flint said. His closest neighbor, Alma Ellison, lived kitty-corner from him down the street. She was smiling as she came to the door. He quickly asked her if she'd seen Maggie.

"I saw her when she arrived at your house. Is something wrong?"

"Did Maggie seem all right?"

"Yes. She waved and I waved back."

"Did you see anyone else?"

Alma thought for a moment. "You know how little traffic we get out here. I did notice a brown van go by. It was driving so slow, I knew the driver must be lost. And there was one of those large dark SUVs. I can't say if either of them stopped at your house since I got busy after that. Is Maggie all right?"

"I don't know. I can't seem to find her," he said. "If you think of anything else..." She promised she would call him.

Back at the house, he told Mark what Alma had said. "Celeste drives a large dark SUV."

"I'm going to have a deputy go by Celeste Duma's house," the undersheriff said.

From the moment he'd walked in and seen the mess and couldn't find Maggie, he'd wanted to race over to Celeste's house and demand to know what she'd done with Maggie. "I'll go."

Mark stopped him. "I'm sorry, Sheriff, but I can't let you do that. With you, it would be confrontational. Please, let me handle this. You called me because you know you are too emotionally involved. This is now considered a crime scene. We're going to treat it as such and pray that we're wrong."

Flint knew Mark was right. It *was* why he'd called him. He'd been afraid of doing something that would put Maggie in even more jeopardy. He listened to Mark on the phone for a moment and then stepped outside, needing the air.

He could tell that Mark was as worried as he was. The question was, where was Maggie now? His hand went to the small velvet box in his pocket. Why had he waited so long to ask her to marry him? What if...? He couldn't bear to let himself even think it. He had to believe that she was still alive and that they would find her, he told himself as he stepped back inside the door. Mark was still on the phone.

"The only deputy close to town is Harp," Mark said, covering the phone with his hand and making an it-will-be-all-right face. The county was large and the sheriff's department was small. It meant stretching law enforcement to its limits sometimes. It was one reason Flint would love to get rid of Harp and get a better deputy.

Flint groaned silently. Deputy Harper Cole was the last person he wanted to depend on right now. He knew why Mark couldn't go himself. He was protecting the possible crime scene—and Flint. If the DCI became involved, the first suspect was always the boyfriend. He listened to him tell Harp what to do at the Duma house.

"Get inside. Be polite. Try to have a look around and see if anything appears amiss. If Celeste and her husband will let you search the place without a warrant, great. Nice if you could check her car. Just listen, please." Mark sighed. "Maggie Thompson is missing. Yes, the sheriff's girlfriend. Now listen. Look for blood. I can't get into it right now. There could have been an accident involving Celeste and Maggie. Call me if there is any question." He turned back to Flint as he disconnected. "Harp is actually the best choice right now. No one takes him seriously. If you're right about Celeste, she won't be concerned about Harp showing up and should let him in without a warrant. That will save us time."

Flint tried to breathe a little easier. "Great. I'm forced to depend on the town hero."

Mark sighed. "It is going to be all right."

A few months ago, Harp had managed to save two people's lives. One of those lives belonged to Flint's brother Darby. The other was Darby's now wife, Mariah Ayers Cahill. Flint had been ready to fire the deputy before that night and would have months ago if Harp hadn't been the mayor's son. He'd given him more chances because of it. But Flint had reached his limit. He'd told Harp that if he messed up again... Then Harp had come through that night and was now the town hero. At least until he messed up big-time again.

And that was why Flint wished it was anyone but Harp going over to Celeste's house. He knew his ex-wife. If she was behind this, she would lie. Flint would know if she was lying. He doubted Harp would.

He raked a hand through his hair as he glanced toward the fallen bookshelf. As crazy as he thought his ex was, he never really thought she was capable of...of whatever had happened here.

"We don't know for sure it was Celeste," Mark said.

Just as they didn't know that she'd vandalized Maggie's salon and almost set her house on fire? "She's certainly capable. But if she did something to Maggie..." Flint couldn't continue.

Mark laid a hand on his shoulder. "We don't even know that the blood is Maggie's. One step at a time. We'll find her."

He nodded, but he knew the statistics. The first seventy-two hours were crucial. But that wasn't if the missing person was injured. He had no idea how badly Maggie had been bleeding. Maggie hadn't been missing long. If they could find her soon... Otherwise, he knew he might never see her alive again.

"Why haven't we heard from Harp yet?" Flint demanded.

"He hasn't even had time to get over there. You need to stay calm. We have to work this one step at a time. Is there anyone else who might want to harm Maggie?"

"No." He'd answered the question too quickly. Mark was looking at him with concern. "I don't know. The only person she's had run-ins with that I know of was Celeste." He realized he didn't know if Maggie had had other problems with anyone. Maggie was so independent. He loved that about her, but now he wondered if she would have told him if she'd had trouble with anyone else.

Celeste was a different story since she was his ex. Maggie seemed to think that he could do something about her. Now he sure wished he had.

The undersheriff looked around the room for a moment. "You keep the doors locked when you aren't home?"

He hadn't wanted to admit it, but he shook his head. "Also,

I've never changed the locks from when Celeste and I lived here together. She probably still has a key."

Mark gave him a disapproving look before he asked, "I'm assuming you didn't touch anything?"

Flint heard something in his voice. "No—you know I didn't. You aren't thinking about kicking me from this case—"

"No, *I* can't. As you know, in the state of Montana, the sheriff is an elected office. Not even the county commissioners can pull you off a case."

"Only the Division of Criminal Investigation," Flint said, suddenly aware of where his undersheriff was going with this.

"I'm hoping to know what we're dealing with before we call in a DCI team," Mark said. "You agree?"

A part of him wanted the criminologists on this as quickly as possible. But once they called in the DCI, the team might decide because Maggie was his girlfriend that he be put on a leave of absence. He'd be off the case. He couldn't bear the thought. Silently, he swore. They had to find Maggie before he was locked out of this investigation. As it was, his house was now a crime scene.

Deputy Harper Cole cruised down the street toward the Duma house. He wondered what this really was about. Maggie Thompson was missing? There had to be more to it than that. He had tried to ask, but the undersheriff had cut him off. Clearly both Mark and Flint still didn't have any faith in his abilities. It pissed him off. He was a hero.

Well, at least everyone thought he was. Everyone but his pregnant girlfriend, Vicki. Why had he confessed everything to her that morning in the hospital after he'd almost died? He'd been feeling guilty, amazed he was still alive, and apparently he'd felt the need to confess to someone. But Vicki?

Now he was stuck with her. She could hold it over his head

for the rest of their lives because if the truth about that night ever came out...

Harp shuddered at the thought. He would be the laughingstock of town instead of a hero. Worse, he'd be fired. He'd have to leave town. He might never get another job in law enforcement and he'd gotten damned attached to carrying a gun and being "the man."

Now he slowed in front of the Duma house. Here he was again, dealing with something connected to the sheriff. Maggie Thompson was allegedly missing? So what was he doing here?

He parked in front of the sheriff's ex-wife's house and warned himself not to screw this up. Reading between the lines of what the undersheriff had said, Mark thought Celeste Duma had done something to the sheriff's girlfriend.

Smiling, he climbed out. He loved this sort of small-town drama, especially when it involved the sheriff. It surprised him Flint wasn't the one coming over here himself. Flint must be going crazy with worry. Why else would he let Mark be calling the shots?

He covered the butt of his gun with his hand as he walked toward the front door. There was no car parked in the drive. As he passed a window in the garage, he peered in. Empty. This was going to be a waste of time. No one was home.

Ringing the bell, he glanced around the neighborhood. It was a much nicer one than where he and Vicki lived. She'd talked him into moving in with her. Another mistake he'd made. She spent most of her time puking her guts out since getting pregnant. She never felt like doing it anymore. He worried this was what marriage was going to be like.

He rang the bell again and then knocked. Total waste of time.

At the sound of a car engine, he turned to see a large dark SUV pull in. Wayne Duma. Now, here was someone who thought a whole lot of himself, Harp thought. Hell, he'd bought himself and his wife *matching* SUVs for one of their wedding anniversaries. How full of himself was that?

Duma was frowning as he exited his vehicle. Clearly he didn't like seeing a deputy on his doorstep. "Can I help you?" the man asked in the same tone he probably used with solicitors at his door. It only pissed Harp off more.

"I'm looking for Mrs. Duma."

"She's not here."

"So I gathered. Can you tell me where she is?"

Wayne looked as if he was losing patience. Harp felt the same way. "What is this about?"

Harp didn't answer. "I need to talk to her. Sheriff's department business."

"She's left town."

"When did she leave?"

"Earlier. I insist you tell me what this is about."

"Where did she go?"

Duma looked as if he wanted to dig his heels in.

"Maggie Thompson is missing. I need to speak with your wife."

The man groaned and looked away. "Not this foolishness again." He turned back to Harp. "My wife has gone to a spa. If Maggie is missing, it has nothing to do with Celeste."

"What spa?"

"I have no idea."

"Was she driving there or flying?"

Duma shook his head. "I didn't ask."

"I'm going to need to have a look around. I'm sure we can get a warrant—"

"That isn't necessary," Duma said, stepping past him to unlock the door. "Help yourself."

Harp stepped in and looked around. "Nice place you have here." He walked through the house. It appeared a housekeeping service had been there recently. It had that smell. It did nothing to improve his mood since he'd never had a place that smelled this good.

"I'm going to take a look upstairs," he told Duma, who didn't bother to answer. He was on his phone. Harp listened as the man left a message for his wife to call him.

Upstairs, he stuck his head in each room. The place was immaculate. He couldn't see Celeste down on her knees scrubbing the bathroom floor to make it shine like that—let alone to wipe up blood. *Rich people*, he thought with a sharp bite of jealousy.

He figured, as clean as the place was, it wouldn't be hard to find blood evidence—if there had been any. But so far, he saw nothing to indicate that there had been anything going on there.

At the end of the hall, he pushed open the door into the master bedroom and felt his pulse shoot up. The room looked as if it had exploded. There were clothes everywhere, on the floor, on the bed, thrown on the closet floor.

He heard Duma behind him. The man gasped and then swore.

"Can you explain this?" Harp asked.

"Apparently Celeste had trouble deciding what to take to the spa."

"Right. Don't touch anything in this room." He pulled out his phone. "The sheriff is going to want to talk to you."

CHAPTER FOUR

At the same time her boyfriend was calling the sheriff, Vicki was doubling over in pain. She clutched the sink next to the toilet bowl. Ever since she'd lost the baby, she'd had terrible cramps at that time of the month. Keeping Harp off of her for the days she was flowing was hard enough. But the lying…

She told herself that she couldn't keep this secret any longer from Deputy Harper Cole, the man she'd fallen in love with. Every day, she promised herself that she would tell Harp that she'd lost the baby. But when he came home, she just couldn't bring herself to confess.

He'll leave you the minute you tell him.

After all, it had been the only reason he'd moved in with her. She hadn't told, thinking she would get pregnant again. But here was another month and no baby. The doctor had said she shouldn't have any trouble getting pregnant again. She'd thought that if it happened soon enough, Harp would never have to know she'd lost the first baby. He never paid any attention to how many months had gone by.

He'd asked her once when she was going to start showing. "Guess you'll be looking like you stole a basketball soon enough. Does that mean we aren't going to be able to do it?"

She'd assured him that they could have sex—the one thing that seemed to make him happy—almost to the end. "But only if you are more gentle."

That had cheered him up. Nothing else about living together had. True, she wasn't much of a cook. Often she was bored and just watched television all day. She missed working at the café, but she couldn't very well go back there without admitting that she'd had a miscarriage early on in her pregnancy.

What was she going to do? she thought as she doubled over again with a cramp. And how was she going to keep this from Harp? She couldn't pretend to have the flu every month for five days. Even Harp would figure that out after a while.

She had to get pregnant again. Otherwise…

Vicki felt the pills she'd taken begin to work on her cramps. Without the pain, her thoughts cleared some. She considered what Harp had told her had happened the night that man had come looking for Mariah Ayers, now Cahill, and had almost killed both Mariah and Darby. Harp had admitted to her that he wasn't the hero everyone thought he was. He'd lied and she was the only one he'd ever told about it.

Now with the sheriff's girlfriend missing and him being put on leave, maybe Harp really did have a shot at becoming the next sheriff. But only if no one ever knew the truth about that night.

She placed a hand over her stomach. Maybe she didn't need a baby to keep Harp after all.

"I can assure you that Celeste had nothing to do with Maggie Thompson being missing," Duma said from a chair in the interrogation room at the sheriff's department thirty minutes later. He was a big man, distinguished, gray at the temples.

"How can you be so confident of that?" the undersheriff asked.

Flint watched through the glass window that acted as a mirror on the other side. Harp had stayed at the house to make sure nothing was disturbed until the state crime team arrived out of Billings. Flint desperately wanted to be the one questioning Duma.

"I need you to let me handle this," Mark had said. "You know you're too emotionally involved."

Swearing under his breath, he'd nodded. "You're right. I'll do whatever you suggest. I trust you, Mark."

"You'd do the same thing in my shoes. The DCI will want to talk to you. After that, you'll need to find somewhere to stay since your house is now a crime scene."

Flint had felt as if his heart would burst when Mark had gotten the call from Harp. "What did Harp find over there? Please, Mark, you have to tell me."

"Nothing to indicate that Celeste had anything to do with Maggie going missing. But she's left town and she was apparently upset before she left. Flint, I told you—"

His heart had started pounding the moment Mark had answered his phone and said, "Bring Duma down to the sheriff's department for questioning."

Panic had made his knees go weak. *"Celeste?"*

"No—Wayne Duma. He says Celeste left town to go to a spa."

"She's lying. You have to—"

"Flint, he's coming downtown. We'll find out what he knows."

"She picked today to leave town? Mark—"

"I know. We have to find Maggie. That's what we're doing."

Flint had nodded, but his heart had been racing. Celeste

had done something with Maggie. This had been building for some time.

"I know you're right, Mark, but I need to know what's going on or I'll go crazy. Starting with what Duma has to say."

Mark had suggested he watch the interrogation. Flint had agreed, although he could feel the clock ticking like a time bomb in his chest. Maggie had been missing for at least several hours now. Statistically, the sooner they found her, the better chance they would find her alive. He feared she'd been taken on impulse. He envisioned the scene back at his house. The two women arguing, maybe getting into a shoving match, and then Maggie getting hurt.

If she was badly hurt, things would have gone downhill from there. Celeste would be scared. She'd do something stupid, like abduct Maggie to keep what had happened from coming out. Things would only get worse from there. Celeste would be running scared. She would realize how hard it was to hide someone. How desperate would she get, all the time not realizing that she was getting in deeper and deeper?

He stared through the glass, wanting to shake the truth out of Wayne Duma.

"How do you explain the condition your bedroom was in?" Mark asked.

Duma rubbed the back of his neck, looking uncomfortable. "Celeste and I had a fight last night. She was still upset this morning."

"What did you fight over?"

"I don't even know. With Celeste..." The man looked away. "We haven't been getting along for some time now. This morning, after another rough night, I suggested we might want to take a break."

"Divorce?"

"I didn't say that, but I think that's the way she took it. I told her we would talk about it later when we were both calmer."

Flint felt his stomach roil. Celeste would have been beside herself, he thought. She might not like the choice she'd made in hooking up with Duma, but she wouldn't want to give up the luxury, the name or the perceived power that came with it. Given the kind of mood she must have been in, anything could have happened.

"I went to work," Duma continued. "I knew she had some meeting she was going to. I almost didn't take her call later that morning when my assistant said she was on the line. I didn't want to continue the argument, especially at work and on the phone."

"But you did take the call."

He nodded. "She was still upset. She sounded hysterical. I honestly thought she might do something to herself if I didn't stay on the line. So I let her talk. She went on about the two of us, the same stuff I've heard before. I don't give her enough attention, that sort of thing." He sighed.

"Did she mention Maggie Thompson?"

Duma looked away for a moment. "She told me that she'd run into Maggie at the grocery store and that her ex and Maggie were moving in together." He cleared his voice. "She was calmer then, I thought. She said she was having trouble dealing with it, that she had some unresolved feelings for Flint and that part of our problem was that she blamed me for their divorce. If she hadn't met me…

"But that she loved me and just needed some time away. She said she was sorry she'd put me through so much. She sounded as if she was accepting that her ex was going to find happiness with someone else. She promised that when she came back everything would be much better."

Much better because Maggie would be out of the picture. Cursing, Flint couldn't believe what he was hearing. He wanted to put his fist through the glass. He'd been married to Celeste. He knew what extremes she went to when she felt she was about to lose something she wanted. There was no telling what she would have done.

"Did she tell you where she was going?" Mark asked.

"No, just that she was packing to go to a spa. She sounded... calm."

According to Harp, Celeste had been anything but calm given the shape of the bedroom where she was packing, Flint thought. Had she gone from there over to his house the two of them had shared and confronted Maggie?

Celeste probably still had her key, not that she would have needed it since she knew he usually left the door unlocked. So she could have been waiting for Maggie. Or worse, he thought with a curse, she could have just walked in and surprised Maggie.

He mentally kicked himself for not getting the locks changed, for not locking his door. But this was Gilt Edge, after all. Aside from a rash of break-ins a few months ago by some teens... The point was that Celeste could have gotten to Maggie—and had.

But then, so could anyone else, he thought and shook his head. It hadn't been anyone else. He knew who had Maggie. He was staring at the person's husband.

"I'm telling you Celeste wouldn't have done anything to Maggie. Yes, maybe she tried to scare her off with some stupid vandalism, but kidnap her?" Duma shook his head. "She wouldn't do anything so..."

"Crazy?" Mark asked.

Duma hung his head. "She was just angry. By now, she's over it. We've had fights before."

He didn't sound convinced they would patch things up, Flint thought. This man had seen Celeste's crazy. He was running scared this time and probably fed up. Flint knew that feeling, having been there with Celeste himself.

"I think my wife has too much time on her hands and..."

Duma looked up at Mark as if pleading with him to agree that Celeste wouldn't have hurt Maggie. "This whole thing is so… frustrating. Yes, my wife might need…help. I've tried to get her to see someone." He put his head in his hands. "It's put a terrible strain on our marriage. I should be more patient with her, but when she calls me at work with this foolishness…"

"Did she mention that she was going over to Flint's house to see Maggie?"

Duma lifted his head. "No. I told you. She said she was going to a spa."

"But she didn't mention what spa or where and you didn't ask?"

"No. I was just relieved that she was going away for a while." He looked guilty, and for a moment, Flint almost felt sorry for him. Maybe if Duma hadn't had an affair with Celeste while she was still married to him, Flint could have worked up more compassion for the man. Instead, he felt as if Duma had gotten what he deserved: one crazy-ass woman who was capable of doing just about anything.

But if Celeste had lost it and done something to Maggie… He clenched his fists tighter. They had to find Celeste. It was too much of a coincidence that she'd left town now—at the same time Maggie had gone missing. Especially now that he knew how upset Celeste had been.

Mark was questioning Duma about other spas Celeste had gone to. Mark had gotten a warrant, so they were checking into Duma's bank and credit-card statements. In the meantime, the state crime team would be arriving and going over Flint's house as well as the Dumas'. Flint had mixed feelings about that. Maybe they would find proof that would help find Maggie. Or maybe they wouldn't find any physical evidence other than Flint's own DNA at the scene and kick him off the case.

"Does Celeste own a gun?" the undersheriff asked.

Flint's ears perked up. Duma raised his head. He looked guilty. Flint swore.

"I bought her a gun when…when she told me that her ex was harassing her," Duma said. "I know now that it wasn't true." He sighed. "But I thought if it made Celeste feel safer…"

Mark asked about the make and model and if Celeste had taken it with her. Duma swore he had no idea if Celeste had taken the gun.

Who takes a gun to a spa? Flint thought.

"The DCI team out of Billings will want to take a look at your house after they finish with the crime scene," Mark said. "I hope you'll cooperate."

Duma sighed. "I want to help in any way I can."

Flint listened as Mark finished up with Duma, who promised to call him with the names of the spas that Celeste usually went to.

He hated the waiting. Worse, hated feeling so helpless. Hours had gone by. Where was Maggie? Unfortunately, he knew firsthand how investigations could take a wrong turn, how law enforcement could spend too much time suspecting the wrong person, how people died while the cops were barking up the wrong tree. He couldn't let that happen. Once they found Celeste—

"Sheriff?" The dispatcher stuck her head into the small room adjacent to the interrogation room where he was standing. "We just got a call. I think you'll want to take it."

His heart took off like a wild horse in the wind. "About Maggie?"

The dispatcher looked embarrassed. "No. I'm sorry. The caller said it was about Jenna Holloway."

Jenna Holloway had disappeared following an argument with her husband, Anvil, last March. Anvil admitted to striking her after she'd confessed to having an affair with another man, but swore she wasn't hurt when she drove away.

What had sent up red flags were Anvil's actions after she'd allegedly left. He'd destroyed a section of Sheetrock with his fist and then he'd cleaned up the kitchen, mopping the floor before washing the clothes he'd been wearing.

When Flint had arrived he'd noticed the freshly scrubbed kitchen, as well as Anvil's bruised and bloodied knuckles. Anvil hadn't been able to repair the section of Sheetrock before he'd called to report Jenna missing. But he'd certainly covered his tracks on everything else.

Over the weeks that followed with no word from Jenna, more facts had emerged. It seemed that Jenna had more secrets than just a lover. She'd become pen pals with some inmates at Montana State Prison, taken up shoplifting and stealing from the family grocery budget. She'd also begun wearing makeup and had bought herself some sexy undergarments— things apparently out of character.

When her car turned up in a gully, Flint had become more convinced that Anvil hadn't just taken his temper out on a wall. The state crime investigators had been called in, but they'd found no evidence to prove that Anvil had killed her.

Since then Flint had been waiting for someone to stumble across her shallow grave. The DCI had gone over the Holloway farm with cadaver dogs and found nothing. Anvil had sworn that he didn't kill her. Not that anyone in town believed him. But with four mountain ranges around the valley and miles and miles of wild country, Jenna could have been buried anywhere.

Flint suspected that someone had finally found her body when he took the call.

"I should have called you months ago," a man said.

"You know something about Jenna Holloway's disappearance? Who am I speaking to?"

Silence. A crank call?

"Kurt Reiner. Jenna's been staying with me."

Flint had to sit down. "Jenna Holloway is with you?"

"I know I should have called, but she was too afraid of him finding her if I told anyone where she was."

"She was that afraid of her husband?"

"*Her husband?* No, man. It was some dude who was threatening her."

He tried to get his head around this. Jenna was *alive*? Had been alive since the night she disappeared back in March? "Where has she been all this time?"

"Sheridan, Wyoming. We've been renting a place down here."

Flint rubbed a hand over his face. "I'm confused. So why did you decide to call me now?"

"A little over a week ago, she saw the man who'd been harassing her back in Montana. He was in town. She'd been telling me that she'd felt as if someone had been watching her. I figured she was imagining things or getting tired of being with me, you know what I mean? Anyway, the next night she freaked. She saw him standing across the street, watching our second-floor apartment. I ran down, but by the time I reached the corner, he was gone, roaring away in his van. So the next day—"

"Wait. A van?" He thought of what Alma Ellison had told him. "What color van?"

It took Reiner a minute to answer after being interrupted in the middle of his story.

"A brown one. So, anyway, a couple days ago I came back to the apartment and…" His voice broke. "She was gone and the place was a mess as if there'd been a fight. And now she's missing. *Really* missing this time."

A brown van. What were the chances it was the same van his neighbor had seen earlier today driving by his house? Sheridan, Wyoming, was about six hours away, no big deal for those who lived in these large Western states. Still, it was a stretch to think it could have been the same van.

"You didn't happen to get the plate number on that van, did you?"

"Naw. It was an older-model panel van."

"Wyoming plates?"

"No, I don't think so."

"Montana plates?"

"I really didn't notice since the back of the van was so dirty. But now that I think about it, they were some different colored plate, not Wyoming or Montana. That's all I know."

Flint raked a hand through his hair. Why did he think there might be a connection? He knew who had taken Maggie and she didn't drive an old brown van. She drove the newest, largest black SUV they made.

Still, both women were from Gilt Edge. Jenna had her hair done at Maggie's shop by the other stylist, Daisy Caulfield, but the two had known each other. He wouldn't be a good lawman unless he checked this out.

"I need to talk to you more about this," Flint said. "Can you come up to Gilt Edge?"

"Sorry, but I finally landed a pretty decent job. Even if I could afford to drive all the way up there—"

"Did you talk to the local police?"

"Couldn't really do that under the circumstances, you know. I kept hoping she'd turn back up. That's why I didn't call until now. I didn't want any trouble with the law." Also, the local law probably wouldn't have much interest since Jenna had pulled this disappearing act already up in Montana.

"I probably shouldn't even have called you," Reiner said.

Flint spoke quickly, afraid now that the man might hang up. "Did Jenna tell you anything more about this man?"

"No. Just said he scared her and wouldn't leave her alone."

Flint thought of the prison pen pals Jenna had been writing before she'd disappeared the first time. Something definitely had been going on with the woman.

"Listen, you did right by calling me." He tried to think of what to do. No way could they send an officer down there. Nor did he think the local law in Sheridan would be much help on this one. And he couldn't go himself. He had to stay here in case there was a break in Maggie's disappearance.

"Tell me what hours you work and where you live. I'll send someone to take your statement."

"I don't know, man."

"I'm not sending a cop. It's a private investigator I know. I'll have him contact you. Don't worry. It's someone I trust with my life—and yours and Jenna's."

Reiner sighed. Flint could tell that he was regretting this call. "Okay."

Flint jotted down the information. "Give me your phone number. I'll get right back to you." He disconnected and called Curry Investigations in Big Timber, Montana. Former Sweet Grass County sheriff Frank Curry answered on the second ring.

CHAPTER FIVE

Flint caught Frank and his business partner–wife, Nettie, just before they were leaving for the day. From his office at the sheriff's department, he filled them in on the Jenna Holloway case. He'd met them both on a state investigation some years ago when Frank was sheriff. A big man, Frank looked like an old-timey lawman with a gunfighter mustache.

He'd heard that Frank had retired and opened his own investigation business with Nettie. He admired the two of them doing that since they were both in their sixties. Most people their age were headed for their recliners.

"I got a call from a man in Sheridan, Wyoming, who says he's been living with Jenna Holloway since March—but that now she has disappeared again," Flint told them. He held the phone tighter. "I'd go check this out myself, but Jenna is not the only one missing. The woman I've been seeing, Maggie Thompson, is also missing. My undersheriff is doing everything possible to find out what happened. The DCI has been called in."

"What can we do to help?" Nettie asked from a phone extension at their office.

"Kurt Reiner believes Jenna was taken by a man in a brown van a couple days ago. A brown van was seen on the same street where Maggie disappeared earlier today."

"You think the cases might be connected," Frank said.

"I think it's a long shot at best. But both women are from here. If this man knows anything about Jenna Holloway and her disappearance..." His voice broke. "I can't leave here in case—"

"We can go first thing in the morning," Nettie said. "Just send us the information."

"I really appreciate this," Flint said. "Truthfully, I don't think Maggie was taken by some man in a brown van. I think my ex-wife did something to her and it scares the hell out of me. But my ex is allegedly away at some spa, and this information on Jenna, who disappeared last March, just came in. When the man mentioned a brown van..."

"I understand. We'll get back to you as soon as we've talked to Kurt Reiner," Frank said.

He swallowed the lump in his throat, unable to voice his gratitude. He trusted this longtime sheriff, having heard nothing but good news about him. Nor was Frank's wife any slouch when it came to investigating, he'd heard.

"We'll start with Jenna," Frank said. "Then we'll see where you are on Maggie's disappearance. We understand time is of the essence. If you need anything..." He read off their cell phone numbers.

"Thanks, Frank. I knew I could count on you. I've emailed everything I have. As soon as I hear from you verifying that Jenna was the woman living with Kurt Reiner, I'll go out to the Holloway farm to talk to the husband. Anvil might have heard from her and just not called me. Or he could be involved. At this point, it's all up in the air."

"We have the photo of Jenna and the information you just emailed. We'll be in touch."

★ ★ ★

Ten o'clock the next morning, Frank sat down across from Kurt Reiner. Reiner was dressed in jeans, sneakers that had seen better days and a ragged T-shirt with a logo of some band Frank had never heard of. Somewhere around forty-five with a neck tattoo of a snake and a variety of other tattoos on his pale skin below the sleeves of the T-shirt, Reiner appeared to be trying to look younger. His eyes were steel blue with thick lashes in a pockmarked face that wasn't quite handsome.

But there was something about him that Frank thought might appeal to a woman either looking for trouble or running from it. A quiet mousy woman who'd married a farmer ten years her elder might have looked at Reiner and thought he had something she'd missed out on. Especially since she'd apparently been drawn toward the wilder side of life before her disappearance.

The first thing Frank had done when he'd met Reiner at a local café was show him the photo.

"Yep, that's Jenna," the man had said. "Except now she's a blonde."

"You wouldn't happen to have a photo of the two of you, would you?"

Reiner nodded. "I figured you'd want proof." He dug out his cell phone and swiped for a photo. It was a selfie of him and Jenna in a bar. While not great resolution, there was no doubt it was Jenna—even blonde.

What struck Frank was that she looked younger than she did in the photo Flint had gotten from her husband. He took a photo of the pair and texted it to Flint to let him know that they had a positive ID while Nettie made polite conversation to distract Reiner.

"So how did you and Jenna meet?" Frank asked after the three of them were seated at a back table out of the way. Reiner had suggested the place, wanting to meet in public.

Frank got the feeling that he was worried a half-dozen cops would be waiting for him.

Now Reiner shifted uncomfortably in his chair and shot a look toward the door. "So you're a private dick?"

"Nettie and I are licensed private investigators, yes," Frank said. "No one is going to arrest you." He'd told him this on the phone but clearly the man had trust issues. He could tell that Reiner wished he'd kept his mouth shut about Jenna.

"You care about her," Nettie said. "That's why you're here. Are you in love with her?"

Reiner blinked, his expression softening as he looked at Nettie. "She was sweet, you know? The kind of woman who takes care of a man."

Frank wondered how she'd taken care of him, but let his wife take the lead. Nettie had a sense for these things. He'd learned to trust her instincts long ago.

"You must miss her."

Reiner's blue eyes filled with tears as he nodded. He swallowed convulsively, his Adam's apple going up and down for a minute. "That's why I called. If some...bad dude has her..."

"Then let us help her," Nettie said. "We're going to need to know everything she might have told you about the man, but let's start with how you two met."

He nodded. "She was writing to my brother, Bobby. He's in prison in Deer Lodge."

Flint had said she'd been writing to prisoners at Montana State Prison, but when she'd disappeared none of those men had been released, so they were cleared as suspects.

"He told me about her and that she needed help, so..." Reiner shrugged. "So I wrote her and we met. I had to help her, you know?"

"But when you met her, there was something about her that stole your heart," Nettie said.

Reiner smiled. It was a good smile. Frank could see how

a woman looking for a radical life change could have fallen for this guy. He had a certain charm.

"She told you about her husband?"

"He seemed like an okay dude. I think she felt bad for hurting him, but she had to get out of there since this other dude had started freaking her out."

"There was someone after her?" Nettie asked.

"He followed her home one day from town, she said. She saw him drive by the farm real slow and then come right back by. She said that if her husband hadn't come back on his tractor when he did..."

"She saw the man again?" Frank asked.

"He drove by the next day and later that night. Then one morning, he drove his van up in the yard. He must have thought that her husband was gone. But he wasn't. Anvil, right?" Frank nodded. "He went outside to see what the man wanted and the dude took off."

"Did she know who he was?" Frank asked.

Reiner shook his head. "She said she never got a good look at him. Just had a bad feeling, you know?"

"Why her, do you think?" Frank asked.

"Who knows how dudes like that pick their targets, but she was terrified of him."

Frank glanced at Nettie. He could tell that she was thinking the same thing he was. Why would the woman be that terrified of someone driving a van who'd possibly followed her home once and drove into the yard another time? He could understand concern. He could even understand fear. But terror? Not unless she had some other reason to fear the man behind the wheel of that van.

Which meant she knew him. And if he was the one who'd abducted her... Well, why else would he come looking for her in Wyoming unless there was more to the story? If that was even what had happened to Jenna. The woman seemed to have a habit of disappearing.

Flint took a shower at the sheriff's office and put on the clean uniform shirt and jeans that Mark had gotten him from his house. He'd been up all night, dozing only a little in the break room at the office. He felt wired, terrified one moment, and confident the next that they would find Maggie alive, and soon.

In the meantime, he knew that if he didn't work, he'd go crazy. While Mark canvassed the neighborhood, Flint was holding down the fort. He kept thinking that someone would call with news about Maggie. By now, word would have traveled around the county. Someone had to spot her.

Mark had called to say that Celeste hadn't turned up. Wayne hadn't heard from her, other than an email from a Paradise Valley spa confirming her reservation for last night. She hadn't shown, though. No one knew where she was, but Mark had a BOLO out on her, as well as Maggie. Someone was going to spot her as well, Flint told himself. They would find Maggie. Then Celeste would spend the rest of her years behind bars for abducting her.

He just prayed that Celeste wouldn't kill her. Mark had called earlier to tell him that it appeared Celeste had taken the gun her husband had purchased for her since it hadn't been found in the house. As hard as he tried to think about anything else, he could feel the clock ticking.

When he'd received the texted photo of Jenna from Frank, he felt sick. All this time, Jenna had been hiding out in Wyoming with a man? He wondered how Anvil would take this news—if he didn't already know. .

On his way out to the Holloway farm, Flint couldn't get the photo of Jenna and Kurt Reiner off his mind. Jenna was smiling in the snapshot. She looked so different from the photo her husband had given him back in March. For one thing, she'd bleached her hair blond and she was clearly wearing makeup. He hoped he wouldn't have to show this photo to Anvil. It was going to be hard enough on the man when he learned that his wife had been shacking up with a lover in Wyoming all this time. He didn't need to see how happy she looked.

He thought about the first time he'd driven out to the Holloway farm. Anvil had called him to say his wife was missing. He'd known little about the couple, since they stayed to themselves and seldom came into town.

He'd seen Jenna in passing in town when she'd made the trip in for groceries, but other than a nod to each other, they'd never even spoken. Jenna had seemed…painfully shy. Now, though, he wondered if he'd misread not only her, but also the entire situation.

It was clear now that Jenna had planned her escape from the farm. From her husband. From even the law. She'd done it systematically. Flint had changed his view of her since seeing the photo of her and Reiner. He realized he needed to know a whole lot more if there was any connection between Jenna's and Maggie's disappearances.

Thinking about Jenna kept his mind off the panic he felt when he thought of Maggie. He told himself that once Mark found Celeste… But he felt wired one minute and exhausted the next. He kept praying that Maggie was alive. That Mark would find her before it was too late.

While he tried to concentrate on doing his job, the thought of Maggie being missing hung at the back of his mind like a physical pain that never went away. When he thought of her, his heart would pound and he'd feel sick to his stomach. Not being part of the investigation was driving him crazy.

He knew he should be glad that there'd been a break in the Holloway case for the distraction. Otherwise he would be pacing the floor at the sheriff's department, waiting for word. Mark had promised to call the moment there was any news.

But he also knew that he was too involved in this one, even if the DCI didn't force him to take a leave of absence. As he pulled up in the yard, the front door of the house opened and Anvil appeared. Worry burrowed the farmer's brows. Anvil held a dish towel in one hand, a cup in the other.

There was a time when Flint would have thought the man was worried that Jenna's body had turned up and he was about to go to prison for murder. But Anvil didn't look worried. He merely looked mildly curious. From the beginning, the farmer had sworn that his wife had run off with another man. As it turned out, he'd been right.

Still, Flint doubted Anvil was ready for this news, he thought as he climbed out of the patrol car and started toward the porch steps.

"Sheriff?"

"I've got some news about Jenna." He pulled his coat around him to ward off the cold wind coming out of the snowcapped mountains. Low clouds hung over the peaks with the promise of a winter storm by noon. Christmas was only days away, and without a doubt, it was going to be white. Just the thought of Christmas without Maggie… He felt his stomach roil. "Mind if we step inside?"

Anvil shoved the door open and moved aside to let the sheriff enter. The first thing that struck him was how clean the house was. Anvil hadn't just cleaned up after the incident with his wife. He'd continued to do so. The house looked spotless. Flint had to wonder if it had ever been this clean when Jenna was taking care of it.

Also, Anvil looked more kept up. He seemed to be dressed better. There'd definitely been a change in the man. Some local women had noticed it after Jenna disappeared. The women were convinced that Anvil had done away with his wife and was looking for another one just because he started wearing jeans instead of overalls. At least the last half of that still might be true, Flint thought.

"Coffee?" Anvil asked as he put down the cup he was holding and moved to the sink to carefully fold the dish towel and hang it over a rack.

"Sure," Flint said, studying the man's back. The news he had was a double-edged sword. He feared it would draw blood from a man who had already been put through the mill over Jenna's first disappearance.

Not only had Anvil found out disturbing things about the woman he'd spent twenty-four years with, but also he'd lost her. The worse part was that most everyone in the county still believed that he'd killed her.

"When Jenna disappeared, what did she take with her?" Nettie asked in the Sheridan, Wyoming, café.

Reiner looked up at her in surprise. "You mean did she take her clothes and stuff?"

"Did she?"

"No." He looked insulted. "She was…abducted. I told you, the apartment was torn up as if she'd struggled. I was at work. I came home and she was gone."

"None of her things were missing?" Frank asked.

The man seemed to consider that. "Her purse was gone, some of the money I kept in the apartment for groceries. I figured that's where she was headed when whoever took her showed up at the apartment."

"How much money was missing?" Frank asked.

Reiner looked as if he didn't want to answer. "She took all that was in the drawer. Maybe a couple hundred. Maybe less." He looked sick. "You're thinking she bailed on me, but you're wrong. She wouldn't have done that. You don't know her like I do."

Frank wondered if her husband of more than twenty years

had told Flint the same thing when she'd disappeared back in March. He doubted either man had really known this woman.

"She ever talk about her past?"

"You mean like her husband?"

"More like old boyfriends before or after her husband," Nettie said.

Reiner seemed to think for a moment. "She mentioned growing up in some hellhole in North Dakota. Her parents were really strict. She said she never saw them touch each other. Seriously, not a hug, a kiss, even hold hands. She wondered how they'd conceived her."

"Where was this in North Dakota?" Frank asked.

"Some wide spot in the road." He frowned as if thinking. "Radville. That's right, because she said it was anything but rad. I thought that was pretty funny. She had that kind of sense of humor."

"Did she say why she left there?" Nettie asked.

He shrugged. "Who wouldn't? She might have said that her parents were glad to see her go. They didn't want her dating. I think they wanted her to become a nun. Not really, but you know what I mean." He laughed. "Jenna a nun? Jenna was the horniest woman I'd ever—" He stopped, his gaze going to Nettie. "Sorry."

"So she had a sexual appetite?" Nettie asked.

"Boy howdy. I got the feeling she hadn't had any in years, if you know what I mean."

Frank thought he did. "She like it kinky?"

Reiner colored and shot Nettie a look before turning back to him. "Seriously?"

"Nettie can handle it," he assured the man. "Jenna like it rough?"

Looking embarrassed, Reiner looked away and said, "I think it was all that pent-up stuff from first her parents and then that straitlaced old man she was married to."

Frank had to smile to himself. He'd called Anvil Holloway an old man and Holloway was nearly ten years Frank's junior. He saw that Nettie was amused since even at their ages there was nothing wrong with either of their own sexual appetites.

"What about friends?" Nettie asked. "Surely she had a friend back home that she kept in contact with."

"Dana," he said with a nod. "Apparently she didn't escape Radville. Jenna felt bad for her, talked about helping her out, you know?"

"Like sending her money?" Frank asked.

"She sent her some. I didn't mind." He looked defensive. "She didn't send much. Like I said, I didn't mind giving it to her."

"She call her?" Nettie asked.

He shrugged. "A few times. But I don't see what—"

"We're going to need Jenna's cell phone number."

"She didn't have one. She used mine."

"Then we are going to need it and your passcode," Frank said. "Sorry. We'll get it back to you as soon as we're done with it. I can give you money for a new phone."

Reiner looked as if he might leap up and make a run for it. But after a moment, he reached into his pocket, brought out the phone and laid it on the table with a gesture that said, "I have nothing to hide." Nettie wrote down the passcode, and turning on the cell, she keyed it in. Seeing that it worked, she pocketed the phone.

"Dana have a last name?" Frank asked.

Reiner shrugged. "I never heard it mentioned."

"What about friends since the two of you have been living here in Wyoming?" Nettie asked. "Friends from work maybe?"

He shook his head. "She didn't have a job. We thought it best, you know, under the circumstances."

"What did she do all day?" Frank asked.

"Hang. Watch TV. She cooked," he said, brightening. "She

was a great cook." He looked at his watch. "I really need to get to work."

"We'll keep in touch, but if you hear from her, call me," Frank said, sliding his business card and a hundred–dollar bill across the table. "You did good calling the sheriff. We'll find her."

Reiner looked like a man badly beaten with regrets. "Right."

"We'll mail your phone to your apartment address," Frank said to the man's retreating back and got a dismissive wave.

"A waste of postage," Nettie said. "You know he's taking off. Won't be hearing from him again." She brought up the photo of the man and Jenna on the cell phone.

Frank sighed. "I think we got all we could from him," he said, watching through the window as Reiner drove away in an old compact car, the back bumper covered with stickers.

The sky was a dull gray as they stepped out of the café and walked toward their SUV. The cold air smelled as if it might start snowing at any moment.

"We need to know more about Jenna," Nettie said as she climbed into the passenger side of the SUV.

"My thought exactly." Frank smiled over at her as he slid behind the wheel. They'd always had this wondrous connection. She smiled back. It still amazed him how much he loved this woman and had since he was a boy. He'd lost her to another man for a while, but getting her back was the smartest thing he'd ever done. She fulfilled him in every way. Having her as a partner in their investigative business was just the cherry on top.

So far their business was doing better than even he'd hoped. Which he thought proved it was never too late. Never too late for love, he thought, looking at Nettie. Never too late to take a chance on something you loved doing. And the two of them loved investigating. That was, he did. Nettie loved snooping into other people's business, he thought with a smile.

"Jenna knew who was after her," Nettie said after Frank called the Gilt Edge sheriff's cell, only to have to leave a message. "This man is someone from her past."

"Some bad history there. You think the man was blackmailing her?" Frank asked, looking over at her.

"Could explain the money she was taking from her grocery budget back in Montana. Might also explain the prison pen pals." She nodded. "Actually, I'm betting she was looking for someone to take care of the problem for her."

Frank chuckled. "Where would a woman go to get help with some man she said was terrorizing her? Prison. I like it."

"Instead she got the brother of one of the men and either decided to leave with him or really was abducted by the man from her past." Nettie chewed at her lower lip for a minute. "Doesn't explain the sexy undergarments or the shoplifted makeup unless… She could have thought that she was going to have to give her possibly ex-con hired killer something, and she didn't have much money, from what Flint has told us."

"You think she was looking for someone to *kill* the man after her?"

Nettie shrugged. "At least threaten him."

As he started the SUV, he chuckled. He loved the way Nettie thought. "That all makes a strange kind of female sense."

"Women are pretty practical thinkers. If we need something, we try to figure out how to get it. Womanly wiles are usually a last resort."

"Then I'd say Jenna was desperate, wouldn't you?"

"Definitely. It would explain why she took off with Reiner. It wouldn't have taken her long to figure out that he wasn't tough enough to take care of the man after her."

"So then what?" Frank said.

"Once she saw the old boyfriend, assuming that's who the man in the brown van is, she realized Reiner wasn't going to take care of the problem for her. So what would she do?"

"Run again."

"Or call his bluff. What do you think the old boyfriend wants?" Nettie asked thoughtfully. "It's got to be more than money."

"Love? Revenge?"

Nettie had wrinkled her nose at the first one. "I'm wondering how he found her in Wyoming when law enforcement couldn't find her even with a BOLO out on her."

"You're thinking she *contacted* him?"

"Or Kurt did. Jenna could have gotten the old boyfriend's number from her friend Dana. She calls it on Kurt's phone. He sees a number he doesn't recognize and calls it, giving away her location. Reiner's definitely feeling guilty about something. It's why he called Flint. But it could be because he didn't protect her. Or it could be because he got scared and didn't want to be involved in whatever happened next. I would love to have seen his face when he realized she'd taken all his money. If either of them called the old boyfriend, it could be on the phone—or at least the bill."

"That would be a stroke of luck, but let's remember we're just assuming this man is an old boyfriend," Frank said.

Nettie chuckled. "If Reiner saw a number on his phone he didn't recognize, called it and a man answered, I'd say that was what he would have assumed, as well."

"Think Reiner would have been angry enough to hurt her?" Frank asked.

Nettie shook her head. "I think he really cared about her. He's the kind of man who would take her back."

"Like the husband. Flint said Anvil had said he just wanted his wife back."

Nettie looked thoughtful as they drove out of town. "Makes you wonder who Jenna really is. Certainly not the woman her husband thought he married. Nor the one Reiner thought he was saving. I hope I get to meet this woman."

CHAPTER SIX

Anvil brought two cups over to the table and motioned for the sheriff to have a seat. As Flint pulled up a chair, he saw that the man's hands were shaking as he put down the cups of coffee. He was reminded that Anvil had said he would take his wife back if she was ever found, no matter what she'd done. He wondered if that was still true. *If* Jenna was found again.

Or if Jenna would go back to Anvil after everything that had happened between them—including him slapping her.

The farmer pulled up a chair. "Is she...?"

"She's been living in Wyoming."

Anvil looked up. "Wyoming?" He didn't seem that surprised to hear this news. But then, all along, he'd believed that she was alive after taking off to meet some man. Apparently, he'd been right. "Not very far away at all."

"I don't have all the facts yet, but my office was contacted by a man who said he'd been living with her since she disappeared from here in March."

"I see."

"The thing is, the reason the man contacted me was because Jenna has disappeared again," Flint said.

Anvil let out a soft breath of air that could have been a laugh. "So you don't know where she is?"

"No, but I sent a private investigator down there to find out what he can. I'll know more when he reports in. But under the circumstances, I have a positive ID, so I wanted to let you know."

He thought about the man in the brown van that Kurt Reiner had told him about. From Frank's message on the phone, he and Nettie were convinced that Jenna had known the man.

"Also, I was hoping to get more information on Jenna's past before you met and married. Did she ever talk about any old boyfriends?"

The farmer shook his head. "I knew nothing about her past." He cleared his throat and picked up his coffee cup to hold it in both of his big rough hands.

"I'm sorry, but I have to ask. How well did you know Jenna when you married her?"

Anvil stared down at the brew for what seemed like a full minute before he said, "Apparently not very well."

"What was her maiden name?" he asked, pulling out his notebook and pen.

"Roberts."

"She wasn't from here, right?"

Anvil shook his head. "She told me she grew up in a small town in North Dakota. Something-ville. I'd never heard of it."

Flint looked on his phone. "There's a Buttzville, but it says it's a ghost town."

Anvil shook his head.

"Radville?" It appeared to be the only other North Dakota town with *ville* on the end.

"That sounds right."

"So you don't know if she dated someone before she met you?"

The farmer met his gaze. "If you're asking if she was a virgin…" He quickly looked away. "There'd been at least one other man. Maybe more. I never wanted to know." He shook his head again.

"Does she have any family back there?"

"She said her parents died when she was young. She was raised by an old-maid aunt who died before she moved to Gilt Edge."

"Did she ever say what brought her here?"

Anvil took a sip of his coffee and Flint could see that he was stalling for time. He took a drink of his own coffee and waited.

"I… I…found her in one of those matchmaking newspapers you pick up at rest stops." The man kept his eyes downcast. His face was flushed and he seemed to be having trouble breathing. "If I'd known what I was getting into…" He finally looked up. "How I met my wife was something I thought I would take to my grave."

"I'm sorry," Flint said, meaning it. He wanted to say that there was nothing to be ashamed of for finding love that way. But whether or not it had been love on Jenna's part was doubtful. One of the last things she'd told Anvil before she'd walked out of this house was that she'd never loved him. He wondered, though, if she'd only told Anvil that so he wouldn't come looking for her.

"Did you happen to see anyone around town or your farm who drives a brown van?"

"A brown van?" The farmer frowned. "Not that I can recall. Is that what the man drives?"

Flint shook his head. "It's something else I'm working on."

Anvil rubbed a hand over his face. "How did she meet the man she's been with?"

"Like I said, I don't have all the facts yet. I'll let you know when I—"

"Don't bother," the farmer said, shoving back his chair and getting to his feet. "I've managed just fine without her. I'd just as soon keep it that way." He walked over to the sink and slumped over it, his back to Flint. "When you find her again, I just need to know where to send the divorce papers."

"If you hear from her—"

"I won't," Anvil said, and Flint let himself out. As he was headed for his patrol SUV, he saw that he had missed another call from Frank. Nothing, though, from Mark. He looked at his watch. Maggie had been missing for almost twenty hours. He felt as cold and bleak as the day. The sky had darkened with the storm. He felt the bite of the freezing day as the first few flakes began to fall. The winter snowstorm had hit. He couldn't bear to think that Maggie might be out in the storm, freezing cold and...

He shook off the panic that had him running scared. He needed to call Frank back but he hated to tie up the line. Maybe Mark had found out something about Maggie.

"I'm starving," Nettie said as Frank drove away from the café.

"We were just in a restaurant," her husband said with amusement.

"That was work, and anyway, I crave Mexican. I thought I saw a restaurant down that way." She pointed to the south.

"I just can't imagine what any of this has to do with Maggie Thompson," Frank said. "From the way Flint described her, a businesswoman, she doesn't have much in common with Jenna, let alone some man in a brown van."

"Flint said the brown van was a long shot. The two cases might not be connected, but I think we should chase down Jenna's friend Dana from back home. I'm betting her number will be on this phone."

Nettie took Reiner's phone out of her pocket, tapped in the passcode and touched Phone and then Recents. "What's the area code of North Dakota?" she asked. "I'm betting it's 701." She smiled as she put the phone to her ear and listened to it ring. Once. Twice. In the middle of the third ring, a woman answered.

"Jenna, oh God, I was so worried about you. When I didn't hear from you, I thought for sure that he'd found you and—" She stopped as if suddenly realizing that Jenna hadn't spoken, not one word. *"Jenna?"* A horrified sound came out of the woman's mouth. "Clark? Oh God. No." The call ended abruptly.

A chill raced up Nettie's spine, making her shiver.

"What?" Frank asked in concern.

"A woman answered." She repeated the woman's words verbatim. It was a gift from when she'd been the worst gossip in the county. She never got what she'd heard wrong, though.

"So if the woman who answered was Dana, she was worried about some man finding Jenna. A man named Clark?"

"Apparently so." She scrolled through the rest of the recent calls on the phone. "If Jenna called the man after her, possibly a man named Clark, she must have deleted it. All the other numbers are local." She looked up as Frank pulled into the parking lot of the Mexican restaurant and pocketed the phone.

Flint returned their call only minutes after they'd ordered. While Frank stepped out of the room to fill the sheriff in on what they'd found out, Nettie stayed and nibbled on the fried tortillas and salsa.

"Well?" she asked when her husband returned.

"No word on Maggie. He wants us to keep investigating."

It wasn't until they'd both devoured large plates of seafood enchiladas that Nettie said, "I've never wanted to go to Radville, North Dakota, more than I do right at this moment. I don't know what happened to Maggie Thompson, but Jenna Holloway is in trouble. If she's still alive."

"I wish I didn't agree."

She pushed her plate aside and pulled out her tablet. "I want to talk to her friend Dana. But first...how old is Jenna?"

"Forty-seven when she disappeared in March," Frank said.

"So what year would she have graduated from high school back in Radville?"

"About 1987," he said. "You think they went to school together?"

Nettie typed Class of 1987 Radville, North Dakota, and scrolled down until she found one marked Classmates 1987. She found the yearbook, clicked on Who's in the Book. The list was alphabetical by last name, but it didn't take her long since there weren't that many graduates. Nor was there many Danas or Jennas, for that matter.

Undersheriff Mark Ramirez rubbed a hand over his face and looked at the clock. The first twenty-four hours were critical in a possible abduction case. And that was what they were dealing with, wasn't it?

No one had seen Maggie—not since a neighbor waved at her from down the street twenty-two hours ago. That same neighbor when questioned again said she'd noticed the older-model brown van go by and thought she heard it slow as if to turn. She thought it could have turned into the sheriff's drive but she wasn't sure. She hadn't been paying attention.

Outside the window, snow whipped around in the wind to form drifts in the parking lot. There was still no word on Celeste Duma, either, but there was a BOLO out on her and the SUV she was driving.

As much as Mark hated to admit it, he was starting to agree with the sheriff that Celeste Duma might have had something to do with Maggie's abduction. Why else hadn't she at least called her husband to let him know where she was? Wayne Duma had left messages for her, but said all of his calls had been going straight to voice mail. Each hour, Celeste looked more guilty.

The state crime team had driven up from Billings and were now finishing up at Flint's house. The preliminary lab tests had come back on the blood found on the floor based on DNA samples from Maggie's house. Not that Mark hadn't suspected it would be her blood. There was just enough blood to know that Maggie was injured. So far, they weren't looking at this as a homicide.

As far as Mark knew, no other evidence had been found at the scene indicating that anyone else had been in the house—except the sheriff. It was his house, so that wasn't unusual.

"The sheriff and Maggie have had an off-and-on relationship," Harp had commented when he'd come in at the end of his shift. "Who's to say it didn't turn violent? She was going to move in with him before and changed her mind." He'd shrugged.

Mark had wanted to punch him, but that was nothing new. There was no love lost between Harp and Flint, so of course he would want the sheriff to be a suspect. "I heard you're getting married," he said, changing the subject.

That shut Harp up. "Guess so."

"Heard you have a baby on the way. Know if it's a boy or a girl yet?"

"Too early."

"Well, congrats."

"Sure." Harp put on his coat with a sigh. "Where is the sheriff, anyway? He could be out there burying her body right now."

"You should get home to your pregnant girlfriend," Mark said as Flint came through the door. Harp tipped his hat to the sheriff and went out, closing the door behind him.

"I hate to ask," Flint said.

"Just Harp being Harp." Unfortunately, he probably wasn't the only one in town questioning the sheriff's innocence. People liked to talk, and while Flint was liked, most people thought the worst when something like this happened.

Flint pulled off his Stetson and shook snow off his coat as he hung it up along with his hat. Through the window, he saw that the snow was coming down hard. This would make finding Maggie more difficult—and also more urgent if she was out in this storm. He silently prayed she was somewhere warm.

"Any word?" Flint asked hopefully.

"We're waiting for Celeste to check in at the spa in Paradise Valley. Apparently, she called this morning and changed her reservation to today because of the storm..." Paradise Valley down by Livingston was a good three-hour drive when the roads were bare. But Celeste had left yesterday. That meant there were already more than twenty-four hours that her whereabouts couldn't be accounted for.

Mark knew that the sheriff thought the spa reservation was merely a ruse and that the woman was wherever she'd taken Maggie. "Her cell phone is turned off, but that's probably because she doesn't want to talk to her husband. I left a message for her, telling her we need to talk to her immediately and that it was urgent."

Flint made a disparaging noise and met his gaze. "You're buying into this?"

"I put out a BOLO on her and the vehicle she's driving. That's all we can do right now. If she doesn't show up..." Mark cleared his voice. Right now they had three missing women: Maggie, Celeste and Jenna Holloway. "How did it go at Holloway's?"

It took Flint a moment. Mark could see that it was next to impossible for him to keep his mind off Maggie. "Anvil wasn't happy to hear that his wife had run away with another man and was now missing again. I did receive more information on Jenna for the PIs I hired."

Mark had been surprised that the sheriff had hired the PIs out of his own pocket. "You didn't think Sheridan, Wyoming, law enforcement could handle it?"

Flint met his gaze. "Normally I would turn it over to them, but if she was taken by a man driving a brown van..."

Mark rubbed a hand over his face again. He hated to see Flint chasing something as coincidental as a brown van. True, it was the small seemingly inconsequential things that often solved a case, but he felt that the sheriff was clutching at straws. Not that they had much else to go on.

"Celeste was never going to the spa," Flint said, sounding exhausted. "She's taken Maggie."

Mark said nothing because there was nothing he could say. Maybe Flint was right. Or maybe he was too close to this. They'd found no evidence at the Duma house that Maggie Thompson had ever been there.

"DCI still at my house?" Flint asked after a moment.

Mark nodded and considered how much to tell him. Flint was still sheriff. He was still in charge. But that could change at any moment. He was waiting for a call from DCI and he had a bad feeling what the news would be. "The blood was Maggie's. Not enough to fear that she was mortally wounded," he added quickly. "So far they haven't found any evidence of a third person at the scene."

"*Third* person?"

"Most of the prints are yours at the house."

Flint groaned and raked a hand through his hair as he dropped into a chair across from Mark's desk. "If you tell me that they think I'm a suspect—"

"You know how this goes. Of course they look at the boy-friend first."

"It's a waste of time."

"They're going to want to know where you were in the hour or so before you came home and found Maggie gone," Mark said.

Flint swore and looked away. "I already told the officer from DCI who called me. I had driven out to the ranch. My father saw something out there a few months ago. The military wouldn't say what was going on, but I found tracks. There'd been men around the missile silo wearing hazmat suits. I wanted to have a look around to make sure everything was okay. I don't have to tell you what my father thinks is going on out there."

"More problems with aliens?" Mark tried to lighten the conversation.

"He doesn't trust the government, either. He's convinced they're keeping something from us."

Mark laughed. "Imagine that." He sobered. "Did you see anyone out there?"

"No. So no, I don't have an alibi. I had turned off my phone. Truthfully, I figured if Celeste had found out that Maggie was moving in, she'd call, and I wasn't up for one of her tirades. When I turned my phone back on, there was the call from Maggie, so I came home. This is ridiculous and you know it."

"I do, but you also know it is going to look suspicious to DCI." His phone rang. He looked at Flint and then picked it up. "Ramirez." He listened, his stomach turning with regret as he did. "I'll let him know."

All the color had drained from Flint's face.

"It's not Maggie," he said quickly. "It was the DCI, though. They think it's best if you're off the case."

Flint got to his feet. "We're already short staffed. We can't afford to lose another lawman, especially right now with Mag-

gie missing and possibly out there in this snowstorm somewhere hurt and—"

"I agree. But you know I have to do this. I'll keep you informed. That's the best I can do and I shouldn't even be doing
that. Flint, we'll find her."

"But will you find her in time?"

"You need to get some rest. For the time being, you'll be
on paid leave. Where will you be staying? I'll get some clothing sent over there. Anything else you need?"

"I'll be at the ranch." The sheriff put his Stetson back on
his head and reached for his coat, looking like a broken man.
Mark's heart went out to him. He'd worked with Flint for
years. He admired the man, trusted him with his life. He
knew in his heart that Flint hadn't hurt Maggie. But with
these types of investigations, DCI called the shots.

And under the circumstances, he thought their call was the
right one. Better for Flint to step off this case.

"I'll be at the ranch with Hawk and Cyrus," Flint said,
his gaze locking with Mark's. "Call me if there is any news.
Any at all."

"You know I will."

Deputy Harper Cole took no small amount of pleasure
when he heard that the sheriff had been put on leave. He told
himself that the DCI wouldn't have done that unless they'd
found something at the crime scene that had made them suspicious.

"What if he's guilty as hell?" Harp had said to Vicki when
he got to her apartment after hearing about it from the night-
shift dispatcher. He still thought of this place as Vicki's apartment even though he lived there now. It had been Vicki's idea
for him to move in to save money. All she talked about now
was baby clothes and high chairs and cribs. It drove him crazy.

"Who's guilty as hell?" she asked distractedly.

"The sheriff. He's been put on a leave of absence. If he's the one who hurt his girlfriend…" Harp couldn't help smiling. "I could be sheriff sooner than I thought. I was going to run against him in the next election anyway, but this is perfect."

She turned to look at him, frowning. "What happened to his girlfriend?"

He shrugged. "No one knows. Right now all of law enforcement is looking for her—and Celeste Duma. The sheriff is convinced Celeste took her."

"Why would she do that?"

Sometimes this woman tried his patience to the point of breaking. "Because Celeste is the sheriff's ex-wife." Vicki still looked confused. "You're burning something on the stove."

She turned around and quickly pulled off the smoking skillet. He shook his head. Vicki was no cook. Nor was she much of a housekeeper now that she was pregnant. Hell, there seemed to be only one thing she was good at.

He got up from the kitchen table to press himself against her backside.

"Harp, I'm cooking."

"No, you're not. You're just burning stuff." He nibbled at the side of her neck. "Turn off the stove and let's go into the bedroom."

"I thought you were hungry?"

"I am and I think you know what I'm hungry for," he said, pressing himself harder against her.

She sighed and he thought fondly of the days when she wouldn't have hesitated. He cupped her breasts. There was more there now that she was pregnant. He tried not to think about that as he tweaked one nipple, then the other before he picked her up off her feet and carried her the few steps to the bedroom.

Vicki was built like a preteen and wasn't much heavier than one. He tossed her on the bed and began to undress.

"Just be more gentle this time, Harp. I don't want you hurting the baby."

The baby. He groaned as he ripped off his uniform shirt and dropped his jeans to the floor without taking off his boots. Grabbing her ankles, he pulled her to the edge of the bed. *Gentle, my ass.*

Flint was on his way to the ranch when he realized he hadn't eaten since breakfast. He saw that there were only a couple of cars parked out front of the Stagecoach Saloon that his sister and brother owned. He didn't feel like being social, so he parked on the side and entered the back door.

"Howdy, Sheriff," Billie Dee sang out when she saw him. "You're in luck. I've still got some shrimp gumbo left. Want me to make you a bowl?"

He smiled at the cook. Billie Dee was a large older Texan with one of those cheerful personalities that radiated out like rays of sunshine. "I'd love a bowl. Mind if I have it back here in the kitchen?"

"Not at all," she said. As she slid the bowl in front of him, he met her gaze and saw compassion. Clearly she'd heard about Maggie being missing. "Can I get you a beer with that? Or are you on duty?"

"I'm…off duty. So I'd love a beer, but I can go get it." He glanced toward the front of the building and the saloon. "My brother working?"

She waved him back into his chair. "Let me. You know those regulars. They'll want to talk your arm off and your gumbo will get cold. You just sit tight." She left and came right back with a cold beer.

"Thank you." It was more than thanks for the beer and they both knew it. He wasn't up to answering questions. He wasn't up to visiting at all.

"It was slow, so Darby sent Mariah upstairs to rest. We got

us some pregnant women runnin' around here," she said as she came back to the table with a small bowl of gumbo of her own and sat down. "All they talk about is babies." She laughed.

Flint took a bite of the gumbo. It was good and hot with both heat and spice. Billie Dee was determined to make Texans out of all of them. He listened while the cook told him about his sister and Mariah.

"They're not even showin' yet and they're busy buying maternity clothes. Sure not like anything I've ever seen," she said with a shake of her head. "I thought the idea was to hide that baby bump. Instead, these tops let it all hang out." She laughed again. It was a warm sound that seemed to fit the woman, the kitchen and the food. He hadn't realized how hungry he'd been until he saw that his bowl was empty.

"You want some more?" Billie Dee asked.

Flint shook his head. "Thank you so much for..." He couldn't finish for a moment, his throat closing. "...everything." He swallowed and picked up his beer to drain the glass.

"You're most welcome," she said, getting to her feet and taking their dishes. "You heading up to the ranch?" she asked, her back to him.

So she even knew that he would be staying with his brothers Hawk and Cyrus.

"Cyrus was in earlier," she said with a laugh. "Heard they were cleaning the house. They're all excited about having a guest."

"I'm hardly a guest."

She turned then to smile at him. "Take it as a compliment that they cleaned. Sounds like they're pleased to have you staying with them."

They were the only ones, he thought uncharitably. But it didn't surprise him that Billie Dee saw a silver lining in everything. He wondered about her past. He'd never heard her mention family or really ever want to talk about herself. How had she ended up in Gilt Edge?

He groaned inwardly. His brother Darby wasn't one for running a security check on his employees. That was how he'd lost money when he'd hired someone he'd thought was the perfect employee who had been ripping him off for months.

Flint figured that his brother and sister had lucked out hiring Billie Dee even though he suspected she'd just shown up one day and gotten hired on. He hated the lawman in him that made him not just curious, but suspicious. Often people who didn't talk about their past had something to hide. The thought reminded him of Jenna Holloway.

"That was the best gumbo I've ever had," he said to Billie Dee now, telling himself he had more to worry about right now than his brother's hires.

The cook laughed. "I'm bettin' that's the first shrimp gumbo you've ever had."

"And you'd win that one," he said, smiling at her. Montana was known for its beef. He'd grown up on it and venison. It was a meat-and-potatoes kind of place, especially in rural areas like Gilt Edge.

"Come back if Hawk and Cyrus's cookin' is what I suspect it is goin' to be," she said. "I'll keep a little somethin' hot for you if you don't mind listenin' to me go on."

He felt a little guilty for even suspecting that Billie Dee had a past that might be worrisome as he thanked her again and left. His thoughts quickly boomeranged back to Maggie and that sick ache in his gut as he drove toward the ranch. *Where are you?* And where the hell was Celeste?

CHAPTER SEVEN

The ranch house was big and rambling. Flint hadn't spent much time there since he bought his house in town right after the law-enforcement academy and getting hired on as a deputy.

But as he parked and got out, he looked up at the three-story house with its huge deck off one side and felt the memory of his idyllic childhood warm him. He'd loved growing up here on the ranch. Also, he had ranching in his blood. Maybe that was why his father could never understand why he'd left it behind to become a "cop."

The front door of the house swung open. "Hey!" Cyrus called down to him. "We were just about to throw some steaks on the grill. Come on up."

Flint took the steps, feeling as if weights had been tied to his legs. Exhaustion pulled at him. For hours he'd been wired, waiting to hear of any news about Maggie. Worry had worn him down. Suddenly just picking up one foot after the other seemed too much for him.

Cyrus had left the door open. He closed it behind him and

followed the smell of potatoes baking in the oven to the back of the house and the large country kitchen. His brother Hawk was sitting at the island. Cyrus had on an oven mitt and was reaching in to see if the potatoes were done.

Neither brother looked like they knew what to say or do. When he'd called to ask if he could stay at the ranch, he'd had to tell Hawk that he'd been put on paid leave because Maggie had disappeared and foul play was suspected. He'd said he didn't want to talk about it and Hawk had simply said, *Come on up to the house. We'll have a room ready for you.*

He'd appreciated that. Neither brother was a big talker. They both spent most of their time on the back of a horse, chasing cattle or mending fences. So he could tell that they didn't know what to say to him now.

"Quite the domestic scene here," Flint said to break the pained silence. "This how it looks every night?"

Hawk laughed. "Cyrus is showing off for you. We don't have guests much. Not that you're a guest..." He looked to his brother to bail him out.

"I make a mean steak, no matter what Hawk says. If I left the cooking up to him we'd be having boxed macaroni and cheese."

Flint smiled at the two of them and felt such a surge of love for them that his eyes burned with tears. "I had a bite at the saloon. If you two don't mind, I just need to get some rest. Which room—"

"Top of the stairs," Cyrus said, closing the oven and taking off the mitt. "We made up your old room. If you need anything..."

He shook his head and headed for the stairs, thankful that his brothers had the good sense not to quiz him right now. All he wanted was to get to his room and pass out. But even as he thought it, he knew he wouldn't be able to sleep.

Where was Maggie? It was the thought that drilled into his skull. Somewhere out in this snowstorm? Cold, hurt, dying?

As sheriff, he was the one expected to save people. He felt as if he'd let Maggie down. She'd told him that she was afraid of Celeste and he'd kept saying he didn't think she was really dangerous.

Now he wanted to kick himself. He should have protected her. It was his job. He should have asked her to marry him a long time ago. There was so much he should have done—and didn't.

Flint tossed his coat on the bed and moved to the window. Looking out at the falling snow, he thought about the first time he'd seen Maggie. He'd been driving down Main Street when she'd caught his eye. She was walking down the sidewalk on a bright spring day, her head high, her face turned up to the sun, her long chestnut hair pulled into a ponytail that bobbed as she walked. She was smiling.

Yes, it was the smile, the joy in it, the feeling it gave him just seeing her.

But he'd been in the middle of a divorce after Celeste had torn his heart out. He'd looked away, but he'd never forgotten that moment or that woman.

It was weeks later that he'd found out her name was Maggie Thompson and that she'd opened a beauty shop in town.

That was all he'd known about her—and he hadn't learned much more in the time they'd been dating, he realized with a start. He told himself that he'd respected her privacy about her past, but now he regretted not asking. He couldn't help but think of Anvil. Like the farmer, had he not asked because he was afraid of what he would have learned?

Flint almost laughed at the absurdity. His past wasn't just known all over town—it had been walking around in expensive heels, still making his life miserable. How much worse could Maggie's past be?

Just the thought of Celeste made him ball his hands into fists. He'd been so sure that she wasn't truly dangerous. That she wouldn't hurt Maggie—just torment her. He'd been wrong and now it was Maggie who would have to pay the price.

That was the thought that stayed with him as he stepped to the bed and sat down. Exhaustion pulled at him. He told himself he'd never be able to sleep as he lay back, too tired to even take off his boots. Celeste had Maggie and as sheriff it was his job to get her back.

Only he wasn't sheriff. Worse, he feared he couldn't get her back.

Maggie woke with a start as she felt something close touch her temple. She tried to shove it away only to find her wrists were bound on each side of her, as were her legs when she tried to move.

Her eyes flew open. She was immediately blinded by a bright light, but she sensed someone was leaning over her. Panic seized her as she tried to pull free of the restraint. *Where am I? What happened?*

She must have voiced the words because she heard a soft chuckle a moment before she felt the needle prick her arm. The room smelled musty and damp. She shivered as she fought to make sense out of what was happening to her, but her brain felt too foggy and slow.

Digging into her memory, she found the last thing she remembered was being in Flint's house and realizing she wasn't alone. Her heart began to pound and she fought her restraints.

She pried her eyes open, trying to see beyond the bright light even as she felt the drug make her eyelids droop. Through the slits she saw shadows that seemed to waver.

Her eyelids drooped and she was pitched again into darkness.

Mark got the call from the spa the next morning. He had every law-enforcement agency across the country on the lookout for Maggie, but he'd heard nothing. Nor had Celeste shown up at the spa last night before he'd finally given up and gone home to bed. He'd left word for the manager at the spa to call him first thing in the morning.

Now as he picked up, he told himself that the news wasn't going to be good. It wasn't.

"I'm sorry, but Mrs. Duma called and left a message. She said she wasn't going to be able to make her appointment with us." He'd learned earlier that she'd ordered the three-day treatment that included everything from seaweed wraps to hot rock massages.

Mark swore silently. Flint had been convinced that Celeste was behind this. Mark had been skeptical. Given the bad blood between the two women, he couldn't see how it would have gone down. Maggie wouldn't have gotten into a vehicle with Flint's ex and Celeste wasn't strong enough to put an unconscious Maggie into her car and abduct her. Unless she'd had help.

That seemed even more far-fetched. Celeste behaved as an upstanding citizen in Gilt Edge—most of the time. It wasn't like she hung out with friends who would help her abduct her ex's girlfriend.

"Did Mrs. Duma say why she was canceling or where she was calling from?" he asked now.

"She said because of the snowstorm. Apparently she'd tried to get down here but had to get a motel, unable to drive any farther yesterday. She didn't say where she was calling from. I got the impression she was heading back home as soon as the roads were passable."

"If you should hear from her again, please give me a call," Mark told the woman. He hung up, then picked up the phone again and called Wayne Duma.

"I just heard from the spa in Paradise Valley—" He'd barely gotten the words out when Duma interrupted him.

"Celeste just walked in the door. I was going to call you."

Mark groaned to himself. Duma wasn't going to call until he'd quizzed his wife. "I'll send a deputy—"

"That won't be necessary. We'll come down to the sheriff's office."

The sound of his cell phone ringing dragged Flint up out of a dark hole filled with hellish nightmares. He sat up, disoriented and heart pounding with a fear he couldn't explain. It took him a moment to realize he was in his old bedroom. It looked so much like it had before he'd moved out that for a moment he was transported back in time. It was as if the past twenty years hadn't happened.

Then he remembered. Maggie was still missing.

His cell phone rang again. He swung his legs out of bed and, rubbing his face to chase away sleep, reached for his phone where he'd left it on his childhood desk the night before. "Sheriff Cahill," he said into it, his voice froggy. He cleared his throat as memory returned. He was on a paid leave of absence. "Hello?"

"Flint," said a familiar male voice.

He almost groaned. What the hell was Deputy Harper Cole doing calling him at this hour? If there was any news, Mark would be calling.

"Harp, this better be good."

"I thought you'd want to know," the deputy said in a conspiratorial hushed tone. "Celeste Duma is back in town and on her way down to the sheriff's office."

All remnants of sleep were gone. Flint got to his feet and looked around for his coat. "Do you know where she's been?"

"No, but Mark is setting up the interrogation room right now. I guess he didn't call you. I would imagine you can't sit in on this but I still thought you should know."

It was so like Harp to suck up at a time like this. "Thanks."

He disconnected and reached for his coat. At the back of his mind, a voice was warning him not to do this. If he went down there and busted in...

But he knew Celeste. He would be able to tell if she was lying when no one else could. He had to look into the woman's face and know the truth. A knot formed in his chest, making it hard to breathe. He would know if she'd hurt Maggie, if she'd done something with her.

And then... He didn't want to think about what he might do if she tried to lie her way out of this. Or if she refused to tell him where Maggie was and what she'd done with her. Or if she'd killed Maggie.

He ran a hand through his hair as he headed for the door. It had been almost forty hours since anyone had seen Maggie. Celeste would tell him the truth if he had to shake it out of her.

CHAPTER EIGHT

Flint went in the back way of the sheriff's department. On the drive in, he'd told himself to keep his cool. But just the thought of seeing Celeste and knowing what she'd done...

"Stay calm," he reminded himself as he walked down to the interrogation room and stopped short to duck into the viewing room. He could see Mark sitting down with Celeste and her husband. Wayne looked as if he hadn't gotten any sleep. Celeste had put on her face before coming down. Just knowing that she'd taken the time to apply makeup when Maggie was missing made his blood boil.

He turned on the speaker so he could hear what was being said.

"I'm telling you I didn't have anything to do with this woman's disappearance," Celeste said indignantly.

Mark said, "But you saw her at the grocery store the day she disappeared."

"Did I? I suppose so. I saw a lot of people."

"Maggie told you that she and Flint were moving in together," the undersheriff informed her.

Celeste raised an eyebrow. "Why would she bother to share something like that with me? I couldn't care less." Beside her Wayne groaned. "Fine, but she didn't *tell* me. I overheard her on the phone with Flint."

"Where did you go after you left the grocery store?"

"I took my groceries home and put them away and then packed for the spa."

Mark shot a look at Wayne, who had his head down. "Your husband said you called him upset."

Celeste didn't look over at Wayne. "I'm sure he's exaggerating. I was probably just harried because I'd checked the weather and wasn't sure I could reach the spa before the storm hit."

Flint saw Wayne close his eyes.

"Harried?" Mark asked. "Is that how you explain the condition of your bedroom before you left?"

"I told you," she said with infinite patience, "I was in a hurry."

"But not so much of a hurry that you didn't drive by your ex-husband's house."

The large dark SUV that Alma Ellison had seen. He fisted his hands, his breathing coming faster. If she lied...

"That's not on your way out of town," Mark pointed out. "In fact, it's out of your way."

Celeste took her time answering. "You have no proof that I drove by his house."

"Actually, we have an eyewitness who saw you heading down the street toward the house where Maggie disappeared from shortly after that." It was a bluff.

"It's my word against your eyewitness's," Celeste said, lifting her chin in defiance.

"In an assault, abduction and possible murder case, I suspect the eyewitness will be enough to send you to prison," Mark said.

"I told you—"

"Let me break it down for you. Maggie has disappeared. We know she was bleeding at the house. If you know where she is, you need to tell us what happened." Celeste tried to interrupt, but Mark kept talking over the top of her. "Here's what I suspect happened. You got into a fight. It turned violent. You panicked. Then what did you do with her? Promise to take her to the hospital? But where did you take her instead? If you let her die, it's murder. So tell me, where is Maggie? The clock is ticking, Celeste. You don't want to spend the rest of your life in prison."

"How many times do I have to tell you?" she screamed as she got to her feet. "I didn't do anything to the woman. Yes, I drove past the house. I don't know why I did, all right? I just did and then I left town. *Alone.* I drove toward Paradise Valley, but the roads got too bad. I pulled over at the first motel I found. You aren't going to pin this on me. I know my rights. I want a lawyer."

Flint couldn't take any more. Celeste was lying through her teeth. He stalked out of the viewing room and burst into the interrogation. His ex-wife's eyes widened in alarm when she saw him. She backed up as he stalked toward her until she collided with the wall.

All that warning himself to be calm did no good. He rushed to her, demanding, "Where is Maggie? What did you do to her, you crazy—"

The rest was a blur. He heard the scrape of Mark's chair as he clamored to his feet over Celeste's scream. All the months of Celeste's tormenting Maggie and doing everything possible to keep them apart came out in a flash of fury.

"You're going to tell me the truth before it's too late!" He grabbed her by the throat and squeezed.

He felt strong hands on him, dragging him back. He could hear Mark telling him to stop. All the years he'd been a lawman, he'd never lost control. It irritated the hell out of his siblings because he was the one who stayed calm no matter what.

Several more hands were on him. Mark had him in a headlock and someone broke his hold on his ex-wife.

"If you hurt Maggie, so help me, I'll... I'll kill you," Flint yelled as the two deputies pulled him off her.

Celeste leaned back against the wall, her eyes wide with fear as she touched her throat where Flint's hands had been only moments before. She was gasping for breath.

"You really do hate me, don't you." She was the only one in the room who sounded calm.

"Get him out of here," Mark said to the other deputy, who quickly ushered him out of the room. He heard Mark say, "Let's all take it easy."

"I want a restraining order against that man," Celeste said, sounding not just calm now, but pleased. "And I want assault charges filed against him," he heard her say before the door closed behind him.

Mark sighed as the door closed behind the deputy and Flint. How had the sheriff known he was interrogating Celeste? Harp, he thought with a curse. He'd been there this morning when Celeste and her husband came in.

"Let's sit back down," he said, worried what was about to happen now.

Celeste looked over at her husband. Wayne hadn't moved during all that. Nor had he said a word. He still had his head down as if studying the top of the interrogation table. "Wayne? Do you hear me? I want Flint fired." She began to cry as she touched her throat. "I want him thrown in jail. I want him..." She glared at Mark. "I want him behind bars. I don't feel...safe."

"I don't condone the sheriff's behavior," the undersheriff said. "But given the earlier stunts you pulled on Flint, I can understand his frustration. He believes you're lying. He believes you have harmed Maggie. He believes you are willing to let her die rather than tell the truth."

Celeste's gaze was tear-free and ice-cold when she settled it on him. "I wish I *had* taken her. I wouldn't have brought her back. It would serve him right."

Wayne lifted his head to look over at her, his expression filled with horror.

As if realizing how damning her words were, Celeste quickly began to cry. Through her sobs, she swore she hadn't taken Maggie.

"This isn't the first time you've threatened Maggie," Mark said. "I believe the words you wrote on the mirror at the beauty shop were 'Die Bitch.' If you had anything to do with Maggie being injured at her house and disappearing, we need to find out before it's too late. If Maggie is found alive before anything else happens to her, things will go much easier on you."

"I told you I don't know anything about the beauty-shop break-in or Maggie disappearing," Celeste said through her tears. "Just because I didn't want Flint getting tied down with that…woman—"

"Celeste," Duma snapped, raising his head again to glare at her. "For God's sake, if you did something to this poor woman—"

Mark could see that they weren't getting anywhere. He didn't have enough to lock Celeste up. Better to keep a tail on her. Maybe she would lead them to Maggie. Or, given the obvious feelings she had for the woman, maybe not. Wherever Maggie was, if Celeste had left her there, he didn't think she'd be going back for her.

"Since you have nothing to hide, you won't mind if we inspect your vehicle," Mark said. "We'll be able to tell how many miles you went since Maggie disappeared and even possibly where you went."

"You'll need to get a warrant," Celeste snapped as she dug in her purse for a tissue.

"You won't need a warrant," Wayne said with a sigh. "The vehicle is in my name. You have my permission to keep it as long as you like. I just had it serviced before Celeste took it, so you should be able to get the information you need easily enough. Also, we have the navigation service. I'll make sure they work with you."

Celeste's eyes flared with anger as Wayne rose to his feet. "I mean what I said," she snapped, turning back to Mark. "I want Flint arrested for attacking me."

"I didn't see anyone attack you," Wayne said, making both Mark and Celeste turn to look at him. "I think you're lying again."

"What?" she demanded, clearly in shock. "He just had to be pulled off of me. You were sitting right here. You saw what happened. You witnessed it."

Wayne smiled. "But it's your word against mine, Celeste."

Her gaze shot to Mark. "You had to have him pulled off me."

He said nothing, waiting to see how this played out.

She clamped her jaw tight, eyes narrowing. "I see what the two of you are doing." Her face was a mask of anger. "I might have driven by his house, but I didn't touch a hair on that bitch's head. However, I do have bruises on my neck that prove that Flint tried to kill me."

"How do we know it wasn't like last time when you hurt yourself to make it look like I abused you?" Wayne asked, his voice deadly low.

All the color drained from Celeste's face.

"I guess we're done here for now, then," Mark said, getting to his feet. "But I have to ask you not to leave town, Mrs. Duma."

She shot him a withering look. "How could I since you'll have my SUV?" Celeste looked indignant as she met his gaze. "Everyone always wants to blame me. But you have to believe me. This time, I didn't do *anything.*"

"This time," Duma said with a groan. He looked at Mark. "I can't let her talk to you again without a lawyer present," he said almost apologetically to the undersheriff. Without looking at Celeste, he started for the door.

"I didn't do anything," Celeste said, practically stomping her feet in frustration.

"If you can't tell the truth, then just keep your mouth shut," Wayne said.

Mark saw her appalled face. There would be hell to pay when Celeste and Wayne got home. He hoped he didn't get another domestic dispute call from that house tonight.

"This isn't over," she snapped and stormed out after her husband.

Flint had his head in his hands and a deputy at the door to keep him from leaving his own office. He couldn't believe what he'd done. What scared him most was that he would do it again if he got the chance. Celeste was lying. He knew it gut deep.

But still, he shouldn't have burst in there. He shouldn't have grabbed her. All the years of problems with her had surfaced in the perfect storm. He'd never put his hands on a woman like that, never thought he ever would. That Celeste had pushed him to that point terrified him. What if the lawmen hadn't been there to pull him off her?

His cell phone rang. He checked it, not interested in talking to anyone but Maggie. But when he saw it was Frank calling, he took it.

"I wanted to update you on what we've gotten so far," the PI said.

He only half listened, even more convinced that some man in a brown van hadn't taken Maggie. He realized that he'd missed something. "Wait—did you just say you're on your way to Radville, North Dakota?"

"Nettie has her heart set on it," Frank joked. "We want to talk to Jenna's friend. Don't worry—this is on the house. We think this Clark person might be the man in the brown van. Reiner said the plates on the van weren't Wyoming or Montana. We're thinking they could have been North Dakota. I know it's a stretch."

"No, that's good. But I'm still paying." He heard Mark coming down the hallway. "I have to go. Let me know where you're staying in Radville. If you can't reach me, call my brother Hawk. I might be in jail for a while." He disconnected as the undersheriff came into the room. "I'm sorry," Flint said, lifting his head when he heard Mark walk into the room. "I lost it. I couldn't help it. I'm sure they're filing charges. I just hope I can make bail."

Mark walked around to his desk and sat down. He motioned for the deputy to leave them alone. "No one is filing charges."

Flint looked up at him in surprise from the chair where he sat.

"I'm as surprised as you are that you won't be spending Christmas behind bars. That is where you should be."

"I don't know what possessed me."

"Sure you do," Mark said, leaning back in his chair. "I wanted to shake the truth out of her too. You've had years of her lies."

That surprised him. If anyone was by the book, it was his undersheriff.

"Celeste wanted you sent straight to prison, but her husband defended you. He said he didn't see anything."

Flint blinked. "Why would he do that?"

"From what I gathered, he still might have some resentment toward her after she called 9-1-1 and said her husband had hit her."

He nodded. "Then later she just happened to remember that Wayne wasn't even in the house and that she must have fallen down."

"You think she purposely injured herself to try to…frame him?"

Flint sighed. "We're talking about Celeste. She will do whatever it takes to get what she wants. I shouldn't have lost it with her, but she's the most lying, conniving woman I've ever met. I wouldn't put anything past her."

"Including attacking and abducting Maggie."

He nodded, feeling the weight of his building grief. "It's been too long. If Maggie's injured…"

"We're following every lead. I'm hoping Celeste's car will give us some idea of where she went."

"You have an eyewitness who saw her in my neighborhood right before Maggie disappeared. Maybe if you arrested her…"

Mark shook his head. "If she took Maggie, she might lead us to her. Also, Alma remembered that the woman driving was blonde and ID'd Celeste. But she's admitted driving past. Unfortunately, Alma can't swear that Celeste pulled in at your house. She did slow down, though, before Alma lost sight of her behind the trees."

Flint swore, knowing he was right. He was glad that Mark was in charge of the investigation. "I'm not thinking clearly. Of course you're right."

"That's why I'm tempted to lock you up for your own good," his undersheriff said. "Another stunt like you just pulled and—"

"I know. I would do the same thing if it was you. I keep thinking about Anvil Holloway when his wife disappeared.

I never appreciated what he'd been going through. All those months..." He shook his head. "You have my cell number if—"

"If we get any word of Maggie, you know I'll call. But, Flint, if you go near Celeste—"

He nodded. "I won't. I can't. I honestly am not sure what I would do if I found out that she has Maggie."

"That is not what I wanted to hear," Mark said.

CHAPTER NINE

Maggie woke as if from a bad dream. She felt sticky with per-
spiration and sick to her stomach. She fought to open her eyes
against the lethargy that made her body feel made of clay.

Her mind felt as thick as her tongue. She licked parched
lips and tried to swallow. So thirsty. That was the thought
that pulled her to the surface.

Her eyes came half-open to reveal what appeared to be ver-
tical metal bars. She was in jail? She closed them again as she
struggled to wake up and make sense of what she was seeing.

A memory of being tied down made her pulse jump. She
blinked, recalling the bright light in her face and someone
putting something on her temple.

Her hand went to her temple. She felt a bandage. Her eyes
flew open as she realized she was no longer bound—but she
was still a prisoner. She was surrounded by thick metal bars.

She struggled to sit up, but felt too weak. Her gaze focused
on the twin bed under her and then the bars around the twin-
bed mattress. There appeared to be a way for the bars to be
lowered on one side like a baby's crib, but as she sat up, she

saw that the latch was out of her reach. She glanced upward, looking for a way to escape, only to see that there were also bars across the top.

Her brain finally kicked in. She was in a cage!

As panic coursed through her veins, igniting her pulse, she grabbed one of the bars and pulled herself to her feet. The bars felt achingly cold in her hands. The cage had been made out of old bed frames bound together. Gripping them tightly, she shook the outside of the cage. It had only minimal give, rattling just a little. It felt too solid. She wasn't getting out of there unless someone unlocked it.

How did I get here? Where am I? Who put me in here? Why?

Her mind whirled as she took in what appeared to be a normal little girl's bedroom—except for this giant bed cage on one side of it.

"Help!" she screamed. "Help! Someone help me!" She screamed until her throat hurt and she was too hoarse to scream anymore.

There either wasn't anyone out there or maybe they couldn't hear her. The thought terrified her. Someone had left her to starve? Now more than ever she needed something to drink. As she thought it, she saw the water bottle at the end of the bed. She dropped down and grabbed it. There was only a swallow in the bottom of it. Had she drunk the rest? Or was this all she was getting maybe ever?

She thought she should save a little of it, but as she lifted it to her lips, she couldn't stop herself. She drank it all down and wished for more. That was when she saw the plastic urinal tucked in the end of the bed.

What else had she missed? She quickly dug, hoping for something to eat, but found nothing else. Angrily, she threw the empty bottle toward the bedroom door and thought about hurling the urinal as well, but stopped herself.

Exhaustion and remnants of the drug pulled at her. Her

gaze went to the sheets. She blinked as she saw the design. With a frown, she noticed that the comforter matched.

When she was little all she'd wanted was a Cabbage Patch doll. For three Christmases she'd asked Santa for one, but she'd never gotten one. That was when she'd realized that there was no Santa. At least not for her, a girl whose mother had died in childbirth and who was now being raised by an elderly aunt.

The message had seemed to be that if she wanted something, she would have to get it herself.

That hadn't worked out well, either. She'd taken a neighbor girl's doll. Her aunt had made her feel like a criminal. After that, she often saw her aunt watching her, expecting the worst.

Since then she'd had to fight for everything, even her own survival at times, and the weight of that unfairness had never been worse than it was at this moment. She stared down at the sheets, realizing that she hadn't even known as a child that they made Cabbage Patch sheets. Not that her aunt would have ever bought her something so frivolous.

Suddenly tears blurred her eyes as Maggie thought of how much she'd missed out on that had nothing to do with dolls or sheets or anything that could have been bought. She was the girl without a mother—or a father, for that matter. An oddity that even her aunt had trouble loving. And now her one chance to be loved, to find happiness with Flint, had been snatched away from her. All the fight going out of her, she lay down on the bed and sobbed.

Harp smiled to himself as he drove away from the office. His plan couldn't have gone better. He'd known Flint would go down to the sheriff's office and make a fuss. What he hadn't expected was for the man to completely lose it.

Laughing, he recalled how shocked everyone had been. Like him, they must have thought Flint had a heart of stone.

Instead, it turned out that the man had more than a little passion in him. If Mark and the other deputy hadn't pulled him off his ex-wife, Flint would be behind bars for murder.

As it was, somehow he'd skated. Why hadn't charges been filed against him? Those Cahills, he thought with disgust.

But he was in too good of a mood to think about them and how Lady Luck seemed to smile on them. Well, most of the time. He reminded himself that Flint's girlfriend was gone, maybe even dead. There was that.

He preferred to think about the scene Flint had made. It would get around town, and when the next election rolled around—if Flint held it together that long—Harp the Hero had a good chance of being the next sheriff.

His smile widened as he considered what he could do to make his chances better. With a groan, he realized there was something he'd been putting off. The county might be more apt to vote for a married man with a family. He nodded to himself at the thought. It was time to marry Vicki before the baby came.

He imagined her surprise when he told her she needed to start planning their wedding. She'd been acting...weird lately. He'd just thought it was the pregnancy.

But what if it was something more? He cursed under his breath as he recalled baring his soul to her at the hospital. What had he been thinking? Now she had him over a barrel for life. Unless... He frowned. Was it possible she didn't want him anymore? Didn't want him to be the father of her baby?

Panic whirled through him for a few moments before he laughed and glanced at himself in the rearview mirror. He was Harper Cole, one of the most eligible bachelors in town, and once he was sheriff...

He laughed again at his own foolishness. Vicki was a former waitress and not even a good one. She couldn't do any better than him. She had to know that. And if she didn't, then maybe it was time he reminded her.

Undersheriff Mark Ramirez studied the information obtained from Celeste Duma's vehicle. Her husband had said he'd had the car serviced the day before she'd left town allegedly to go to a spa in Paradise Valley.

He checked the mileage on the car the day it was serviced, then the mileage now. Celeste had driven over seven hundred miles. It took him only a minute to check the mileage from Gilt Edge to the Paradise Valley spa. Only three hundred and eighty miles round-trip—and Celeste had said she'd never reached it, but had stopped on the way and stayed in a motel.

So how did she explain the more than three hundred extra miles on her car?

She'd lied about where she'd gone.

Mark swore. No wonder Flint had lost control and tried to choke it out of the woman. Celeste had been lying—just as the sheriff had said. But did her lie have something to do with Maggie Thompson's disappearance? That was the question he needed answered.

He picked up the phone and called the Duma house. Wayne answered. "We've checked the mileage on the car. Unfortunately, the navigation system had been turned off. But it appears that Mrs. Duma didn't go where she said she did. I'm going to need to talk to her again."

He heard Wayne swear before he said, "I see."

"I'd like her to come back down to the sheriff's department."

"And if she refuses?"

"Given the other things we know she's done to Maggie, I'll ask Judge McDonald to sign a warrant for her arrest."

Flint felt lost as he stopped at the saloon. He'd been driving around for hours, checking every old barn, every old build-

ing, every place he'd ever been with Celeste that might make
a good place to hide a person—or a body.

His work was such a part of him that without it, he didn't
know what to do with himself. Everywhere he looked, he
saw Christmas decorations. Not that many hours ago he'd
been planning his and Maggie's first Christmas together as
an engaged couple.

As time passed with no word of her, he couldn't bear the
thought of the holidays without her. He'd been raised to pull
up his boots and tackle whatever life threw at him. Celeste
had done her best to destroy him, but he'd survived her and
thought that he could withstand just about anything after that.

But this... He considered meeting Frank and Nettie in
North Dakota. Not that they needed him. They'd found Jenna
Holloway's best childhood friend. Now he just had to wait
and see what they learned. Anyway, he was on paid leave. He
wasn't supposed to be working *any* cases.

The waiting, though, was killing him. He felt as if he was
coming apart at the seams. And the one thing he couldn't
do was go near Celeste. He'd gotten off easy the last time.
He wouldn't count on it again and he would be of no use to
Maggie behind bars. But he was of no use to her right now.

"You look terrible," his sister, Lillie, said when he walked in.

"Thanks."

"Seriously, is there anything we can do?" his brother Darby
asked. Hawk and Cyrus had made the same offer.

He shook his head as he pulled up a stool at the bar. "Thanks,
really, but there is nothing any of us can do. Mark is doing everything he can to find Maggie. All we can do is wait."

Lillie sat down beside him and put her arm around him.
"We're going to find her."

He nodded, not sure he believed that. Too much time had
passed.

"You want a beer or something stronger?" Darby asked.

"Just a cola."

"What about something to eat? I'm sure Billie Dee—"

"Thanks, Lillie, but I'm not hungry." Silence filled the saloon. He looked around, surprised the place was empty. He hadn't even noticed when he'd walked in. "Where is everyone?"

"Probably Christmas shopping," Darby said. "It will pick up later."

"I'm worried about Maggie, but I'm just as worried about you," his sister said. She exchanged a look with her twin brother. "We heard what happened at the sheriff's department."

He'd known word would travel fast, especially if Harp had anything to do with it. "I lost control. It's not like me."

"No kidding," Lillie said.

"Who could blame you under the circumstances," Darby said. "You really think Celeste took Maggie?"

"I know she's lying about something. Maybe the answer will be in her car. If she took Maggie somewhere, we might be able to find her before it's too late."

"What do you mean, *if* Celeste took her?" Lillie asked. "Of course she did. Look at all the other things she's done to her."

"There is no proof that she did any of those things," Flint said with a sigh. "She's been careful so far and made sure she didn't leave behind any evidence. Maybe we'll get lucky. Maybe she slipped up this time."

"I have to go," Lillie said as her phone buzzed. "Doctor appointment." She patted her stomach. "Please take care of yourself," she said and hugged him so tightly that he thought he might burst into tears.

And all this time, he'd thought he was holding up so well.

"Lillie's right. It has to be Celeste," Darby said. "Who else would want to harm Maggie?"

The question played in his head. Yes, who? That was just it—he had no idea. Why had he never pushed Maggie for more information about her past? Because it had been clear she didn't want to share it. Something bad had happened. He knew that much. And it had involved a man.

Flint felt a prickle of doubt run over the back of his neck as he took a sip of the cola Darby set in front of him. What if he was wrong? What if Celeste was telling the truth for once in her life? What if she hadn't taken Maggie?

He heard a sound and turned to find Mariah had come in and stopped in the middle of the room. He hadn't heard her enter the saloon. Darby had said she was upstairs resting. He saw her expression. "Mariah?"

She had one hand over her stomach, fingers splayed out. The other was over her mouth. Her eyes were closed, but tears were leaking from beneath her eyelids.

"Mariah?" She was scaring him. He said her name softly as he slid off his stool and stepped toward her, but still she flinched.

Darby, seeing that she was in some sort of pain, rushed to her. "What is it? Mariah? Is it the baby?"

She shook her head, her dark eyes slowly opening. They focused on Flint. He saw her swallow. "Maggie..." Her voice broke.

He felt his blood turn to ice. He heard his sister's voice in his head. *Her grandmother was a fortune-teller. Mariah says she doesn't have the sight. But I think she's afraid of it and pretends she doesn't know things. Isn't it cool? We have a psychic in our family.*

It was hard for him to even say the words. "Mariah, if you know something..." Flint saw her start to shake her head. "Or even sense something, please. Anything will help."

She took a deep breath and let it out. She looked to her husband. Darby nodded and took her hand in both of his. "I can't even be sure it's Maggie. But when I saw you sitting there, I felt...something."

"Please." All his pain came out in that one word.

"If it's her, she's alive. Her head hurts." She closed her eyes again for a moment. "She's somewhere damp and dark." She frowned. "Not above ground. Maybe a basement? She's... alone and...scared. It's quiet there. No traffic." Mariah shook her head. "That's all I feel and I'm not sure you can trust it. But I had this strong sense of...aching love and regret."

"Thank you," Flint said, his voice barely a whisper. He'd never believed in any of this. He knew other police departments often called in psychics. But right now he desperately wanted to believe that Mariah was right and Maggie was alive. They just had to find her.

His cell phone rang. He quickly checked it. Mark. His heart began to pound as he took the call. *Let Maggie be found alive and well. Let what Mariah said be true.* "Cahill." His voice broke.

"I'm bringing Celeste back in for questioning. Do not show up."

"I won't. What did you find?"

He listened as Mark filled him in on what they'd obtained from her SUV. "She went seven hundred miles, so she's lying about driving toward Paradise Valley," Mark said. "That's only a little over a three-hundred-and-eighty round-trip and she never made it that far, according to her. Any idea where she might have gone?"

His pulse drummed in his ears. Celeste had lied about where she'd gone. She *had* taken Maggie, just as he'd thought. "Did you find her gun?"

Mark seemed to hesitate. "We found it in the car."

So maybe he was right and it was premeditated. He hoped Celeste burned in hell for this. "I have no idea where she might have gone." He thought of what Mariah had said. "But my sister-in-law..." He hesitated. "She sensed something about Maggie. She says she's somewhere damp and dark belowground. Somewhere quiet. Somewhere like a grave. When you ask Celeste, she's going to lie."

"I know. But if she does, I'm going to arrest her."

CHAPTER TEN

Seven hundred miles? Flint drove back to the ranch, staring out at the falling snow and imagining Celeste behind the wheel of her big SUV. She couldn't have gone that far without stopping for gas at least a couple of times. There would be a record, but that would take time to track down. Unless she used cash.

If she'd had that much cash, then it would mean all of this had been premeditated. He tried to get his head around it. Had she been following Maggie for weeks? Possibly. Maybe the run-in at the market had been planned. That thought shook him. He and Maggie had thought that his ex had backed off and all this time she'd been stalking Maggie?

Originally he had thought Maggie's abduction had to have been spur-of-the-moment. Celeste had been upset about Maggie moving in with him. She'd driven by his house, seen Maggie's car, pulled in. She hadn't planned to hurt Maggie.

But she had taken the gun Wayne said he'd bought her. So she could have been armed when she went into the house. The two had argued—that much was obvious. But then what?

Had she pulled the gun on Maggie? Was that why Maggie had gotten into her vehicle and left with her?

He still believed that Celeste had panicked and had no choice but to force Maggie to go with her. He could hear Maggie telling him that he underestimated just how vindictive Celeste could be. He'd tried to give her the benefit of the doubt. No wonder for a while Maggie had thought he still felt something for his ex. He just didn't want to believe that he'd married such a woman.

Seven hundred miles. He kept coming back to that. How far would Celeste have been able to get? Gilt Edge was practically the center of the state. If he were to mark off three hundred and fifty miles radius... He grabbed an old atlas from downstairs and made a circle around Gilt Edge with a pen. If Celeste went three hundred and fifty miles one way from Gilt Edge, it would take her to Canada, North Dakota, clear to Wyoming and... He slowed as he was circling through Western Montana and quickly checked the mileage on the atlas chart.

He let out a curse. Flathead Lake was three hundred and thirty miles from Gilt Edge. Hadn't he heard that Celeste and Wayne had a lake house on Flathead? A lake house with a basement?

Deputy Harper Cole couldn't believe what a fool he was. He was driving down the main drag headed for the shitty apartment he and Vicki shared, when it hit him. He couldn't just ask Vicki to marry him. He needed a ring.

"It's time you started taking responsibility for your future," he said to himself, mimicking his father's stern voice as he swung into the local pawnshop parking lot.

Just the thought of his father, the mayor, made him grind his teeth.

"What are you going to do about this woman you've...

impregnated?" the mayor had demanded the last time they'd spoken.

"You make it sound so romantic," he'd quipped.

His father had rolled his eyes in response.

"I don't know yet. Maybe I'll marry her."

"You probably could do worse."

Nice, he thought now. Well, he'd show his old man. He would step up. He'd show the whole town. Almost dying had made him a new man. That and everyone in the county thinking he was a hero.

The idea of being a family man appealed to him more than he ever thought it would. He now saw it as a fresh start. People would forget about the old Harper Cole—not that he saw anything wrong with him.

But if he hoped to be sheriff, he had to look good. He felt a shiver of excitement because he'd finally made up his mind. He could see his future, the wife and child at his side as he was sworn in as sheriff. This baby could be the best thing that had ever happened to him. Harp Cole, a family man.

He smiled to himself as he pushed through the pawnshop door. "I need an engagement ring," he said to Larry Wagner, the owner.

Larry raised a brow before he let out a bark of a laugh. "What would you need that for?" He and Larry had gone to school together. That was back when Larry's father had run the shop—and run Harp out a couple of times, accusing him of stealing.

"I'm getting married," Harp said defensively. "It happens."

"Not to you."

He shrugged. Larry had gotten married right out of high school to Shirley Dale. Harp had never told Larry that he'd been with her only weeks before she and Larry had eloped. Everyone figured she had a bun in the oven and they were right. He'd always wondered if Larry Jr. didn't look more like him than Larry Sr. But he'd been smart enough to keep his mouth shut.

"So what ya got?" he asked, stepping up to the counter. "I don't have a lot of money."

"Imagine that," Larry said as he pulled out a tray of diamond rings.

Harp considered his options. Almost all of them had either small diamonds or bigger fake diamonds. Vicki would know it wasn't real if he gave her a big one. Also, given how small her hands were, one of the smaller, cheaper rings would look bigger and better.

"She has really small hands," he said as he studied the rings.

"So you're marrying that waitress down at Sue's Diner."

"Vicki. Yep, she's a sweetheart."

"I'll bet. How far along is she?" Larry asked with a chuckle.

"I resent that," Harp snapped.

"Settle down. It happens to the best of us." He pulled a ring from the tray. "This is a small size. Does that look like it will fit her?"

He had no idea. "That's the smallest you have?" he asked, checking out the price taped to it.

"I can give you 10 percent off. For old times' sake." Larry met his gaze in such a way that he felt a little uncomfortable. "We're almost like family." Was it possible that Shirley had told him about them?

"Okay. You take a check?" he asked, reaching for his checkbook in his hip pocket. "Maybe you could throw in a little box for it?"

Larry made a rude sound. "You haven't changed. One of the richest kids in town and one of the cheapest."

The depiction of him came as a shock. Was that what everyone had thought?

"My *grandfather* has money. I never saw any of it and neither did my mother. The Mayor—" as he called his father "—has done okay, but it isn't like he's ever cut me any slack. He said he earned his money and I should do the same."

"Really?" Larry looked surprised. "You lived in that big house—"

"My grandfather bought it for my parents as a wedding present. The Mayor says it costs an arm and a leg just to heat it, but my mother loves it."

"Well, at least the mayor bought you nice clothes," Larry continued as if he hadn't spoken.

"That was my mother's doing. She didn't want me to suffer just because my father is a miserly old bastard."

Larry said, "Huh. Guess that explains why I always had to buy the beer at the parties. And I thought you were just cheap."

Harp watched him work the price off the ring and bit his tongue. He'd just shared a dark family secret his mother had worked hard to hide and this was the jerk's reaction?

"How's Shirley?" he asked, thinking maybe it was time to share *Larry's* dark family secret with him.

Larry finally got the tape off the ring and now held it up to the light for a moment before his gaze shifted to Harp. "Fine."

This time there was no doubt about the look. No reason to update the man. Larry already knew. Or at least suspected. The tension seemed to suck all the air out of the shop. He was reminded of the night Larry kicked the shit out of a football player from a neighboring town. He'd almost killed the guy before they'd pulled him off. Larry had a hair trigger and seemed to like to draw blood. Harp would be a damned fool to poke this rabid bear.

"Glad to hear everything's fine," Harp managed to say into the deathly silence. "So how much do I make the check out for?"

Larry gave him a number, and then dug under the counter and pulled out a red box covered in plastic. "This work for you?"

"Great," he said as he filled out the check, his hands shaking a little. He just wanted this transaction over with. He handed Larry the check and Larry handed him the little red box. "Nice doing business with you." Larry said nothing.

He popped the box open like he would when he asked Vicki to marry him. The diamond caught the light and sparkled. He could just imagine her face when he gave it to her. His earlier excitement returned. "It's perfect."

"Congrats," Larry said, sounding as if he didn't mean it.

"Thanks." He checked the man's expression. Larry had just made a nice sale but he didn't look as happy as he should have been.

Harp put the box in his pocket and started out of the store. At the door, he almost turned and said something smart. But fortunately, good sense followed him out to his cruiser.

As he slid behind the wheel, he looked up to see Larry watching him from the front window. It wasn't over, he thought. If Shirley had confessed…

He started the cruiser, reminding himself who he was. Deputy Harper Cole, soon to be sheriff. Not a man you wanted to mess with. Larry might be tougher than old buffalo meat, but Harp carried a gun.

He smiled and flipped Larry the bird as he drove away. He hadn't forgotten that he'd almost died a few months ago, not because he was anyone's hero, but because of his own arrogant stupidity.

But he told himself that he'd put the past behind him. He was a changed man with a bright future. Screw Larry Wagner.

Mark sat down at his desk and pushed the stack of mail to the side. Exhaustion pulled at him. He hadn't gotten but a few hours' sleep since Maggie had disappeared. He rubbed the back of his neck and told himself he was doing every-thing possible to find her, but it felt as if he was swimming through quicksand.

"Celeste Duma is here," the dispatcher said over his in-tercom.

He sighed, not sure he was up to another bout with that woman. But if Celeste had taken Maggie... "Take her and her lawyer into the interrogation room. I'll be right there."

When he found her waiting, he was surprised to see that she'd come alone. No husband. No lawyer. "Are we waiting for your attorney?" he asked.

She shook her head. "He gets paid too much to sit and listen to your inane accusations. Anyway, I have nothing to hide."

Mark didn't believe that for a moment. He smiled, shocked by her arrogance. She thought she was above the law. Flint was now on paid leave. Was that what she'd wanted all along? To hurt him?

He turned on the video camera, gave the date and time, and introduced himself and Celeste Duma.

"Is that really necessary?" she asked, nodding toward the device.

He wanted to laugh since just moments before she'd taken out her compact to check her hair and makeup. It took all his patience not to say something smart about it. He just hoped this wasn't a huge waste of time. There was still no word on Maggie.

Mark felt as if he could be doing more anywhere but in this room with this woman. He doubted Celeste could tell the truth if she had a gun to her head. If this woman had taken Maggie, then Maggie was as good as dead. He had a man tailing Celeste, so he knew that she hadn't been any-where but here since returning home. If she'd taken Mag-gie, then like she'd said, she wouldn't be returning her. Nor would she be returning to wherever she'd taken her to give her food and water.

"I'm curious," Mark said. "Why do you hate Maggie Thompson so much?"

Celeste gave him a wry smile. "My lawyer said I don't have to tell you anything." Her chin went up in naked defiance.

"Then what are you doing here and without your lawyer? You really must hate her. Rather than help us find her, you're doing everything possible to hurt her."

"How can you say that?" she demanded.

"If you really had nothing to do with Maggie's disappearance, then why are you wasting our time and resources to find out where you've been since she disappeared? Is all this just because you can't stand the thought of your ex-husband being happy?"

"Maggie wouldn't have made him happy."

"Interesting that you're talking about her in the past tense."

Celeste shrugged and looked at the camera. For the first time, she seemed nervous. "I just meant...if someone took her, then she's probably dead." Her gaze returned to him. "Isn't that the rule? If you don't find her in the first twenty-four hours, she's probably dead?"

He shuddered inwardly at her lack of empathy. "I'm not sure that's a rule, but yes, it's important that we find Maggie as quickly as possible." He was tired of playing games with this woman. It was time to take the gloves off. "Look, if this is about ruining Flint's life, haven't you already done a pretty good job of that?"

She looked aghast. "He *loved* me. What we had together was—"

"Was so special that you left him for another man. So that's it. You just don't want him to love anyone else."

"He doesn't love her the way he does me."

He raised a brow. "You think he still loves you?"

"I meant the way he *loved* me."

"How can you be so sure he doesn't love Maggie more?"

She gave him a horrified look, then laughed. "That's ridiculous. She's…she's a nobody, a beautician."

"Then why are you so intimidated by her?"

Celeste shifted uncomfortably in her chair. "I'm not. I just know that she's all wrong for him. I don't want him to make the biggest mistake of his life."

"I'm pretty sure he already did that."

She looked like she might erupt.

He quickly cut off the explosion. "Why do you think you have the right to tell him what to do or not do?"

"Because I still care."

"Maybe, but if you did, you'd give him your blessing and you'd help us find Maggie."

"I already told you—"

"Tell me where you went after you drove by your ex-husband's house and saw Maggie."

"I *didn't* see her. I saw her car. I saw that she was moving in."

"And you stopped to confront her."

She met his gaze. "No. I stepped on the gas and sped out of town."

He swore and slammed a hand down on the table between them, making her jump. "Where did you go? The truth this time. You hated her. It was killing you to have the two of them move in together. You were mad and you had already warned her and she hadn't listened. You decided to stop her."

Celeste met his gaze. What he saw made him feel dirty. There was so much malice in those eyes. "I *was* angry and hurt and I hated her. But I knew that if I stopped…" She pulled her gaze away and bit down on her lower lip for a moment. "I was afraid it would get ugly, so I kept going. I drove toward Paradise Valley."

"That's the same lie you've been telling me. It's three hundred and eighty miles round-trip to the spa, which you never reached. You drove over seven hundred miles in that SUV. Now stop lying to me."

"I might have taken some back roads. I don't know. I just drove."

"I've had it with you and your lies. For whatever reason, you can't let go of your ex-husband and you have proved what lengths you will go to in an attempt to keep him and Maggie apart. What you wrote on her mirror at her beauty shop pretty much says it all. 'Die Bitch.' We already know how you felt about her since you're the one who left the message for her."

"Yes, I wanted her gone, but you have no proof that I—"

"You couldn't stand the thought of her moving in, so you killed her. Why else won't you tell me where you went? You have something to hide and we all know it." Mark got to his feet. He'd lost all patience with this woman and said as much. "Celeste Duma, you are under arrest for the abduction and assault of Margaret 'Maggie' Thompson, as well as obstruction of justice. Get on your feet."

"No!" she cried. "You can't do this."

"Actually, I can," he said and began to read her her rights.

Radville, North Dakota, sat hunkered down in the middle of windswept prairie miles from anywhere. A tumbleweed cartwheeled in front of the pickup as Frank and Nettie reached the city-limits sign.

As Frank slowed, Nettie read the rusted sign. Someone had scratched out the original number of residents, changing it from 211 to 209. But she figured it was less than that, given how faded the lettering was.

A neon light flashed Vacancy at what appeared to be the only motel in town. It was one of those single-level U-shaped motor courts that had seen better days.

Frank drove past to what appeared to be the center of town, passing a convenience store of sorts with two sad-looking gas pumps outside. Beyond it she saw a casino sign flashing at the Mint Bar. That had to be the most popular bar name since they'd passed four other ones on their way to Radville.

They drove by an old service garage, now deserted, then an old theater, long boarded up, before she spotted a café in the middle of a block of empty buildings. In the distance, she saw what looked like a school. As Frank approached it, she noticed the windows were decorated with artwork made by young children. The colorings were faded and there was a padlock and chain on the wide double doors.

"I think that city-limits sign was a lie," Nettie said. "No way do 209 people live here."

"Maybe we should get a room first, freshen up before we go see Dana Stevens," he said.

"I doubt there's going to be a run on motel rooms. I just have a feeling that we shouldn't put this off. You know the town clerk called Dana the minute we hung up after getting her address."

"I doubt she's going to skip town, but I'd go with one of your feelings any day. I think I passed her street. Second, right?"

"Yes. It's in the third block."

He laughed as he turned down Second. "There's nothing past the third block." Ahead she could see a blue clapboard house sitting at the edge of town. "Wanna bet that's it? There're enough toys out front that it could be a day care."

"The toys don't look like they've been used for a while," Nettie noted, seeing the rust, the flat tires on the bikes, the dirt that had blown into the cracked plastic sled. As Frank parked, she saw a curtain move, then fall motionless. "She knows we're here. Let's see if she answers the door," Nettie said as she got out.

The woman who eventually came to the door was small and pale with lifeless brown hair and chipped blue-painted nails. Dana wore baggy jeans and a sweatshirt with faded lettering on it. "Yes?"

"We're here about Jenna," Nettie said.

Fear widened the woman's brown eyes. She looked like a woman in her late forties who'd had anything but an easy life. "Is she all right?"

"We don't know. That's why we're trying to find her before someone else does," Frank said.

Nettie saw understanding dawn on her face. "Can we please come in?"

Dana hesitated, but for only a moment. She opened the door wider and ushered them into a house that had seen the wear and tear of the children who'd once played with those toys out in the yard. From the photos on the walls, it appeared that she'd had her children early in life and they were now all grown and gone. Nettie wondered where they'd ended up. Probably scattered to the wind since she couldn't see much opportunity in Radville for them.

"I'm Nettie Curry, and this is my husband, Frank. We're investigators," she said as she took a seat.

"You mean like detectives?"

"Private detectives," Frank said and showed his ID.

Dana barely glanced at it as she sat down on the edge of a chair across from them and fidgeted with the hem of her sweatshirt. "I don't know where Jenna is."

"When was the last time you talked to her?" Nettie asked.

"Last week." She looked even more nervous.

"Did she tell you then what was going on?" Frank asked.

"I don't know what you mean."

"I think you do. Who is Clark?" he asked.

Dana started, eyes widening, but she said nothing.

Nettie tried a different approach. "Dana, we're afraid Jenna is in trouble and we know you're worried about her too. That's why we need your help."

The woman rose and moved to the window to peer out. She looked scared. Nettie remembered hearing a series of locks being released before the woman had opened the door to them. Whatever had Jenna afraid apparently had this woman just as fearful.

"You're the one who called yesterday, aren't you?" Dana asked, turning back to them. "How did you get her phone?"

"From a friend of hers."

"The man she was living with," Dana said.

"He's worried about her too. You need to tell us about Clark. Who is he?"

The woman hugged herself, her expression darkening. "He's my older brother."

"Why is he after Jenna?" Nettie asked.

Dana set her jaw.

"Do you want to help her or not?" Frank asked. "Jenna took off the first time because she was afraid of him. Now she's disappeared again."

"Except this time we think she might have decided to end this," Nettie said. "Did she tell you what she planned to do? That she was going to tell him where she was?"

Dana looked horrified at the thought. "No, she wouldn't do that unless…"

"Unless?" Nettie asked.

The young woman glanced out the window. She seemed even more afraid now. "The only way she would have contacted him was if he…" She swallowed and shook her head.

Nettie leaned forward and lowered her voice conspiratorially. "We know you've been keeping her secret. Something you promised never to tell. But Jenna needs your help now more than ever. Why is your brother after her?"

CHAPTER ELEVEN

Vicki had to tell Harp the truth. She didn't need a baby to get him to marry her. He loved her. Why else would he have shared such damaging information with her that day in the hospital?

At the sound of his patrol car pulling up outside, she felt her heart begin to race. What if he was angry with her and blamed her for losing the baby? What if he was glad the baby was gone because now he wouldn't have to marry her?

Suddenly she wasn't so sure that anyone would believe her if she told them what Harp had confessed that day. Suddenly she wasn't so sure of anything.

She could hear his footfalls on the stairs. She'd been so sure this was the right thing to do. Now, though, she was scared.

His key turned in the lock, the door opened and she knew she had to decide. Now!

As he came through the door, she saw his expression and felt her heart drop like a rock. He knew. Somehow he'd found out that she'd lost the baby. That she'd been lying. Why else was he grinning at her like that? She couldn't move. Couldn't breathe. He stalked toward her, grabbed her and spun her around.

"Harp, I can explain," she said, just wanting to get this over with. But she was getting dizzy, her head swimming. Why hadn't she told him months ago that she'd miscarried?

He was laughing and she could feel a current running through him. "Explain what?" he asked as he set her down on her feet again.

"I feel like I'm going to throw up," she said, meaning it.

"Oh, sorry. I forgot. The baby."

She looked into his face, expecting to see sarcasm.

"You all right?" he asked when she didn't make a run for the bathroom.

Her head was still spinning, but her earlier nausea had passed. Was it possible he didn't know? Her tongue was glued to the roof of her mouth. *Confess*, she screamed inside her head. *Just get it over with.*

"Sit down. You look green around the gills," he said, taking her arms in his big hands and gently settling her on the edge of the couch. "I've got a surprise."

She hated surprises since she'd yet to get a good one. Worse, he was nervous, making her even more jittery.

Harp swallowed, rubbed his hands down the thighs of his jeans and took a breath. He let it out slowly as he dropped to one knee.

She stared in shock as he reached into his pocket and pulled out a small red box. This was his surprise? She wanted to scream. She couldn't marry him with this lie between them.

Vicki looked into his handsome face and her heart broke.

"Will you marry me?" he asked, his voice breaking as he popped open the box to reveal the prettiest little diamond engagement ring she'd ever seen.

It didn't take Flint long to find the location of the Duma lake house. After all, he was still sheriff. He pulled out his cell phone, then reconsidered calling Mark after reminding himself that he was on paid leave. He knew what Mark would say. That was if he didn't try to stop him.

Mark would want to call someone in Flathead to check out the lake house. Flint didn't trust anyone to do this but himself. If he found anything, he would call Mark.

The problem was that the department was short staffed under normal circumstances. With him on leave, it would only put more pressure on manpower. Add to that the winter storm still putting down snow…

Again, Flint reminded himself that he was on paid leave. He'd been pulled off Maggie's case because he was a suspect. Not to mention, he was too close to it. He'd proved that earlier when he'd attacked Celeste. He still couldn't believe he wasn't behind bars. Investigating on his own was a fool thing to do.

For years he'd always gone by the book. He was a straight-arrow guy who didn't believe in cutting corners. But now the woman he loved had been taken. It almost scared him to think what extremes he might go to. But he had no choice. He had to find Maggie. Wherever she was, he worried that she was cold and afraid, hurt and possibly dying. He shoved that thought away, refusing to imagine her in some horrible basement somewhere.

Not that the basement at the Duma lake house would be horrible. Unless there was no heat.

He pocketed his phone, knowing that Mark would try to talk him out of this or, worse, try to stop him. He'd go, he'd check out the lake house and then… *And how exactly are you getting in?*

Flint wasn't going to worry about that now. He had a long drive ahead of him. He'd always gone with his gut instinct partnered with sound evidence, and it had never let him down.

But this time, he couldn't count on it. This was the woman

he planned to spend the rest of his life with. He had to find Maggie, and the one thing he felt soul deep was that the clock was ticking down.

Maggie woke to find a paper bag beside her. The smell alone had her sitting up and reaching for the contents. She was starved and couldn't remember the last time she'd eaten.

She ate the burger and fries as if she hadn't eaten in weeks. Maybe she hadn't. She'd lost all track of time and had no idea how long she'd been here since most of the time she'd been drugged.

Her stomach groaned and for a moment she thought she might be sick to her stomach. She closed her eyes, wishing she hadn't devoured the meal so quickly. After a few minutes, it seemed the food would stay down. She was relieved since she didn't know when she would get fed again.

Not just that. She needed to get her strength back if she ever hoped to get out of here. That thought surprised her since a part of her knew there was little chance of that happening. Whoever had taken her had been planning this for some time.

She pulled herself up and tried the bars again, hoping that she would find them not as sturdy as she had before. But they were just as strong, just as secure. She moved around her prison, looking for a weakness somewhere in the design. The bars definitely rattled more on the side where they opened.

Maggie stopped rattling the cage around her as she heard a sound beyond her room. At first she couldn't distinguish what it was. It sounded like a woman crying.

She wasn't the only woman being held here? Every horror story she'd heard about women captives being held for years against their wills came to her in a rush. Terror filled her.

The effects of the drug still made her lethargic and muddled her thinking. She had no idea where she was or even who had taken her. She felt as if she'd been drugged for days, but there was no way to tell time here.

As she took in her prison, she noticed that the walls were concrete. No windows. Reaching through the bars of her cage, she touched the concrete wall. It was ice-cold. Drawing back her hand, with a horrible start, she realized why. She was underground.

Her legs felt like rubber. She sank to the mattress, dropping to her knees as she clung to the bars. As she felt a full-blown panic attack coming on, she sat back and tried to calm herself. She had tried screaming and crying and pleading. She'd suspected that she wasn't alone, wherever she was, but she hadn't seen anyone. How was that possible since clearly someone had come in to leave her food, water and to drug her? She looked at the half-empty bottle of water at her feet and recalled the chalky taste of it as she felt her eyelids already growing heavy.

Fear sent her pulse pounding. She tried to stay calm, but it was impossible. Who had done this to her? There was only one person who wanted her away from Flint so badly that she would do something this crazy. Celeste.

Just the thought of the woman made her angry. Her pulse slowed some. She caught her breath. If she had any chance of getting out of there, she had to think. Panicking would get her nowhere. Panicking was exactly what Celeste would want.

And yet she could feel the drug working through her system. She dropped to the bed even as she tried to fight the drug, tried to think. Why a bed that looked like a child's? Why a cage that, when she thought about it, looked like an adult crib? Maybe Celeste was crazier than even she thought.

She felt rising panic again and pushed it back down. Eventually Celeste would show herself.

"I know who you are!" she yelled. "Show your face, you coward!" She listened and thought she heard the sound of footfalls overhead. Bracing herself, she prepared to face her abductor, but the drug was too powerful. She lay over on the bed and was asleep when her door opened again.

Celeste jerked free of the undersheriff's grip as he tried to get her to her feet. "I'll tell you. But you aren't going to like it."

He would bet on that. Celeste was beginning to look as tired as he felt as she dropped back into her chair and met his gaze head-on. "You want the truth, right?"

Mark sighed, and without sitting back down, he crossed his arms and leaned against the wall, waiting. "I'm all ears."

"It was just like I said. I drove past Flint's house, actually the house that I once shared with him. I saw her car. I even saw her digging around in the back of her car and coming out with a bag. She was moving in." Her voice broke. "Yes, I hated her. I didn't want her with Flint. The truth is… I've never gotten over Flint."

The admission seemed hard to make and yet Mark wasn't going to be taken in by this woman. Celeste was one hell of an actress and a consummate liar. He waited, wondering what she was up to.

"I think I made a huge mistake." Tears welled in her eyes. "I know I'm the one who left him," she said quickly. "But I needed…more, and Wayne…" She ducked her head as if embarrassed. He thought she should have been.

"You mean money."

"Money. Things. Status," she snapped. "I hated being a sheriff's wife. I thought once I had those things I'd be happy."

"But you're not."

She shook her head without looking up. "I'm miserable and I can't bear the thought of Flint moving on. Especially with Maggie."

"Why *especially* with Maggie?"

Silence. Then in a small voice, Celeste said, "Because I can tell that he's in love with her."

Mark felt his heart begin to race. "So you stopped when you saw her moving in."

Celeste licked her lips and looked up at him with those big luminous green eyes, and he thought, *oh hell, here it comes. She's finally going to confess.* He couldn't wait to get her behind bars in one of their orange jumpsuits. This woman—

"I wanted to stop, but like I said, I knew it would go badly. Just think, though, if I had, maybe I could have saved her."

Mark let out a bark of a laugh. "You could have saved Maggie?"

She narrowed her eyes at him. "Yes, because as I was driving past, I saw a man come out of the pines and head toward the back door."

"And you didn't think this was an important tidbit of information to tell us before *now*?" He wanted to shake the woman until her teeth rattled. How had Flint put up with her as long as he had?

"No, I didn't think it was important because I recognized him. I'd seen him with her before. He was an old boyfriend who was trying to get her back. I thought if he was this persistent, maybe he'd succeeded this time."

"Why wouldn't you have told us this right away?" Mark demanded.

"I wanted to give them time together."

He shook his head, fighting to control his temper. "Do you have any idea what you've done keeping this from us? We've lost valuable hours on this case because of you."

Celeste flipped her hair back and looked impatient. "How do you know even now that Maggie didn't run away with him?"

Mark shook his head. "Because she was injured in a struggle."

"They could have made up," she argued stubbornly.

"Wait—what do you mean, maybe he succeeded in getting her back *this* time?"

"Because like I said, I'd seen him with her before."

He gave her a disbelieving look. "Where?"

"In Billings. About three weeks ago. It was at this seedy bar on the wrong side of the tracks."

Did he believe this story? "If it was that seedy, what were *you* doing there?"

"I was with friends, a bachelorette party. We were hitting all these awful bars…" She must have seen that he didn't care about that. "Maggie was sitting at the bar with this man. It was clear that they knew each other well, if you know what I mean."

"No, I don't. How is it that she didn't see you?"

"It was incredibly dark in there and I was sitting with friends in a far corner and they were at the bar. Also, Maggie wasn't looking around. She and the man had their heads together, trying to keep their voices down, but anyone could tell they were arguing. At one point, he grabbed her and kissed her hard. She slapped him and he slapped her back. It got uglier and the bartender told them to leave. The man refused, so the bartender called the cops. Maggie talked the man into leaving before the cops came. They went outside to the parking lot."

"You *followed* them?"

"No. The bartender went to the door and held it open to watch. I guess to make sure that the man didn't hurt her before the cops arrived. I could see them still arguing. It was clear that there was history between them."

"Did you hear what they were arguing about?" he asked, still questioning whether he believed this.

"He wanted her back. That he'd changed, that he didn't want to live without her, that sort of thing. She was saying she couldn't, that she'd moved on, that he needed to leave her alone. But it was obvious that they knew each other from before."

"Before Maggie came to Gilt Edge?"

Celeste shrugged. "That's my guess since I've never seen the man before."

"You're sure she didn't see you?"

"She had her hands full with her old boyfriend."

"And you never told Flint?" He had a harder time believing she wouldn't have gone straight to Flint with what she'd seen.

"I thought about it," she admitted. "But I don't have the best track record with him."

"Or with the truth."

She mugged a face at him. "I thought maybe this man might win her back, so I kept quiet. But I was prepared to tell if Maggie and Flint moved in together."

"Did Maggie leave with the man at the bar?"

"I was watching through the open door. She left in her own car. The man was furious over whatever was going on between them. I didn't see what he was driving just then. But he spun out when he drove away because I heard gravel pelting the side of the bar right before I could hear a siren in the distance. So he'd probably heard it too."

"But you saw what he was driving later?"

"After we heard his tires throwing gravel, I looked out and I saw an older-model van go by."

Mark blinked. "What color?"

"Brown."

Nettie listened as the story came out in starts and stops. A terrified Dana Terwilliger Stevens kneaded her hands as she talked, her gaze often going to the window as if she thought her brother might appear at any time.

"You have to understand. Clark always had…problems." She looked away, shame and guilt marring her features. "My mother tried to protect him, refusing to believe there was anything wrong with him."

"What was wrong with him?" Frank asked.

"He was…different. He would lie and make up stories. If he didn't get his way, he would be furious and mean. He liked to hurt things, hurt people."

"Did he ever hurt you?" Nettie asked and saw the answer in the way the woman's gaze shifted away. "Did you tell your mother?"

Dana let out a laugh. "Like she believed *me*. Clark said I was just trying to get him in trouble. She said he was special and that I needed to be nice to him. She thought I was jealous and maybe I was. Mother loved him more." She shook her head.

"Did he hurt Jenna?" Frank asked.

Dana's head came up. Tears filled her eyes. "I tried to protect her, but I couldn't. He became obsessed with her. He said she was his and always would be. He made up stories of how their life would be. It was crazy. He followed her, went into a rage if she talked to anyone, especially a boy at school."

"How old were you and Jenna when this happened?" Nettie asked.

"Thirteen. But he'd been crazy about her since she was little. He said she was his little baby doll. He…he was always touching her. I thought he wouldn't hurt her, but…" Her voice broke.

"Did he rape her?" Nettie asked.

Dana nodded, head down as she stared at her hands in her lap. "I was at school. I had detention. Jenna forgot and stopped by the house. My mother…left them alone."

"Did Jenna tell anyone?" she asked, knowing the answer.

"No. But shortly after that, Clark got into trouble with the law and was sent away."

Nettie saw a revengeful satisfaction in Dana's expression that told her Clark's run-in with the law hadn't been bad luck.

He'd been set up by his sister. She'd put up with him abusing her, but when he'd hurt her best friend...

"So why is he after Jenna now?" Nettie asked.

Dana chewed at a cuticle for a moment before she answered. "He's been locked up for years. When he'd get out, he'd look for her, but get in trouble and get sent back up. When he was released the last time, he came back here looking for her and I could tell that he'd gotten even worse. He had this idea that she was his wife and..." She shuddered. "He went crazy when he couldn't find her and got locked up again for a while."

"But he's back out," Frank said.

"There's more to the story, isn't there?" Nettie said.

Nodding, Dana said, "I'm afraid that he's heard somehow."

"Heard what?" Frank asked when she didn't continue.

Dana swallowed. "That Jenna had a baby nine months after... That she'd had his baby all those years ago and kept it from him. Kept it from everyone."

CHAPTER TWELVE

Harp had pictured the scene all the way to the apartment. Vicki would be surprised. Delighted. She would probably shriek, cover her mouth with her hands, cry. He would slip the ring on her finger. It would fit perfectly, proving that they belonged together.

She would then throw herself into his arms and they would make love like they'd never made love before.

That was why he was so taken aback when she simply stared at the ring. He thought maybe it was too much of a shock for her with her hormones raging and all. So he pulled out the ring, grabbed her hand and slipped it on her finger.

The ring was way too big. It slid around her slim finger, the small diamond disappearing from view. He tried to fix it, amazed how cold her hand was, but she pulled it back, took one look at him and cried, "No!" She turned and ran into the bathroom, locking it behind her.

Harp stared after her as he heard her crying in there. What had just happened?

He realized he was still holding the stupid cheap box Larry

had put the ring in. He flung it at the bathroom door, furious with Vicki for ruining the perfect picture he had in his mind of this moment. This was what they were going to tell their child?

Storming over to the bathroom door, he pounded on it.

From inside came the sob-choked "Go away!"

"Have you lost your mind?" he demanded. "I just asked you to marry me."

"I know." More bawling.

He really didn't need this. Hauling back, he slammed his fist into the door. It was a hollow core, so the first layer of wood splintered. From inside the bathroom, Vicki screamed. He wanted to scream too as he pulled his fist out. His knuckles were bleeding and several of his fingers hurt like hell. He'd broken something for sure.

"Look what you made me do!" he yelled, then kicked the door. It shuddered but his boot toe only made a dent in the door.

"Stop," Vicki cried. "You're going to ruin the door."

"*Ruin the door?* You think I care about the damned door?" he yelled back.

Someone pounded on the wall from the other apartment and said they had called the sheriff's department.

"I *am* the sheriff's department, you dumb—" The rest was lost in the sound of sirens.

Mark tried not to let his surprise show. "What bar was it?"

Celeste didn't remember but described where she thought it was on the south side of Billings.

Mark stared at Celeste as she finished. "Why wouldn't you have told us about this when Maggie went missing?"

"I thought about it, but like I told you, I wanted to give Maggie time to get away since I think she left with him."

"I could hold you in contempt for this."

"Nor did I think you would believe me." She narrowed her eyes. "You're not even sure you believe me now. Anyway, it was clear that the man was crazy about her. Why can't you believe that he simply talked her into going with him?"

"Or *forced* her. You didn't stick around long enough to see him leave?"

"I didn't have to. As I was driving on around the corner, I looked back and I saw him come out, so he wasn't in there long."

"Maggie wasn't with him?"

"No, but he could have been going to get his vehicle."

Mark couldn't believe this. "This man could be the one who hurt her. Don't you get that? Tell me what he looked like," he said, sitting back down as he pulled out his notebook and pen.

"Big, blond, light-colored eyes, tattoos all over his arms."

"You said you thought he drove a brown van. Did you see him get into it and leave?"

She shook her head. "But I took that road behind Flint's house. I saw the van parked in the pines. It was pulling out. I figured he'd either failed to convince her to come back to him or that he was driving around to pick her up at the house. I thought I'd just wait and let it all shake out." She shrugged. "I'm still betting Maggie is with him right now."

Mark rubbed his hand over his face. Exhaustion pulled at him. Did he really believe anything out of this woman's mouth? "You still haven't told me where you went after that."

She looked surprised that he wasn't going to let it drop. "I told you about the man—"

"Either you explain the missing hours and over seven hundred miles on your vehicle or—"

"I was with someone." Her gaze met his. "A man."

"What man?" he asked with an impatient sigh and waited for another story.

She shrugged. "I honestly don't know his name. It's true. He was just some man I met in a bar."

"*What* bar?" He couldn't help sounding skeptical. He couldn't even be sure that the story she'd told him about the man in the bar in Billings with Maggie was the truth.

She named a bar. He wrote it down. "Where?"

"Bigfork."

He looked up. "What were you doing over in the Flathead?"

"After I got upset about Flint and...and Maggie moving in together, I left town. I didn't get very far when I realized I didn't feel like going to a spa. So I decided to drive over to our house on the lake."

"Did you make it?" he asked, hoping for something he could prove was true.

"No. I ended up spending time with this man until I got the messages from Wayne...and I turned around, drove back as soon as I could, but with the storm..."

"Where did you spend the night?"

"In the man's trailer."

"I suppose you wouldn't know how to find him or the trailer."

"It was late, dark, and I was...was drunk." She raised her eyes until she was looking right into his. "You can understand why I didn't want anyone to know."

Mark studied her. He'd always thought he was good at catching a lie, but Celeste was in a class of her own. He wanted to believe the Billings story about the man in the brown van, but Wayne could have told her about the van that was seen in Flint's neighborhood since he'd been questioned about what colored vans he owned with his many businesses.

"I'm going to let you go for now," he finally said. "But if I find out that any of this is a lie..."

"It's not. I swear."

He looked at her, wondering how many times she'd sworn something was the truth as she lied through her teeth.

But what if this time she was telling the truth? If Celeste hadn't taken Maggie, then maybe an ex-boyfriend had.

After Celeste left, Mark walked back to his office. How much did Flint know about Maggie Thompson's past? It was time he found out.

It was late by the time Flint reached the Flathead Valley. The lake, the largest freshwater lake west of the Mississippi, shimmered in the moonlight. He forgot how beautiful it was here. That he and Celeste had come here on their anniversary only made this trip more painful. It was the perfect place for his ex to hide the woman he now loved.

There was little traffic this time of the night as he drove the narrow road that skirted the east side of the lake and the steep Mission Mountain Range. Signs offering Flathead cherries caught in his headlights as he drove the winding road. The cherry stands were all closed this time of year. In fact, much of the place looked closed for the winter. He doubted Wayne and Celeste used their lake house more than a few weeks in the summer—if that.

He was guessing that it had been something she'd asked Wayne for. Just another way to turn the knife in Flint's back. When they'd come here on their honeymoon, Celeste had said her dream was to own a place on the lake—knowing they would never be able to afford one on his sheriff's salary.

Every once in a while as he drove, he would catch sight of Christmas lights in one of the lake houses below the highway. The decorations made his heart hurt. He couldn't bear to think about Christmas this year if it was without Maggie.

His navigation system in his pickup told him he was almost there. Just another quarter mile. He slowed, watching for the turn. It still came up almost too quickly. He was glad there wasn't any other traffic as he hit his brakes and pulled off.

The road through the pines dropped radically toward the lake. He drove slowly, his navigation system telling him that he'd arrived at his destination. He turned it off, his nerves already on edge. His headlights cut through the darkness of the night and the pine trees as he told himself Wayne probably had installed some kind of security system. There could even be a caretaker. Or at least a close neighbor who would report seeing someone at the house.

But as he reached the end of the road, he saw that there were no close neighbors. The house sat on a point. He couldn't see another light nearby. All he could see was the lake in the moonlight and remember one night on his honeymoon of walking along the shore thinking that he was the luckiest man in the world.

He cut the truck's engine and was instantly surrounded by the darkness of the trees. Only a little moonlight fingered its way in. He opened his pickup door as quietly as possible and stepped out, closing it softly. He'd brought some tools to break in, but he decided to have a look around before he dug out more than a crowbar.

The boardwalk from the parking pad to the house was bathed in moonlight. A breeze came up off the water, putting a chill in the winter air. There were patches of snow around, but nothing like Gilt Edge this time of the year.

As he reached the back door, he noticed that the boardwalk went on around the front of the house. He took it, even though it exposed him. The house wasn't as large and ostentatious as he'd expected. In fact, it looked like something he would have bought if he could have afforded it. The deck out front was wide and hung out to the edge of the water. He could imagine the view from there in the summer.

He walked the rest of the way around the house, trying

doors as he went. All of them were locked, just as he'd suspected they would be. He tried seeing inside but the drapes were drawn. Behind the house, he spotted a shed.

With crowbar in hand, he headed for the shed, all the time praying he wouldn't find Maggie's body inside. The door was padlocked. He used the crowbar, and it didn't take him long to break in.

As he opened the door, he turned on his flashlight, and taking a shuddering breath, he shone it inside. The shed was filled with the usual lake accoutrements, lawn chairs, floats, water skis, leaf blower and barbecue. No body.

Flint took a breath and waited for his heart rate to return to normal before he turned toward the house. On his walk over, he'd decided which door would be easiest to break in through, but as he neared it, he changed his mind, and with the crowbar he smashed a small window next to the door and reached in and unlocked it.

It was cold inside the house. He could see his breath as he moved quickly from room to room. From the outside he had seen that there was only a partial basement. He found the door to it, turned on the light and stopped to listen before descending the steps.

The basement was smaller than it appeared from the outside of the house—only enough room for the furnace, hot-water heater and a little storage. Maggie wasn't being held down here.

Upstairs again, he looked around before taking the stairs to the second floor. He found a sitting room, several more bedrooms. He was about to give up, telling himself that this trip had been a waste of time, when he came to a door that was locked.

Locked? Why would a room be locked? He glanced behind him, thinking of all the expensive stuff he'd seen around the house for any thief to pick up. So why lock this one room?

"Maggie?" His voice came out a croak. "Maggie?" Her name had such a lonely, lost sound in the empty dark house that he couldn't bear to say it again.

He stopped to listen, pressing his ear against the door, but could hear nothing over the pounding of his heart. He tried the knob again and then, using the crowbar, broke the knob and pushed open the door. Cold musty air rushed back at him as he shone his flashlight into what was clearly a child's room, and he felt his heart drop.

Mark had enough to do without dealing with this. "A domestic dispute?"

Harp didn't look up. He was cradling his swollen, bruised and bloody hand in his lap. "I asked her to marry me."

"And she said no?"

"She didn't say *anything* at first. Then she yelled no and locked herself in the bathroom. I was trying to talk to her—"

"With your fist?" The undersheriff shook his head. "We're already short manpower and now this? How bad is your hand?"

"I think something's broken."

Mark swore. "Great. Go to the emergency room. All I need right now is a deputy on medical leave." But as he considered which deputy it was, he thought maybe it was for the best. Harp was trouble, hero or no hero.

"I'll still be able to work," Harp said as he lumbered to his feet.

"How do you figure that? Can you pull your gun and shoot it? If they cast your hand, you might not even be able to drive legally. Let me know what the doctor says. Now get out of here and be damned happy that you didn't get through that door and lay a hand on your...possible fiancée or you'd be behind bars right now."

"You mean the way the sheriff is behind bars?" Harp muttered under his breath.

Mark bit down on his tongue. He didn't want to get into it with Harp. He hadn't slept and with each passing hour was more worried that they wouldn't find Maggie alive. "Don't push it, Harp. You'll lose." Fortunately, Harp had the good sense to keep going.

After Harp left, Mark reached for the mail distractedly. He was still bowled over by what Celeste Duma had told him—and still wasn't sure he believed a word of it. He remembered that he'd been about to call Flint when Deputy Harper Cole had come in.

He tried his number. It went straight to voice mail. He frowned, suddenly worried. Flint had been adamant about being kept in the loop. He left a message for the sheriff to call him as soon as possible.

As he started to push the mail aside again, he noticed one envelope in particular that jumped out at him. There was no return address. No postage stamp. His name was printed on it and the word *PERSONAL* in caps.

He had a feeling about it. Feeling a little foolish, he pulled a pair of latex gloves from his desk and reached for the letter opener. Carefully he tore it open, turned the letter out on his desk and swore.

Flint stared at the little-yellow-chicks wallpaper, the crib with its tiny quilt thrown over one side, the bassinet against one wall and the white rocker with a bookshelf beside it and a dozen children's books all lined up. Everything was brandnew.

The room smelled more musty than the rest of the house. He stared at it, seeing what it meant. He could feel the disappointment like an ache in this room. Had Celeste been pregnant? Had she lost the baby? Or was this just wishful thinking?

No, he thought. This wasn't a room about hope. This was a room for a child she'd already come to love. A child she must have been carrying.

He hadn't known. Somehow he thought he should have. So if she'd lost the baby... Had she also lost all hope of having another one? But why not pack all of this up? Why keep a reminder of what could have been?

Flint felt physical pain at the thought of Celeste coming into this room, leaning over the crib railing to pick up the stuffed teddy bear, to grieve.

His phone rang, making him jump. He quickly closed the door and tried to shake off the compassion he felt for a woman he'd recently wanted to kill.

"Cahill," he said into the phone without checking the caller ID.

"Where are you?" his undersheriff asked.

It took him a minute to find his voice. "Is it Maggie?"

"No, we haven't found her, but I need to see you. Can you come down to the office?"

"I'm not in town." He didn't want to admit where he was. He'd felt no guilt for breaking a window to get into the Duma house to look for Maggie. But seeing that room felt like a violation.

"Flint?"

"I'm fine. Tell me what's happened."

"We have another suspect. What do you know about Maggie's past relationships?"

He swore under his breath. "Nothing. She didn't... That is, I know there was a man and it wasn't good. Are you saying an old boyfriend might have taken her?"

"He might have been at the house that day. He also might have been driving a brown van."

Flint closed his eyes and leaned back against the wall. The lake house suddenly felt very cold, the darkness heavy with a density he hadn't felt before. He pushed off the wall and started walking toward the door, needing to get out of there, needing to get home.

"I have no idea who he might be," he said as he exited the house and headed for his pickup.

"Well, we have a lead we're following up on, but there's more."

Flint heard the hesitation in the undersheriff's voice. It was something he hadn't wanted to get into on the phone. It made him stop just feet short of his pickup. His blood ran cold, the night closing in on him. "What?"

"I just received a ransom demand for fifty thousand dollars for Maggie's return."

CHAPTER THIRTEEN

The bad news was that several bones in Harp's hand were broken and Mark wasn't going to let him be on duty. He'd screwed up again and was furious with himself. No surprise, the undersheriff hadn't taken it well. Add to that the pain and having his hand in a cast clear up to his elbow. On top of that, he'd had to stay in a motel, since when he'd called Mark, the undersheriff had told him not to go back to Vicki last night.

So even with the pain pills, he'd had a rough night with little sleep. He kept going over it in his head, trying to figure out why the woman had acted the way she had. It made no sense. She was the one who'd been talking marriage, babies, all that female crap that made his stomach roil.

And when he'd finally decided to bite the bullet, that was the way she reacted? As far as he knew, she was still locked in the bathroom.

Last night he'd definitely thought about ignoring Mark's order and going over to her apartment and demanding to know what the hell was wrong with her. But he suspected it would end up in a fight. If the friggin' neighbors called the sheriff's department again...

He'd thought about calling Vicki, but Mark had also warned him not to do that, either. *Sleep on it. Trust me, it's the best thing you can do. Everything is much clearer in the morning.*

Harp had hoped that was true. But this morning, he had other things on his mind. He'd had plenty of time in the emergency room of the hospital to think about his future. He'd screwed up. Again. But he'd been thinking there might be a way to fix it.

He'd find Maggie Thompson.

The sheriff's department was a madhouse with DCI. He walked in as if he knew what was going on. He hadn't realized how out of the loop he was until he heard the FBI might be called in because a ransom note had been received.

He found his inside source on her break. "What's going on?" he asked as he took a chair next to her. Gail Anderson was in her late fifties and the night dispatcher. She liked to bowl, drink beer and carry tales, so the two of them had always gotten along.

She filled him in, just as he knew she would, keeping her voice down and their heads together.

"What are you doing here?" the undersheriff asked, suddenly sticking his head in the break-room doorway.

"I was going crazy just sitting around," Harp said. "Isn't there something I can do here?"

Mark shook his head. "You'll just be in the way. Go home." With that, he left.

"You get a raw deal around here," Gail said.

"I just need to prove myself to them," he said. "What do you think happened to Maggie?"

"I'd go with the former boyfriend, though the sheriff's ex is definitely a piece of work. One or the other has her. But the question is, where would you hide someone? We have a tail on the ex-wife, so if she took Maggie, she can't go take her food or water. Of course, she could have an accomplice. A woman like that can probably talk a man into doing just about anything."

"Or maybe she acted alone. I get the feeling from what I've heard that she'd just as soon see Maggie dead anyway. So if she wasn't planning on going back to wherever she hid Maggie...she wouldn't be worried about getting caught."

Gail agreed. "She's the kind of woman who would eat her young."

Harp gave a little laugh, thinking about his own kid. He wasn't sure having it with Vicki was the best idea. She didn't seem real...stable.

"Did they get a plate number on that brown van that was seen in the neighborhood, the one they now think the ex-boyfriend was driving?"

She shook her head as she wadded up her lunch sack and stood to toss it in the trash.

"What about the bar where the two were seen together?"

"*Allegedly* seen together," Gail said and chuckled. "Bud's Bar and Casino. It sounds nicer than it is, I heard."

Right now, a cold beer sounded good, and since he had time to kill, why not drive to Billings?

On the drive back to Gilt Edge, Flint went over everything Maggie had ever told him about her past. He knew little. He'd always thought there was some man who she'd gotten away from, but she'd never said it in so many words. It had been more of a feeling. Now he blamed himself for not asking, but at the same time, he knew she hadn't wanted him to know.

This old boyfriend? How dangerous was he? If he had Maggie...

He still wasn't convinced that Celeste hadn't taken her. But Mark seemed to have changed his mind. Flint thought that was foolish. Unless Celeste had come up with an alibi. But a ransom note? That did not sound like Celeste. Unless she was trying to cover her tracks.

"It's got to be a hoax," Flint said to himself. "Just someone thinking they can cash in on this." He'd driven most of the night, pulling over at a truck stop to get something to eat and some coffee. He knew he was too tired to make any sense out of this, especially when he knew so little.

The sun was up and climbing as he reached Gilt Edge. He swung by the sheriff's office, not surprised to find Mark behind his desk. The undersheriff looked as exhausted as Flint felt.

Mark motioned him into a chair. "Where have you been?"

The two of them knew each other well enough that Mark wouldn't believe he'd just left town for the heck of it. Also, he wasn't going to keep anything from the undersheriff.

"I went over to the Dumas' lake house. I thought Maggie..." Mark swore. "You're determined to get thrown in jail."

Flint shook his head, remembering the baby's room. "She wasn't there. I would have told you, but it was something I needed to do myself."

Mark sighed. "I talked to Celeste again. She *was* headed for the lake house but apparently ended up getting drunk and going home with a man at the bar outside of Bigfork, and yes, her alibi checks out. The bartender remembers her and knows the man she went home with. She was with him until she returned to town."

He shook his head. "It sounds like a planned alibi to me. It still doesn't mean that she didn't have Maggie with her and stashed her somewhere."

"We've had a tail on her ever since she returned," Mark said. "She hasn't left the house except to come down here to the sheriff's department for questioning."

Flint felt his heart drop at the thought of Celeste hiding Maggie somewhere and just leaving her there to die. "She must have someone working with her."

"I considered that," Mark said noncommittally.

"You know how Celeste is. She could easily have met some man and gotten him to do her bidding." Mark looked even more skeptical. "She would have told him it was a practical joke or whatever. Maybe she offered him money. You have to understand, there isn't much this woman wouldn't do to get what she wants, and she wants Maggie out of my life."

Mark nodded. "Then you are going to love hearing this. Three weeks ago, Celeste says she saw Maggie with a man at a bar in Billings. The two, according to her, seemed to have a history and were arguing, the man trying to get her to come back to him. Celeste thought he might have driven a brown van."

Flint shook his head. "You aren't buying into this, are you? She's just trying to save her own neck."

"Maybe, but we're looking into it."

"Wait. Are you thinking the same thing I am? If Celeste tracked down this man, she might have gotten him to help her."

"It crossed my mind after what you just said," Mark agreed.

Celeste was a known liar. He couldn't believe anything she said and neither should his undersheriff. "Wait. When was this alleged meeting in the bar?" he asked after Mark finished telling him everything Celeste had said about this old boyfriend of Maggie's. "This could all be a lie."

"Three weeks ago."

He looked out the window, thinking how much he hated this time of year. It was still snowing, and after several days of it, he felt as if it might never stop. Days like this made him want to move to Arizona. He craved the sun, needed that warmth right now because he felt chilled to the bone.

Three weeks ago. The words played in his head. At first he thought he could prove that Celeste was lying, that Maggie couldn't have gone to Billings. This had to be just another Celeste story.

But then he remembered. Three weeks ago Maggie had

gone to a product show in Billings. But Celeste could have found that out. Celeste could have… He swallowed. Celeste could have come up with this whole story. But the lawman in him was reminded of the neighbor who'd seen the brown van go past. Another little detail Celeste could have added for good measure.

Flint thought back to three weeks ago when Maggie had returned from Billings for what she said was a salon product meeting.

So three weeks ago they'd been dating, but he wouldn't say they'd been all that close. Weeks before that, Maggie's salon had been broken into and someone had started a fire on the back porch of her house. Celeste, but unfortunately, he had no proof of that.

He'd seen Maggie before she'd left for Billings and after she'd come home. She hadn't kept the trip from him. Something about salon products. Or at least she'd made it sound like that. And maybe that was what it had been. Maybe she hadn't lied. Maybe she'd run into the man while down there. Or maybe she'd been planning to meet him the whole time.

He hadn't questioned her about the trip. Because he'd trusted her. Before this moment, he would have said Maggie was the last person on this earth who would lie to him.

Now he shook his head at how naive he'd been. He'd seen a change in her before she went and when she'd come back. There'd been a distance. But he'd blamed it on the things they'd been through with his ex, when maybe the whole time, it had been the old boyfriend.

Maggie wouldn't have liked keeping it from him. Other than that, she wouldn't have anything else to hide, he assured himself. It wasn't like she had been considering going back to the man.

Or had she? Was it possible that after Celeste saw him at the house, Maggie had left with the man?

He shook his head. From what Celeste had reported that she'd overheard of the conversation, the man had been trying to get her back and Maggie wasn't having it.

"If he was trying to get her back..." Flint said and stopped. Maggie had definitely argued with someone and gotten hurt. "You think he abducted her?"

"Possibly."

"She wouldn't have left with him." He saw Mark's expression and he knew that, like him, he was thinking of Jenna Holloway. A woman could sometimes leave with the worse man for her.

"If Celeste and this man joined forces..." He could see that happening, Celeste offering to help the man, telling him that Maggie wasn't serious about some sheriff in some Podunk Montana town. "Where would he have taken her? Billings? Is that where he was living? Or somewhere closer to Gilt Edge?"

"That's what we are looking into," Mark said. "Once we know who he..."

Flint nodded. "Celeste swears she doesn't know? What did the man look like?" He listened to the description. As far as he knew, he'd never seen the man. If the man even existed. Silently he cursed his ex-wife. She lied about so much. This could be a lie, as well. Another dead-end lead that would keep them from finding Maggie.

"Have you been able to verify this incident at the bar?"

Mark nodded. "I talked to the bartender, a man named Brian Bateman. It's the kind of bar where this happens more often than not, but he remembered because of Celeste and her friends. He didn't want any bloodshed with them in the bar. He could tell that they weren't the usual clientele."

"Had he seen the man before?"

"Yes, said he comes in after work sometimes but was never a problem before that. The bartender's description matched Celeste's. Also, his description of Maggie matched."

Flint put his head in his hands for a moment. "If this man has Maggie, and Celeste orchestrated this whole thing…"

"You have to remember that he was reportedly trying to get her back. So there is a good chance he won't hurt her—if he has her."

Flint wondered about that.

"She never mentioned this man?" Mark asked.

"No," he mumbled into his hands, then lifted his head. "That's not true. I think he was the reason she came to Gilt Edge. In order to get away from him."

Mark nodded. "It could be the same man, but we don't know that." The undersheriff sighed. "Then there is this." He handed him the bagged ransom note.

The sheriff read it twice and looked at his watch, having lost track of time.

"How soon do I have to come up with the money?" There was no way he could raise that much money on his own.

"I'm waiting for the kidnapper to contact me again."

"It could be to throw us off who really has Maggie," Flint said.

"Maybe. Or this person might have her. I suspect, like you said, it could be someone who doesn't know where Maggie is, trying to cash in."

"Even so, I can't raise fifty thousand dollars, not unless I got the family to put up the ranch. I can't ask them to do that."

"We need to ask for proof of life first."

Proof of life. He bit the inside of his cheek to fight the pain. He wanted to argue that a kidnapper didn't have Maggie. That Celeste and this old boyfriend of Maggie's had thrown in together to do this. But he couldn't.

It was all supposition with no proof. He was still a lawman. The truth was he had no idea where Maggie was or who had taken her or even if she was still alive.

CHAPTER FOURTEEN

Bud's Bar was pretty much what Harp had expected. He'd been smart enough to buy himself a change of clothes when he got to Billings. That seemed easier than going back to the apartment and Vicki. He didn't know what he was coming home to anymore.

Now he wore jeans, boots and a checked shirt. He'd driven his truck down since his patrol car was now at the sheriff's office until he could go back to work. This wasn't the kind of bar he wanted to walk into in uniform anyway.

It was dark and smelled of stale beer. He let the door close behind him and waited a moment to let his eyes adjust to the dim light. The place was small—just big enough for the large U-shaped bar at its center and a half-dozen poker machines against one wall and some tables and chairs against the other wall.

Bud's looked like a rough place that had seen better days. The floor tiles were of an indiscriminate color and worn thin. As he stepped in and found an empty bar stool, he noted the vinyl seats were cracked and torn, and had long since lost their cushioning ability.

He ordered a draft and looked around. There were people in front of all but one of the poker machines. He could only see the backs of their heads and the glow of their faces in the screens. None of them fit the boyfriend's description he'd gotten from his friend Gail at the office.

The bartender was a big thirtysomething guy with dark hair who looked like he lifted weights. After Harp ordered a draft, the man shoved a draft in front of him and took his money without a word. For this time of the afternoon, Harp was a little surprised to see how many people were bellied up to the bar.

Several of the men on the other side of the bar were arguing. The bartender made a beeline for them. Harp couldn't hear what he said to them, but they quieted right down.

Gail had told him that the bartender who'd been on duty the night Maggie had been there was named Brian Bateman. He heard one of the patrons say, "Bri, we could use a couple more down here."

Bri as in Brian? Harp had just taken a sip of his beer when the door to the bar opened, throwing in a shaft of bright sunlight from outside. Like everyone else, he turned and was momentarily blinded.

The man who entered was big and blond.

Harp shot a look at the bartender, who had also turned toward the door. One look at Bri's expression and he knew that the man who'd just entered was Maggie Thompson's old boyfriend. As the man walked past to take a freshly vacated seat two stools down, Harp noticed he had tar on his boots and jeans. Brian went over to get the man's order with the same diffidence he'd shown Harp.

But after he'd placed a beer and a shot in front of the man, he headed to the back. Harp saw the bartender on the phone and had a pretty good idea who he was calling.

Unfortunately, the big, blond man also noticed.

"If you just called the cops on me again…" the man said as

he shoved to his feet. He picked up his half-empty beer and hurled it at the bartender's head.

Harp wished now that he'd brought his stun gun. He slipped off his bar stool, thinking he was going to have to improvise. The boyfriend was much bigger than he'd expected. As the blond man headed for the door, Harp picked up his bar stool and swung it, catching the man in the back.

The man was big and tough. He spun around, looking for a fight. Things would have gotten ugly if the bartender hadn't leaped over the bar to give the man a tap with the baseball bat he kept behind the bar.

The blond went down like a ton of rocks and was out cold.

"I'm with the sheriff's department up in Gilt Edge," Harp said. "I'm assuming that's who you just called?"

Bri nodded.

"Mind calling them back and telling them it's covered?"

While the bartender made the call, Harp checked the man's wallet. His name, according to his Montana driver's license, was Gary Long, forty-two. The address was one there in Billings. Other than a couple of credit cards, the wallet held a twenty and some ones, along with a pay stub from a roofing company.

"Could I get a couple of you fellas to help me take him out to my rig?" Harp asked.

Flint drove to the Stagecoach Saloon as if in a fog. From the moment he'd walked into his house and seen the overturned bookcase, he'd been out of his mind with worry. It was almost at the crucial seventy-two-hours point. After that, a case was considered cold and chances of getting the victim back alive had dropped considerably.

The worry had worn on him night and day until now he felt like a zombie. He wasn't even sure he was thinking clearly.

Earlier, he'd felt some strange hope that Maggie was okay, but that hope was quickly fading. Had he lost his mind? He'd actually been relieved that Celeste and some old abusive boyfriend of Maggie's could have taken her? He'd been afraid when he'd heard that Celeste hadn't been anywhere since returning. All he'd thought about was who was taking care of Maggie, who was feeding her, who was making sure she was warm and dry and not out in the winter storm?

But if this former abusive boyfriend had Maggie, if he was the one she'd come to Gilt Edge to escape from and now the man had her...

He felt sick to his stomach. Worse, he couldn't be sure that some unknown person hadn't kidnapped Maggie for fifty thousand dollars. All he knew was that he had to do whatever it took to get her back—even if it meant asking his family for help.

As he entered the bar and café, he felt his heart breaking. He'd prided himself on being able to handle his problems himself, probably because he hated asking for help.

"Any news?" Lillie asked as she ran to him and threw her arms around him.

"Nothing yet."

As she pulled back, Darby joined them to put an arm around his shoulders. "Would a drink help?"

He was already choked up. Their sympathy was killing him. "It can't hurt at this point." They all moved to the bar. Lillie pulled up a stool next to him while Darby went behind the bar to get them something to drink.

"We got a ransom demand," he said after a moment, his voice breaking.

Darby froze behind the bar. "How much?"

"Fifty thousand dollars."

Flint saw his siblings exchange a look.

"We'll raise it. How much time do we have?" Lillie asked.

He shook his head, finding himself close to tears. His family. He couldn't have loved them more than he did at that moment. "The kidnapper will get back to us. I guess. Mark just got the one letter making the demand."

Darby swore under his breath. "We need to call Hawk and Cyrus. We'll have to put up the ranch but it belongs to all of us."

"I can't ask you to do that," Flint said, but neither Lillie nor Darby seemed to be listening.

Lillie was on the phone to their brothers. "They're both on their way," she said as she disconnected. "It's going to be all right," she said, putting a hand on Flint's.

He nodded, but in his heart he feared it was already too late for Maggie.

"Where am I?" Gary Long said twenty minutes later when he regained consciousness inside his house after Harp had gotten the address off the man's driver's license. "What the hell's going on?" he demanded as he found himself duct-taped to a dolly that Harp had found in Long's garage and wheeled into the kitchen. It hadn't been easy binding the man with only his one good hand. Getting him out of the pickup, though, had only been a matter of pulling up next to the garage, opening the door and shoving him out in the snow. He'd then rolled him unceremoniously onto the dolly, taped him and stood him up.

"Where is Maggie Thompson?"

"Is that what this is about?" The man snorted and tried to get loose only to find that his ankles were also bound to the dolly. "Why? Have you lost her?"

Harp caught him before he tipped the contraption over and fell face-first to the floor. "You were seen at her house. Tell me about you and Maggie."

Gary shook his head. "Kiss my rosy red—"

"Look, I can turn you over to the sheriff in Gilt Edge or you can tell me what your connection is to Maggie. Or we can talk about the meth I found in your bedroom."

The man swore. "If Maggie says I did anything to her, she's a liar."

"So you two dated?" he asked.

Gary laughed. "*Dated?* Is that what she told you?" He shook his head. "We shacked up for a while. That's all it was."

"Then why were you trying to get her back?"

A muscle jumped in the man's jaw. He struggled to get loose before finally giving up. "What's it to you, anyway?"

"I'm a sheriff's deputy. You were seen with her at Bud's and then later going into her house in Gilt Edge."

"Oh yeah? So what? Anyway, it wasn't her house. It was some cowboy she was moving in with."

"She told you that?"

"Maybe I figured out a few things on my own."

"So you've been following her."

Gary said nothing. "What happened when she saw you at her boyfriend's house?" Harp asked.

"What do you think happened?"

"I think you hurt her."

Gary shook his head as he looked away. "Is that what she told you?"

That was the second time he'd said something to that effect. Harp was beginning to wonder if they had the wrong man. When he'd gotten Gary out to his pickup, he'd taken the man's key, expecting it to go with a brown van.

But there was no brown van in the parking lot at Bud's. Instead, the only vehicle key on Gary's ring went with a small, older-model two-wheel-drive pickup. Harp had also searched the man's house and found no sign of Maggie.

But what he had found was meth in one of the drawers in the bedroom that he knew he could use as leverage.

"Maggie didn't tell us anything. She's missing."

That got the man's attention. *"Missing?"*

"If you know anything about what happened to her—or about the meth I found in your bedroom…"

Gary groaned. "Okay, I saw her that day at the cowboy's house. I surprised her. The house was open, okay? I didn't break in. She wasn't happy to see me. We argued. I might have pushed her."

"And she might have fallen and smacked her head on the edge of the bookcase?"

"Look, when I left she was fine. She was pissed and threatening to call the cops if she ever saw me again, but that was it."

"What did you do then?" Harp asked.

"I told her I was done. Move in with her cowboy. I didn't care. And I left."

"That was the last you saw her?"

"Yeah, I wanted her back. I love her, all right? I thought maybe we deserved a second chance... I've changed."

Harp doubted that, but he said nothing.

"She made it perfectly clear that she's moved on. So that was that. I told her that the cowboy can have her. Now she's missing? I swear I know nothing about that. She was fine other than a little blood on her temple, but otherwise was fine when I left."

Harp got the feeling that he was telling the truth. "Did you see anyone as you were leaving?"

Gary shook his head.

"You didn't notice another vehicle parked nearby?"

He started to shake his head again, but stopped. "I saw an old brown van parked in the trees behind the house. If anyone was driving it, I didn't see them."

Frank turned onto the road to the Roberts North Dakota farm, feeling as curious as Nettie was about meeting Jenna's parents. In the afternoon light, the place sat on a wind-scoured plot devoid of trees or even snow. Old farm equipment rusted in a nearby field and a windmill clanged as it turned slowly in the breeze. He and Nettie climbed out.

There were no Christmas lights or decorations to be seen.

If not for the faded curtains at the windows and the pickup parked out front, he would have thought the farm abandoned.

"This place gives me the creeps," she said as they started toward the porch steps.

"You can stop right there!" a strident female voice announced. "Whatever you're selling, we aren't interested."

Frank looked up to see a thin, weathered elderly woman in a faded housedress standing on the porch, holding a shotgun. He stopped walking and so did Nettie. The woman looked as if she knew how to use the firearm.

"Mrs. Edith Roberts?" Nettie asked.

"Like I said—"

"We're here about Jenna."

The shotgun wavered in her skinny arms for a moment. "Don't know anyone by that name." Her voice broke, though, as she said it.

"We're afraid your daughter is in trouble," Nettie persisted. "We're hoping you can help us find her."

"That doesn't come as much of a surprise. You the law?"

"Private investigators," Frank said.

The woman licked her thin lips. "Like I said—"

"We know Jenna is your daughter. We also know that she gave birth to a baby thirty-three years ago," Frank said. "We're afraid that the father of that baby now has Jenna and plans to hurt her."

"Clark Terwilliger?" Edith Roberts said the name like a curse, lowering the shotgun to one hand as she reached for the porch pillar with her free hand for support. Her gaze went to the horizon. "Les will be back soon. If he catches you on his property—"

"We can make this fast," Nettie said. "Please, let us come in."

The woman hesitated. Her brown eyes looked as washed-out as the land. "The moment we hear his tractor coming up the road..." Seemingly weak from the news, she stepped away from the pillar. The shotgun thumped against her stick-thin legs as she led the way inside.

They followed her into a living room with a worn sagging couch, two threadbare recliners and an ancient television. There were religious sayings on the walls and pictures of Jesus.

"We need to know what happened to your grandchild," Nettie said.

"I don't have a grandchild," Edith snapped as she stood the shotgun by the door and motioned for them to sit down. She stayed standing by the wall, her arms crossed over her flat chest. Frank could see that the woman had her ears nervously peeled for the sound of the tractor. He wondered what would happen if Les Roberts found them there asking about Jenna.

"What happened to the child that Jenna gave birth to?" Frank asked.

"It died."

"I don't think so and neither does Clark Terwilliger. We heard he's been looking for the baby."

"I wouldn't know nothin' about that. A midwife took care of it."

"Here at the house?" Nettie asked.

Edith shook her head. "Over at my sister's in Turtle Lake. I didn't want to know. I just wanted it done. God's will that it died. Jenna came home and we put it behind us best we could."

Frank doubted Les Roberts had put it behind him, especially given what Dana had told them about Jenna's parents. "How long before Jenna left here after that?"

The woman seemed upset by the question and maybe a little guilty. "Run off at sixteen."

"Have you seen her since?"

Edith looked away for a moment. "Called once a few months later. Needed money. Les…"

"You didn't send her money," Nettie said. "Did she say where she was calling from?"

"Didn't ask. That's the last we heard from her."

"Then you didn't know she'd gotten married to a farmer in Montana?"

Edith looked almost pleased to hear that, but then said, "You say she's in trouble now, though."

"The father of the baby, Clark Terwilliger, is apparently after her and might have already found her."

The woman shuddered at the name as if it was one not spoken under this roof. "Don't know how I can help. Like I said—"

"Why would Clark think the baby survived?" Frank demanded.

"How would I know what a man like that thinks?"

"Mrs. Roberts," Nettie said. "If the child survived—"

She shook her head. "You're wastin' your time."

"Let us at least talk to your sister," Nettie pleaded. "What is her name?"

"Edna. Edna Burns, but she is goin' to tell you the same thing I did."

But there would be a birth certificate—and a death certificate, if she'd really died, Frank thought.

At the sound of a motor engine, he saw Edith tense. "You have to get out of here." Fear made her rigid.

They'd been sitting on the edge of the couch and now rose quickly. "Here is my card," Frank said. "If you think of anything else that might help us…"

She took the card and shoved it deep into the pocket of her dress as she turned and hurried to the door.

They both stepped out into the blinding light. Frank blinked. He could see a tractor coming across the flat surface of stubble field, still a good half mile away. He and Nettie hurried down the porch steps and into the SUV. He glanced at Edith standing board-straight on the porch, her face a mask of fear.

"He won't hurt you, will he?" Nettie asked as she whirred down her window.

"Go! Please! I'll be fine."

Frank started the engine and drove down the road. The tractor passed in the field next to them. From beneath bushy white brows and a dark stained baseball cap, Les Roberts glowered at them as he slowed the tractor. And then they were past him.

He glanced in the rearview mirror as the elderly man pulled up to the house and climbed off the tractor before heading toward the porch, where his wife was waiting.

"I feel like I need a shower," Nettie said. "You think she's all right?"

He saw her glance back. "Our staying would have made it worse. I suspect she's had plenty of experience dealing with him."

His wife shuddered. "I can't imagine being that terrified of a man."

Frank reached over and took her hand. "You would have killed him in his sleep years ago."

She squeezed his hand, and when he glanced over at her, he saw tears in her eyes. "I hate to think there are still women who live like that. Poor Jenna, growing up in that house, let alone coming back to it after…" She looked away, wiping at her tears.

Exhausted after his meeting with the family, Flint had gone back to the ranch. He knew he needed sleep. Upstairs in his room, he lay down on the bed and stared at the ceiling. His mind whirled. *Maggie, where are you?* Was she also somewhere lying on a bed, staring up at a ceiling? He just hoped she was all right.

He thought of the ex-boyfriend. Mark would have a name soon. The Billings cops would pay him a visit. If he had Maggie... He thought of what Mariah had said. Maybe a basement. Maybe soon he would get the call that she'd been found alive and well and was on her way home. Home.

Flint thought of his house, of the two of them living there. He thought again of the Christmas tree he planned to get from the mountains. He had envisioned the two of them decorating it together, holiday music in the background, a crackling blaze in the fireplace. He could almost smell a beef roast cooking in the oven.

And then a terrible thought would hit him that Maggie was never coming back because Maggie was dead. He tried to push away the dark thoughts, but they loomed over him, following him about like a black cloud. He could feel his heart pounding. He stared out at the falling snow, wondering when it was ever going to stop.

Closing his eyes, he tried to get back the Christmas scene, but it refused to come. Determined not to let his mind go down another dark hole, he instead recalled their first kiss.

They had both been so wary about falling in love. They'd both wanted to take it slow. Or at least he had. Maggie had agreed. So they'd spent many hours getting to know each other.

Those were the most wonderful days, he thought now. They had gone on picnics and hikes. They'd swum in the creek, taken bike rides and ridden horses. They'd been like kids and he'd felt himself falling hard for her.

Their first kiss was after one of those horseback rides. They'd ridden up into the mountains after saddling up at the ranch. It had been a beautiful Montana summer day, the sky a blinding blue without a cloud to be seen. The air had smelled of fresh water and flowers and pines. Everything was green and alive.

They'd gotten off their horses to walk down to the creek's edge. When he couldn't stand it any longer he'd grabbed her and kissed her with a passion that neither of them had expected.

He'd wanted her right then, but the kiss had scared him. He'd had passion with Celeste—the wild, untamed type that ran like a race between love and hate. He didn't want that again. And at the time, he'd thought that was the only kind there was.

Months later, after several attempts that were blocked by Celeste and his job, they'd finally made love. It was sweet and slow. At least at first. Then it was filled with passion and love and tenderness. He'd realized that was the way it was supposed to be.

Just thinking about that night made him ache. If he'd had any doubts about him and Maggie, they'd ended that night. He loved her and she loved him. He'd found himself wanting all the things he had yearned for when he'd married the first time: a home, children, a life filled with joy and love.

With Maggie, he really believed that they could have it all. And yet he'd dragged his feet because of Celeste, because of that disastrous marriage, because of those broken dreams.

He reached over and picked up the small velvet box with the engagement ring in it. If only he'd asked her before... He opened the box. The diamond flashed brightly as if mocking him. He closed it and put the box into the top drawer of the nightstand, fearing it might stay there forever.

Why hadn't he asked about old boyfriends? If he had, he might have a name, and Mark would know now and have found the man. Maybe have found Maggie. If Maggie was with the man... Wasn't that better than some stranger who wanted Maggie for some other godforsaken reason?

He closed his eyes, his head aching. As he lay there, he told himself he would never be able to get to sleep.

When his phone rang, he jerked awake.

CHAPTER FIFTEEN

Maggie held her breath as what seemed like hours later, she heard footfalls. As they stopped on the other side of her door, she opened her eyes.

She fought the remaining effects of the drugs as she stared at the doorknob. It slowly turned and the door began to open. Her gaze shot up and she flinched in horror. She'd been so sure she was going to see Celeste's face that she reared back at the sight of a man she'd never seen before.

He was big and easily filled the doorway with the kind of muscles and tattoos that shouted former prison inmate. He was strangely handsome, almost boyish, with short blond hair and big brown eyes fringed with dark lashes. He stepped into the room carrying a shopping bag. It wasn't until he drew close that she realized he was older than she'd first thought, closer to his midfifties than forties.

"I see you're awake," he said, smiling at her.

"You have to let me go. You've made a mistake. I don't know who you are, but I shouldn't be here." Her voice sounded strange even to her ears. "Please, let me go." The words came out on a sob.

"Don't be silly," the man said. "This is where you live now."

No! She thought of news stories about abducted women who'd spent years being locked up in shacks behind some crazy's house or trapped in a basement. She looked past him and saw that he'd left the door standing open.

"Help! Help! Someone help me!" she screamed.

He moved so swiftly that she only caught his image out of the corner of her eye as he reached through the bars. She didn't stop screaming until she felt the slap. It knocked the air out of her. She fell back, banging into the metal bed rail. Her head swam.

"I won't hear any more of that," he scolded. "Now you behave, young lady, or I will turn you over my knee. You have this beautiful room all to yourself. You should be more thankful. I don't want to have to spank you, but I will if you make me."

She stared at him, his words filling her with horror. Spank her? He was talking to her as if she was a child. His words echoed in her head, making her heart race with terror. *This is where you live.*

"I brought you something pretty to wear," he said as he dug in the shopping bag. "But promise me you'll keep your dress nice. If you do, then you can come into the kitchen and eat with us."

Us? She again looked toward the door, remembering that she'd thought she'd heard a woman crying before. How many other people were here in this house? Was it a house, though? Was it a basement apartment? It didn't feel like it. It felt as if someone had tried to make it look like a real house. To fool her? To fool the others? If there really were others.

"Promise?" he asked.

All she could do was nod, her cheek still stinging from where he'd hit her.

He reached through the bars with an item of clothing. She thought about grabbing his arm, jerking it through the bars and…and then what? Even if she broke his arm, she couldn't see how that would get her out of the cage.

She took the clothing he handed her, all the time her mind racing. What did this man want from her? "Please let me go." It came out almost a whimper.

"I'm warning you. Unless you want to go to bed without any dinner…" Her stomach growled in answer and he laughed. "That's what I thought. Now get dressed. Just call when you're ready, and if you behave like the sweet girl I know you are, then you can sit at the table."

She could get out of this cage? It was the only way she would ever stand a chance of escaping. "I will," she said in a small, timid voice that seemed to please him.

The moment he left she looked down at the items of clothing he'd brought her and felt a shudder move through her. The dress was something for a six-year-old but in her size and the shoes were saddle oxfords. Had anyone worn those in the past fifty years?

"Is there a problem?" he asked from the doorway, startling her.

She shook her head.

"That's my girl." He smiled. "Daddy doesn't want to hurt you."

Daddy? Maggie fought the tears that burned her eyes. She swallowed and nodded because she was too scared to speak. Too horrified.

She waited until he left the room again before she took off her jeans and shirt and put on the dress. It was pink and white with pink bows and clearly secondhand. It looked ridiculous on her. The socks he'd brought her were white with pink lace around the top. She sat down and pulled them on with trembling fingers, terrified of what would happen next. She'd just finished lacing up the shoes, which were also used but in her size, when she sensed him in the doorway again.

"Good girl. Ready for your surprise?"

Harp knew he'd broken every law in the book by taking Gary Long the way he had. Except, he hadn't acted as a sheriff's deputy. He'd merely taken the man home, immobilized him for a while so he could get the truth out of him. He liked to think of it as a citizen's arrest.

More to the point, Gary Long wouldn't be filing any charges against him, given what he'd found in the bedroom.

It was easy to rationalize what he'd done. If the man had kidnapped Maggie, it would probably be hard to get a conviction and he'd be in hot water again.

But if he'd saved Maggie, he really doubted the sheriff would have cared. As it was, he had found some crucial evidence. That had to account for something.

He took Gary Long's statement about what happened the day Maggie disappeared, warned him not to leave town and, after cutting him loose, headed back to Gilt Edge. Gary wouldn't call the cops on him for his "unusual" style of interrogation.

He had been feeling good as he drove north, his headlights cutting through the darkness. Turning on his radio, he'd rocked out. He had even looked forward to seeing Vicki. With luck, she would be up for sex. He'd be gentle. He had to think about the baby now.

Harp had been about fifteen miles outside of town when a pickup with Gilt Edge county plates went past on the other side of the road. It had looked vaguely familiar, which was why he'd glanced in his rearview mirror as it tore by. With some concern, he'd seen the driver hit his brakes, pull off and swing back onto the highway headed in his direction.

He'd watched with growing apprehension as the pickup had come roaring up behind him a few minutes later. He hadn't been able to see the driver behind the wheel, not with the pickup's headlights on high beams.

The jackass had stayed right on him all the way into town. It wasn't until they'd reached the town limits that the fool had roared up beside him. Harp had glanced over as the truck had come alongside him. Behind the wheel, Larry, the pawn guy, had flipped him the bird and then had taken off.

Harp had felt his heart racing. His hands had shaken as he'd driven the rest of the way to the apartment. Was that about the other day at the pawnshop? He had cursed himself for flipping Larry off. It had been childish. Or was it about years ago? He'd had a bad feeling from the look on Larry's face that it went deeper than a simple hand gesture a few days ago. He should have known that Shirley couldn't keep her mouth shut.

He'd thought that, being the law, it would keep Larry from doing anything stupid. But he should have known that a guy like Larry Wagner wouldn't have any respect for a badge. He hated to think what would happen if he met Larry Wagner in a dark alley.

Instead of going home last night, he'd gone to a motel, too shaken to even think about dealing with Vicki. This morning, he'd put Larry out of his thoughts and gone straight to the sheriff's department.

After he made the call that had awakened the sheriff, Mark waited until Flint arrived before he ushered him into his office, where Deputy Cole was waiting. He still couldn't believe what Harp had done. If he'd had his way he would have fired him on the spot. But he was leaving that to the sheriff.

Harp told his story, no doubt leaving out parts of it that

would make him look even worse. As soon as he finished, Mark could tell Flint was as incensed by the deputy taking things into his own hands while on medical leave.

"I talked to the bartender this morning," Mark said. "You hit Long with a bar stool."

Harp nodded. "He's a big dude and he would have gotten away if I hadn't. But the bartender tapped him with a baseball bat. That's really what took him down."

The undersheriff shook his head.

"But I got important information out of him as a private citizen—not as a sheriff's deputy because I was on medical leave. Come on—you know we have to find Maggie Thompson as quickly as possible. If I hadn't done what I did, how long would it have taken to clear the ex-boyfriend and narrow down the search?"

Flint groaned. He'd always gone by the book, but Mark could see that the sheriff just wanted Maggie back—whatever it took. "How do we even know that Gary Long didn't lie to you?"

"He was telling the truth. He didn't know Maggie had disappeared. But he admitted to having a confrontation with her about three weeks ago at Bud's Bar—and again at your house. He admits to pushing her, but he swears she was fine when he left."

"And he says there was a brown van parked in the woods behind my house?" the sheriff said. "You didn't feed him that information accidentally?"

Harp shook his head with impatience. "I'm not a fool."

That was debatable, Mark thought as he rubbed a hand over his face. "I'm going to have Gary Long picked up and questioned by the Billings police. I won't mention the meth you found in his house. If he wasn't smart enough to get rid of it... We'll see what they get out of him."

Harp shrugged. "Whatever. But the person we're looking for drives a brown van, right? It isn't Gary Long."

Mark got on his computer for a minute. "The only vehicle I can find registered to Long is a 1979 Ford two-wheel-drive small pickup."

"That's right," Harp said. "White where it isn't rusted out."

"And Long has no idea who might have been driving the van?"

"Nope," the deputy said. "He knew Maggie was dating a cowboy," he said, flicking his gaze at Flint before turning back to Mark. "And he knew where Maggie lived. He admits he was there, followed her from her house to Flint's and had gone in to try to talk her into coming back to him. They argued. He pushed her…" He waved to the document he'd submitted this morning. "It's all there."

Mark looked over at the sheriff. "I'll have Billings law enforcement check to see if Long has been at work since Maggie was taken. You say he's a roofer?" he asked Harp.

"When he came into the bar, I noticed the tar on his boots and jeans," Harp said. "He'd come straight from work. Also, I found a pay stub in his wallet."

Flint raked a hand through his hair. He looked as if he hadn't had a good night's sleep since Maggie disappeared almost four days ago. He also looked like he wanted to fire Harp. Mark was glad to see Flint was still acting like a lawman instead of a vigilante.

"You do realize that we'd have played hell getting a conviction because of the way you handled this?" Flint demanded of the deputy.

Harp attempted to look chastised. "I cleared him as a suspect. You said the clock was ticking. I had to take things into my own hands."

"We'll talk about this when Maggie is found," Mark said.

"Also, so much for the theory that Celeste and Long had thrown in together."

"I wouldn't be that quick to clear Celeste," Flint said.

The undersheriff shook his head. "I don't know, Flint. Celeste and Long both told the same story about the brown van. We have everyone looking for it. Once we find the van..."

"But as many people have reportedly seen this brown van, how come one of them didn't get a plate number? Even one?"

"This time of year most cars are dirty from the winter roads—including the license plates. It wouldn't surprise me that the driver made sure it wasn't easily noticed."

Maggie felt her heart rate soar. *"Surprise?"* She hated the way her voice cracked. Waking up underground in a cage had been enough of a surprise. She couldn't bear to think about what the man had planned for her.

"Didn't I tell you? Your mommy is joining us for dinner. She hasn't been herself but I know she's looking forward to seeing her little girl."

"My...*mommy?*" she repeated, feeling as if she'd fallen down a rabbit hole. This had to stop. She'd done everything the man had asked her to do. She had to try to get through to him, even if it meant being slapped again.

"My mother is dead. She died in childbirth. My father was killed in the Gulf War. I was raised by an aunt."

He smiled at her as if she was a child. "You look like her. I wondered who you'd taken after. But I can tell by your stubbornness that you take after me a little too."

Maggie couldn't speak. What kind of sick joke was this? He wanted to pretend that he was her father? And now her mother would be joining them? She felt as if she might throw up. Where had he brought her? How far underground were they? Was that why he hadn't been worried that someone would hear her screaming earlier?

"You want to see your mommy, don't you?"

She looked down at her shoes and reminded herself that the only way she could escape was if she was out of the cage. She mumbled a yes. But told herself to be very careful. This man was clearly insane—and mean. She'd seen it in his eyes when he'd hit her. He wouldn't hesitate to hurt her—if she crossed him.

It was imperative that she found out as much as she could about her situation before she risked an escape. She hated to think who he'd chosen for her "mommy." She didn't think she would be getting any help from whoever it was. All her instincts told her she was on her own, and yet she couldn't help thinking about the woman she'd heard crying.

Her own birth mother was dead. She had the sudden frightening thought that there would be a mummified body at the table with them. She shuddered, afraid of what she might be facing when he let her out of the cage.

She reminded herself to play along until she knew what she was up against. Raising her gaze, she looked the man directly in the eye and felt herself shudder. Her chances of getting out of there seemed to diminish when he struggled to open the latch that had her locked in. Even more when he picked her up and lowered her to the floor.

He was too big and strong. How could she ever hope to get away from him?

"That a girl," he said.

It felt so good to be on solid ground again, but her fear of what she would find waiting for her in the next room had her feeling light-headed—that and the effects of the drugs he'd given her.

"I know you always wanted your mommy and daddy to be together as a family and now we can be. But if either of you misbehave…"

He didn't have to finish. She had a pretty good idea what

misbehaving could get her—and probably worse than she could imagine. He pointed to the door, indicating he wanted her to go first. She braced herself as she walked slowly, feeling him within reach behind her. She sensed he was dangerously close to the edge of sanity.

As she came around the corner, she saw what looked like an old apartment kitchen and an open doorway that appeared to lead out into a dark and dirty unfinished basement. It gave her little clue of where she was. But in the darkness, she thought she had made out stairs that led up to the next floor.

Her gaze moved from the door and possible escape to the woman bound and gagged at the table, and she felt her heart drop.

Flint's cell phone buzzed. He pulled it out to check the screen. "I need to take this," he said, excusing himself as Mark tore Harp a new one. Not that Harp would be fired. He'd actually been trying to help. It was definitely something new for the deputy who'd been trying to do as little as possible since taking the job.

He wondered about the change in Harp as he took the call.

"We think we know who is looking for Jenna and why," Frank said into the phone without preamble. "Jenna was raped by a friend's older brother and had a child when she was fourteen."

Flint swore under his breath.

"She was pulled out of school, kept on the farm outside of town until she was shipped off to an aunt in the middle of North Dakota. The whole thing was kept a secret by parents who apparently blamed her and weren't about to make it public."

"And the baby?"

"Mother swears it died but we have reason to believe the infant survived. The father of the child is trying to find not just this offspring—but Jenna. Apparently he hadn't known the rape had resulted in Jenna becoming pregnant all those years ago. He's spent most of his time in one prison or another."

"Let me guess. He's out of prison now."

"Afraid so. His name is Clark Terwilliger. He was last seen driving a brown van with Missouri plates."

A brown van. Flint felt his pulse go into overdrive. He glanced at the undersheriff. "Just a minute, Frank. I'm at the sheriff's office. I'm going to put you on speakerphone. Mark, can you see if there is a brown van registered to a Clark Terwilliger? Missouri plates."

Mark moved to his computer, tapped on the keys and said, "A Clark Terwilliger doesn't own a brown van. In fact, I couldn't find any vehicle registered to him."

"Could be stolen," Flint said.

"Try his mother," Frank said on the other end of the line. "Nancy Terwilliger. Apparently she gave him anything he wanted, including Jenna."

"Bingo," the undersheriff said. "A Nancy Terwilliger of Lake City, Missouri, owns a brown Chevy van."

"He's driving his mother's van," Frank said. "Makes sense. Missouri is the last place he was locked up. According to his sister, he's furious that Jenna kept her pregnancy from him and now he is bound and determined to find not just her— but his kid."

"So the friend thinks he wants to hurt Jenna?" Flint was asking.

"Sounds like a love-hate situation," Frank said. "Clark has apparently been obsessed with Jenna since she was really young. Probably looking at a variety of mental problems, from what I've learned."

"So the baby could have died and he just isn't accepting it," Mark said.

"Possibly, but what is interesting is that Jenna was also

looking for her child at one point, so it makes me doubt the baby died," Frank said. "If the infant survived, Jenna might have found her."

Flint thought of the man Jenna had been with in Wyoming and Frank's theory. If Frank was right and Jenna had contacted her rapist wanting to end this, then... "You think she might have made a deal with Terwilliger?" He swore. "Wait—did you say maybe found *her*?"

"The baby was a girl."

CHAPTER SIXTEEN

When he reached the highway after leaving the Roberts farm, Frank had stopped to call Flint first. Then he placed a phone call to Edith Roberts's sister, Edna Burns. He explained that he was a PI looking for Jenna Roberts Holloway.

"Edith said you might be able to help us."

"She did?" The sister sounded surprised by that.

"We need to find out what happened to the baby Jenna gave birth to thirty-three years ago," he told her.

"Oh my," Edna said. "There must be some mistake. The baby died."

He looked over at Nettie. "Was the baby delivered at the hospital there?"

"No." He heard the hesitation in her voice. "She gave birth at home with a midwife."

"I'm going to need to talk to her."

"I doubt the midwife is even still alive."

Frank thought for a moment. "But you must have known what she planned to do with the infant—if it had lived."

Silence, then, "Well, yes, I guess. The midwife thought she knew of a couple who would take the child."

Why would the father of the baby be looking for her if she'd died at birth? Something was wrong here. "If the baby died, then there will be a death certificate."

Silence on the other end of the line.

"I suppose," Edna said, sounding like she wished she hadn't taken his call. "Really, I can't tell you any more than I have."

"Just tell me what the baby's name was on the death certificate."

More silence. He thought she might have hung up. "You say you're a private investigator?"

"That's right. I'm trying to find Jenna. We fear she is in trouble and thought it had something to do with her baby."

"Oh, that is horrible."

"If we have the name on the death certificate..."

"I don't know. I'm sorry." The woman seemed to break down. "Please leave me out of this." She hung up.

Frank looked over at Nettie. "What now?"

Nettie was looking at her phone. She showed him the North Dakota map she'd pulled up. "It isn't that far to the town where Edna Burns lives. There is more to the story."

He smiled. "I think something's strange too. We need the whole story and I suppose there is only one way to get it. But it's late. We should wait and go first thing in the morning."

"My thought exactly. I think it will be harder for her to lie to our faces."

Frank hoped she was right. The drive the next morning to Turtle Creek took only a couple of hours. The landscape by that time had become monotonous. They'd played a word game to keep themselves occupied, but he was never so happy to see the city-limits sign.

Edna Burns lived in a newer subdivision on the edge of town. The door was opened by an elderly, gray-haired woman wearing an apron over a jogging suit. As she opened the door, Frank caught the scent of a baking apple pie.

Frank introduced himself and his wife as Edna merely stared at them.

"We wouldn't be here if it wasn't urgent. Please, Mrs. Burns," Nettie said. "You have to help us. Jenna is in trouble."

"I have to get my pie out of the oven," she said and turned back into the house. They followed her as far as the living room before Nettie stopped to point at a photo on the mantel. For a moment, he thought the girl in the photo was Jenna. She had Jenna's dark hair and eyes and a smile that seemed to light up the room.

In the kitchen, they found Edna kneading the bottom hem of her apron nervously in her hands. "I knew this day would come."

"Don't you think there have been enough lies?" Frank asked.

The timer went off on the oven and Edna busied herself getting the apple pie out. As she set it down, she looked at them with obvious resignation. "I have coffee," she said. "And pie."

They sat down at the kitchen counter while Edna continued to busy herself in the kitchen. She cut them each a hot piece of apple pie and filled cups with coffee. Nettie noticed how immaculate the house was.

"Widowed?" she asked.

"For almost twenty years now."

"I take it you don't see your sister much," she said.

"No. Her husband..." Edna seemed at a loss for words.

"We've met him," Frank told her.

"Then you understand."

Nettie took a small bite of the cooling pie. "What we don't understand is why you let your sister believe that Jenna's baby died," she said after she'd complimented the woman's baking.

"When my sister called me hysterical and told me that Jenna

had been…tainted by some older boy and was pregnant with his child, I didn't know what to say or do. She pleaded with me to help Jenna. I'd never laid eyes on the girl before that. I hardly ever saw my sister, but I couldn't turn Edith down. So they sent Jenna here to have the baby, which was to be given up for adoption since the girl was only thirteen."

Edna stopped to take a sip of her coffee with trembling hands. She hadn't sat down, seemed too nervous and upset. "She was a sweet thing. I felt so bad for her. It became obvious that the older boy had…forced her and it had happened only once. I couldn't understand my sister treating the child like this. Jenna was so homesick and scared."

"So she had the baby here?" Frank asked.

Edna nodded. "I found a midwife since Edith insisted the child be born at home. Jenna had a terrible time. She was so small and the labor was for hours. She finally passed out as the baby emerged. A little girl." Edna smiled. "She was beautiful. Looked just like her mother."

"She was alive," Nettie said. "So why lie?"

"It was my sister's idea. She thought it would be best if the baby was dead."

Nettie felt her stomach roil. "But surely Jenna knew."

Edna dabbed at her eyes with a lace handkerchief she pulled from her apron pocket. "She'd fainted from the pain, and when she woke up, the baby had already been taken away."

"You told her the baby had died."

"I tried to convince myself it was for the best. Jenna could put it all behind her—just as her mother wanted."

"So the baby was adopted," Frank said.

"No. The family changed their mind. I couldn't keep the child. My husband had already been diagnosed with cancer. I had my hands full. But I had a friend. I talked her into taking the infant. I helped financially and babysat when I could. I got to see my great-niece grow up."

"And you never told anyone, including Jenna?" Frank asked.

"I almost did a couple of times. I felt so badly for her that she'd never get to know her daughter. It broke my heart. I would have taken that precious little thing, but under the circumstances, I couldn't."

"If you never told, then how did the father of the baby find out that he had a child?" Frank asked.

"I told you that I thought Jenna had fainted? Well, apparently she knew the baby hadn't died. She'd gone along with it for years, but one day she called me." Edna cleared her throat. "By then my grand-niece had grown up and left here. I thought maybe it was safe to tell Jenna since I knew she wouldn't tell her parents the truth."

"What did she want to know?" Nettie asked.

"Everything. But especially her daughter's name. Apparently she'd seen some woman in a beauty salon and thought it might be her daughter."

Nettie shot a look at Frank. "Where was this?"

"In Billings, Montana. So I told her the name we'd given my great-niece. Margaret Ann. That's the name Jenna said she wanted to give the baby if she was a girl and if she got to keep her. Of course, she couldn't have kept the child. She was a child herself."

"And the last name you gave the baby?" Nettie asked, feeling a shiver run the length of her spine.

"Thompson."

Flint tried not to look at the clock on the wall. They were coming up on eighty-six hours since Maggie was last seen. It was all he could think about. Maggie out in this blizzard. Snow had been falling for days now. Some of the roads around Gilt Edge were closed.

He was doing his best to cling to a thread of hope, but

with each passing hour, he became more terrified how this was going to end.

"I've got a BOLO out on Clark Terwilliger and the brown van with the Missouri plates," Mark said, interrupting his thoughts. "At least now we know why he's looking for Jenna." He looked up from his computer. "So you think this is more about the kid? Wait. Kid? If Jenna had the infant when she was thirteen or fourteen and she is now forty-seven…"

"The daughter would be thirty-three," Flint said and heard Mark make a surprised sound. He met Mark's gaze as he felt what seemed like a bolt of lightning strike him.

"Isn't Maggie thirty-three?" Mark asked.

Flint sat back in his chair, goose bumps racing across his skin. He'd been looking for a connection and it had been right in front of him this whole time? "I've been so worried about Maggie that I… Is it possible?" he said more to himself than Mark.

"And your PIs believe that Clark has Jenna and possibly their daughter?"

Flint nodded, his blood running cold as he heard a text come in on his phone. He glanced down and saw that it was from Frank, along with a photograph of a girl with dark hair and eyes. "Oh God, it *is* Maggie."

Maggie stared at the woman bound and gagged at the small kitchen table as if she was seeing a ghost. Jenna? The woman's hair was now bleached blond and she looked different, but there was no doubt. It was Jenna Holloway.

Shocked and thrown off balance, Maggie began to tremble, her legs threatening to buckle under her. If the man hadn't grabbed her arm, she might have slid to the floor.

Jenna's eyes widened when she saw her and quickly filled with tears. Her face was badly bruised. Jenna Holloway had been missing since March. The thought that she'd been held down here all this time with this man...

"You sit here," the man said as he led her over to what looked like an adult high chair, only it was short and squat and looked cobbled together. His fingers bit into her arm when she didn't move quickly enough. "Don't give Daddy a hard time now. You don't want Daddy to hurt Mommy again, do you?"

Maggie shook her head and sat down in the chair, her body shaking like a leaf in the wind. He reached in the back and flipped the tray part of the chair over her head so it trapped her there. Not that she could move before that. She felt too shocked, helpless with fear and confusion.

Jenna's gaze had followed her and now turned to the man, pleading in her eyes.

"Is Mommy ready to behave now?" the man asked in that annoying singsong tone. He stepped over to Jenna. She nodded without looking at him and he reached over and ripped the tape from her mouth.

Jenna let out a small cry, but quickly smothered it as she raised her gaze to his. "Don't hurt her. Please, Clark."

"See, that's why you've been in so much trouble," he said. "What is wrong with you? Why would I hurt our precious daughter?" He stepped to the stove.

"Are you all right?" Jenna whispered.

All Maggie could do was nod. They were both far from all right. This man was crazy. He'd abducted her and Jenna to pretend they were a family?

The man Jenna had called Clark came back to Maggie, carrying a plate that he set down in front of her. He put a child-sized spoon next to the plate.

Tears welled in her eyes as she saw what was on the plate. It was a child's plastic plate with three small piles of what appeared to be baby food. She could feel him waiting, feel him getting impatient. She picked up the spoon.

He leaned toward her and she did everything she could not to flinch as he placed a kiss on top of her head. "That's a good girl."

"Clark, is this really necessary?"

The man shot her a warning look. "I missed our daughter's entire childhood. Yes, Jenna, it's necessary."

"So did I." Jenna sounded like she might cry.

"Exactly. And whose fault is that?" He suddenly spun toward Maggie. "I told you to eat."

Maggie stuck the spoon into one of the piles, telling herself she could do this. She didn't want him hurting Jenna anymore. She also didn't want to give him any reason to turn his cruelty on her, either. But she didn't want to eat this.

She didn't understand what was going on. Seeing Jenna here had thrown her. None of this made any sense.

"If you are a good girl, Daddy will give you a treat. Now eat, sweetheart."

Maggie didn't think she would be able to swallow a bite. Anything she put in her mouth right now was going to come back up. But she could feel him staring at her, that terrifying darkness coming into his eyes.

"Don't make Daddy hurt you," he said so quietly that she almost didn't hear him over the pounding of her heart. "Or hurt your mommy."

She nodded and took a bite, fighting not to gag on what could have been creamed peas. As starved as she was, it was the most vile-tasting thing she'd ever ingested.

"That's a good girl. You must be hungry. You slept so long. Now eat up and show Mommy that everything is going to be all right now that we are a family."

Mommy and daddy and baby? Goose bumps rippled over her skin. She was in a nightmare that she feared she would never wake from. Who was this crazy man who'd abducted her and taken Jenna?

She managed to swallow the spoonful of baby food. As she scooped up some from the white pile, she glanced again toward the open doorway into the rest of the basement. It didn't appear to be a regular house. There was too much darkness beyond. Where were they?

And how did they get out? She glanced toward the hallway back to her room. That must be where Jenna was being kept. If there was a way out, wouldn't Jenna have found it by now? The thought that the woman might have been trapped here with this man since her disappearance in March made her shudder.

Maggie couldn't stand another hour here, let alone the thought of being kept here for months. Even years.

All she could think was that this was some sick fantasy on the man's part. Surely he would tire of this. And then what?

Her chest hurt from the fear that seized her. So far he'd been acting as if she were a child and he really was her... daddy. She shuddered at the memory of the slap and swallowed the bite from the baby spoon as she saw the way he was smiling at her.

All her instincts told her that things were going to get much worse.

CHAPTER SEVENTEEN

Maggie watched as Clark went back over to the stove. He returned with a sandwich for himself before he went around behind Jenna and released her left hand from the restraints. When he put down Jenna's dinner in front of her, Maggie let out a cry of shock.

Jenna, though, merely looked down at the dead mouse on her plate for a moment, then raised her gaze to look at him as he took his seat again. "Clark, how long are you going to do this?"

"As long as it takes. Eat your dinner, Mommy. You don't want your daughter to see you punished, do you?"

"You know I'm not going to eat this," Jenna said. "You're just looking for an excuse to hit me, so get it over with."

He reached across the table and backhanded Jenna so hard that she almost fell out of her chair and would have if she hadn't still been partially restrained.

"Don't!" Maggie cried.

"See what you've done?" he demanded. "You've upset our daughter." And just as swiftly as he'd hit Jenna, he turned on

Maggie. "You don't speak unless you're spoken to or you'll get some of this."

"No," Jenna said. "Don't take it out on her."

"Why not?" he demanded. "You took everything from me. Well, now I have it back and by damned you're going to play along or I'm going to beat you senseless. Do you understand?"

Jenna rubbed her cheek. "It was taken from me as well, Clark, or don't you want to hear the truth?"

"And now I have it back." He smiled then, cheerful again. His mood swings terrified Maggie. She had no idea what he was going to do next. She wasn't sure he did.

"We can't get it back," Jenna said. "And this…this is…ridiculous and you must know that, unless you're crazier than I remember."

Clark looked hurt. He and Jenna had locked gazes. Maggie could hear the hum of a motor somewhere in the building, the tremulous pounding of her heart. What did any of this have to do with her?

"I don't understand what's going on," she whispered into the deadly silence that had fallen between Clark and Jenna.

"Why don't you tell her, Jenna?" he said without looking at Maggie. "This is all your fault, after all."

She looked to Maggie, her eyes filling with tears that spilled down her cheeks. "He's right. This is my fault. You wouldn't be here if it wasn't for me."

Clark laughed. "I had a little something to do with it back then—and now."

Jenna shot him a pained look, then swallowed as if trying to find the words. "Thirty-three years ago, Clark…" She glanced over at him again. He shook his head back and forth very slowly, that mean warning look back in his eyes. "…we had sex and I became pregnant…with you."

"*What?*" Maggie stared at her, telling herself all of this

was a lie to appease this crazy man. "That's not possible. My mother died. I was raised by my aunt."

"The woman who raised you wasn't your aunt. She was my aunt Edna Burns's best friend."

Maggie blinked. Her eyes felt itchy under the bare bulb overhead, her throat dry. She felt sick to her stomach. She'd known an Edna Burns growing up, a kind lady who lived down the block who'd taught her to bake and sew and—

"I was fourteen when I gave birth to you. I desperately wanted to keep you, but my parents would never have allowed it. So everyone was told that you died at birth. It was a lie we all lived with for years."

All this was too much. Maggie shook her head. "Why are you saying these things? If he's making you—"

"Clark didn't know I'd had a baby," Jenna said. "When he found out..." She glanced in his direction. "...he was very angry and determined to find not just you, Maggie, but me to make us a family."

"And he did," Clark said with a laugh. "And now we're together, just as we should have been all those years ago." He glared across the table at Jenna. "If you had told me—"

"What would you have done?" Jenna demanded. "I was *fourteen*, Clark. I went home to parents who couldn't even look at me. I left home at sixteen, unable to stand another minute in that house."

"You knew our baby hadn't died."

Jenna let her gaze drop. "I couldn't even take care of myself. Let alone a child."

He sneered at that. "You could have contacted me for help."

"Right. How much help would you have been in prison?"

The meanness came back into his eyes and Maggie feared he would strike Jenna again in the tense silence that followed. Her mind was racing. All of this had to be a lie and yet...

"You knew about me when you came into my salon?"

Maggie asked, feeling betrayed when she saw Jenna's guilty expression. "Why wouldn't you have told me who you were?"

Jenna looked again at Clark, her eyes narrowing. "Because I didn't want Clark to know about you. Everyone had been told that you died at birth. It was…safer that way."

Clark shook his head, shoving his plate with his half-eaten sandwich away in obvious disgust. "*Safer?* Safer that I was kept in the dark about my own child?"

"You were in *prison*. My parents didn't want people to know that I was pregnant, especially given the circumstances," she said. "I'm sure even you can understand why."

"You *wanted* me," Clark bellowed as he pushed off the table to get to his feet. The dead mouse on Jenna's plate flew off and onto the floor. Plates clattered.

For a moment Maggie thought he would throw himself across the table at Jenna.

"You wanted me," he repeated in a low voice strangled with emotion. "I loved you. You knew I loved you. If you and my bitch of a sister hadn't gotten me arrested, I would have married you. We would have been a family. *This family!*"

He swung his gaze to Maggie. "Finish your food."

She obeyed, quickly scraping her plate clean as he came toward her, afraid of what he would do now. He lifted the tray to let her out of the chair and she stood, her gaze going to Jenna.

Jenna was her mother and this crazy man was her father? Her mind reeled. It wasn't possible. Just when she thought the nightmare couldn't get any worse.

"Say good-night to your mommy," Clark said.

Her throat constricted and for a moment she couldn't get the words out. She looked at Jenna, silently pleading with her to tell the truth and not make up things to appease this man.

But as her gaze met Jenna's, she saw that this *was* the truth.

Maggie looked away. They had to get out of there. But it

seemed hopeless given that they were both captives of a mad-man who wanted to play house.

"Good night, Mommy," she said as Clark grabbed her arm, his fingertips biting into her flesh.

"That's my good girl."

As he steered her toward her room, Jenna began to cry in gut-wrenching sobs.

"Please don't hurt her," Jenna called after him. "Please, Clark. I'll do whatever you want."

When Frank called, the news no longer came as a shock. "Maggie is Jenna's daughter," Frank said. "That's the con-nection, along with the brown van. Also, I talked to Clark Terwilliger's sister Dana again, hoping she might know of a place he would take them."

Flint had been hit by so much since that phone call from Maggie saying she was moving in. "Did she come up with anything?"

"Not yet. But we'll keep trying. We're checking out some places around here," Frank said.

"Thank you." He disconnected and looked to Mark. "We have to find Terwilliger."

"We haven't gotten a hit on his brown van even though we have the plate number now," Mark said. "He's holding them somewhere. Otherwise, he would have surfaced by now."

Or they were both dead and Terwilliger had dumped the van, gotten another ride and was on the move far from there.

"He's gone to a lot of trouble to find Jenna—and their daughter," the undersheriff said, clearly trying to assure him. "He wouldn't do that just to kill them."

Flint raked a hand through his hair. "I hope you're right. At some point, they are going to become more trouble than they're worth, though."

"At least now we know the connection. You had no idea?"

"None," the sheriff said. "Maggie couldn't have known. When Jenna went missing, she would have said something. She would have shown more concern."

"I guess we won't know until we find them. Jenna disappeared before Maggie was taken. Where around here could he hide them and himself?"

Maggie let Clark take her back into the bedroom and help her into her cage. She'd thought about trying to get away, but he was too big and strong for her. Even if she could escape him, there was Jenna. But the biggest reason for not trying anything was the strong feeling that he was expecting it.

She'd seen the way he'd slapped Jenna. He liked to hurt people and Jenna was afraid he wanted to hurt the daughter he'd said he'd wanted so badly.

That thought sent a dagger to her heart. She told herself that Jenna couldn't be her mother because that would mean that Clark was her father. She shuddered at the thought, since from what Jenna had tried not to say outright, Maggie knew that Clark had forced himself on her.

But it answered a lot of her questions growing up. That feeling of being flawed. Of people talking behind her back. They knew about Jenna's pregnancy, about the rape. They knew that Clark's blood ran through her veins.

The thought made her shudder again as he locked her in and left, closing the door behind him. She listened, hoping he didn't hurt Jenna any more than he already had. But she didn't hear anything. No raised voices. No cries. No sound for a long time until she heard a door slam. Shortly after that, the lights went out and whatever made that humming sound went out, as well. A generator?

Exhausted and still hungry, she lay down on the bed, curling into a fetal position, feeling like a child again. She'd never felt loved until Flint. That thought brought the tears she'd managed to hold back during dinner.

And now she might never see him again.

It tore her heart out.

When Clark didn't return at the sound of her crying, she let it all out. Sobbing for what might have been. Sobbing out her fear and her regrets. Crying mostly for the childhood she could have had—but didn't. Life could be so unfair. She'd always just pulled up her bootstraps, determined not to let it get her down. But this?

Finally, she couldn't cry anymore. She sat up sniffling. That was when she heard it. A scratching sound, then a voice.

"Maggie? Can you hear me?"

She turned to look at the vent near the floor next to her bed. The memory of hearing someone else crying rushed back at her. She wiped her eyes and lay down on the bed so she was closer to the vent. "I can hear you."

"I'm so sorry."

Maggie was too choked up to answer for a moment, her emotions all over the place. "I still don't understand why you didn't tell me," she said finally.

"I was…ashamed. And you were doing so well at the salon. I was so proud of you."

She had to swallow the lump in her throat. She'd never heard those words from the woman who'd raised her. Now she realized that the woman she'd thought was her aunt had always looked at her sideways as if waiting for her to turn out like her father.

"Do you know where we are?" Maggie asked.

"No. I was out most of the drive."

"What are we going to do?" Her voice broke.

"I have a plan, but I'm going to need your help."

"Anything. Just tell me what to do."

"Shh," Jenna whispered. "He's coming back."

★ ★ ★

Mark had gone home this morning to change clothes when he got the call that a letter with no return address, no stamp, had apparently been left for him. He'd been wondering when he was going to hear from the kidnapper again.

He grabbed a quick bite, since he'd pretty much been living at the sheriff's department and hadn't been home in days.

As he ate standing up in the kitchen, he thought about Flint and Maggie. He'd been so happy when he'd realized the sheriff had fallen in love. Everyone in town knew about the sheriff's first marriage and the trouble he'd had with Celeste since then. Mark had thought that Flint was finally going to get a chance for happiness.

Being a confirmed bachelor himself, he had wondered how love would change Flint. Now he knew. Love had definitely taken the starch out of the man. Having Maggie abducted had left Flint bereft. He tried to imagine loving a woman with that kind of intensity and couldn't. Maybe it was just as people said, that he hadn't met the right woman yet.

He scoffed at that as he finished his sandwich, anxious to get back to the office and open the letter that had been left for him. As he drove back to work, he hoped the letter writer and the kidnapper were one and the same and that Flint Cahill got the happy ending he so deserved.

Unfortunately, he'd been in law enforcement long enough to know that happy endings often only happened in fairy tales.

His office called again. Deputy Harper Cole needed to see him immediately. He swore and said he was on his way.

At his office, he carefully opened the letter and read the contents before turning it over to one of the lab techs to check for fingerprints. If these were coming from Clark Terwilliger, then they might be able to find some of his DNA. And since his DNA was available because of all his run-ins with the law...

But all of that took time.

He reread the copy of the note he'd made, thankful to see that a drop site and date and time had been included. Tonight he would find out who was behind the ransom demand.

Mark called Flint and caught him before he left his brother and sister's saloon. "I'm going to need some money—not all of the fifty-thousand-dollar demand. Just enough to catch a kidnapper."

"Where is the drop?" Flint asked.

"Sorry. I can't let you in on this."

"When?" Flint asked.

"Tonight. So one way or another, it will be over soon."

"If it's him and he's arrested, then what happens to Maggie and Jenna if he refuses to tell where they are?"

"Don't buy trouble. This could be what we need to find them."

"Or not."

Mark could hear the pain in his friend's voice. "At least now we're pretty sure who has Maggie and why. We're going to find them. You have to keep believing that."

"I'm trying, but as the days go by…"

"I know. Maybe you could have one of your brothers bring the money by. Stay away, okay? I'll call you later."

Flint couldn't stand to sit around and wait for the call. It was still early in the day. His brothers had promised to get the money to Mark. He couldn't bear simply killing the hours until the ransom drop. He'd done too much waiting. He had to look for Maggie. If Clark was the kidnapper, then he would have to leave Maggie and Jenna to come pick up the money. It would be the perfect time to get them out while he was gone.

But he had no idea where Clark might be holding them. The winter storm had dumped over a foot and a half of snow. Many of the roads were impassable, several closed to through traffic.

"Maybe that's why Clark's van hasn't been seen," he said to himself as he left the saloon and climbed into his pickup. "Maybe he can't get out. Which means he can't get out for supplies, either." But how could he pick up the ransom money if he was the one who'd sent the kidnapping demand?

He tried not to think about that as he looked to the mountains. The simplest explanation was that Clark had them in a house somewhere. He could have rented one. But that would have taken some planning in advance. Also, it would leave a paper trail.

He tried to think like a man determined to kidnap his daughter and the woman he professed to love. Once Clark knew where Jenna was, it was just a matter of abducting her and taking her to wherever he planned to keep the both of them. Flint reminded himself that he was assuming Clark would have wanted to keep them both alive. At least for a while.

Once Clark had Jenna, he would want to put her under lock and key as quickly as possible so he could go to Gilt Edge and get Maggie.

His heart began to pound a little faster. He wouldn't drive Jenna all the way back to Gilt Edge. Too much of a chance someone might see her bound in the back of his van, especially if she was conscious. No, he would want a place close to Sheridan, where Jenna had been staying with Kurt Reiner.

All this time, Flint had been looking around Gilt Edge. If he was right, Maggie and Jenna were being held closer to Sheridan. He told himself that he should wait until he heard from Mark tonight, but he would go crazy waiting for the call.

He swung by the ranch and threw some clothes and supplies into a duffel bag, and then, taking his rifle and several small firearms, he headed for the door.

"I hate to ask," his brother Cyrus said when he saw him come out the door with the rifle.

"I'm going looking for Maggie."

Hawk came up from the barn just then. "We should go with you."

"No," Flint said. "I appreciate it. But it's too dangerous. I can't involve you. It's enough that you've put the ranch up to raise the ransom. Anyway, you need to stay here and take the money to Mark."

They both started to argue.

"I need you both here to make sure that the rest of the family is safe," he said. "Also to get me out of jail if I call since I have no authority to be doing what I'm about to do."

Cyrus laughed. "Anyone seen my by-the-book brother Flint?" he joked. "You know, the one who's arrested our father how many times? I don't know about you, Hawk, but I like this new Flint Cahill. Also, I have to admit, there is something about seeing him behind bars that has its appeal."

Hawk shook his head at his brother as if this wasn't the time for humor. "Call if you need help. You don't always have to do things alone."

Flint placed a hand on his brother's shoulder. "I know. I'll call. Mark said you were bringing him the ransom money? Thanks again."

He brushed past them, wading through the deep snow to his pickup. It was a six-hour drive to Sheridan and he had no idea where to look when he got there. He just had a feeling in his gut that told him he was on the right track and that he'd know what he was looking for when he saw it.

CHAPTER EIGHTEEN

Harp pulled out his phone with his left hand and fumbled with it until he heard it ringing. He'd taken the undersheriff's advice and stayed away from Vicki but he was tired of staying alone in a motel room. It was time to go home. If he still had a home to go to.

"Hello?" Vicki answered in her usual tentative, quiet way.

Today it annoyed the hell out of him. "It's me," he said as if she didn't know that. Silence. "So what was that about the other night?"

"We need to talk."

"Apparently so. I thought you wanted to get married, give this baby a name. I thought..." Oh no, she wasn't crying again, was she? "Look, I'll come home if you aren't going to lose it again."

"I won't," she said and sniffled.

"Okay, I'm on my way." As he hung up, he was having his doubts. Did he really want to marry this woman? Did he really want to get married at all? He thought about his job. He'd done good with Gary Long, even if he had been reprimanded for the way he'd gone about it. He could be sheriff. He could be anything he wanted.

But he'd like a woman waiting for him at home who appreciated him. Not one he'd have to worry about when he walked in the door. He questioned if Vicki was stable and what that would mean for their kid.

He thought about the things that drove him crazy about her. He'd never known what a clean freak she was until on his day off he'd had to sit there watching her scrub. He told himself it must have something to do with those hormones she was talking about because when she wasn't cleaning she was crying. Before that, the house was a total disaster and she was throwing up. Was there no happy medium with that woman?

Either way, he wasn't sure how much more he could take as he parked out front of the apartment, took a deep breath and climbed out of his truck.

Vicki dried her eyes as she heard Harp's heavy tread on the stairs. She promised herself she wouldn't lose control again as she glanced toward the ruined bathroom door. Listening, she heard him turn his key in the lock. The door opened and the first thing she saw was his haggard face. Then her gaze went to the cast on his hand.

She leaped up and went to him. "Is it broken?"

He nodded. "Since I can't shoot a gun, Mark put me on leave." He tossed his hat on the coffee table as he moved past her into the apartment.

"I'm sorry." She wiped her damp palms on the thighs of her jeans. "It's all my fault."

He turned to look at her, and for a moment, she thought he was going to agree. "No, I was the one who lost it. Vicki, what happened? I was so excited about the ring and asking you to marry me."

"I was…overwhelmed. It was what I'd wanted for so long,

but when it actually happened…" She could feel his confused gaze on her. *Tell him the truth.* She'd only made things worse the other night. "It's the hormones," she heard herself say. "I'm not myself."

He stepped to her and took her left hand in his. The too-large ring had slid around her finger. He straightened it so the diamond was up. "We'll get it sized," he said. "I got the smallest size they had. But it will be all right." He met her gaze. "We're going to be a family, you and me and the baby."

She nodded, unable to speak around the huge lump in her throat. *Tell him the truth.*

"We should set a date," he said. "You know, to get married. We'll keep it small because I've heard weddings are real expensive. But you should get a nice dress. Maybe not white," he said with a laugh and quickly sobered. "Unless you want white because you can have whatever you want." He drew her into a hug.

She couldn't breathe. Her tongue seemed rooted to the top of her mouth.

"I love you, Vicki, as nuts as you make me."

The wind whirled the freshly fallen snow, obliterating everything in front of the pickup. Flint gripped the wheel, swearing silently as he tried to see the highway. He'd been driving too fast, feeling an urgency born of knowing now who he believed had Maggie. Clark Terwilliger was a criminal with a rap sheet as long as Flint's arm, not to mention the man was apparently out for revenge.

He caught glimpses of the highway through what he called "snow snakes" as the wind blew the snow across the pavement in hypnotizing stripes. Speeding up, he glanced at his navigation system. He was still some miles from Sheridan, but he wanted to take the back road in, starting with a place called Decker, Montana.

The exit came up fast. He hit his brakes, skidding a little

on the icy road, but getting the pickup back into control as he turned off. The snow had frozen to the pavement, making it more slick than it looked.

Now that he was off the interstate and driving along the Tongue River, the wind wasn't quite as bad. The narrow road was snow covered and icy, and he drove slowly so he could look for whatever it was he thought he'd know when he found it. An old barn with tracks into it? An abandoned house? Any place out here away from everything where a man could hold two women and not be heard or seen, for that matter.

From the snow on this road, it was clear that it got little use. But he reminded himself that there could be a dozen roads like it around Sheridan. Except this one was still in Montana. For a man like Terwilliger, who'd spent most of his adult life behind bars, he would know that taking Maggie across state lines would be a federal offense. Not that it might make a difference to him at this point.

Flint saw one old building after another, but no tracks in the snow indicating that anyone had been in or out of the property since winter had begun. He reminded himself that Terwilliger hadn't been on the move in the van or he would have been spotted. But out here in the boonies, he doubted anyone even knew he was wanted by the law.

The man would only get caught if he went into town. It was afternoon and he would be losing light soon. Flint was thinking he was wrong about Terwilliger staying in Montana when he saw a building ahead through the blowing snow. The old roadhouse looked as if it had long since been closed. Most of the windows, as well as an old loading-dock entry at basement level, had been boarded up.

He slowed, seeing what appeared to be an old two-car garage in the back. His heart began to pound even before he saw the vehicle tracks through the snow into the out-of-the-way property. It was all he could do not to go racing in, guns blazing. As he drove by, he noticed the tracks in front of the garage where someone had been using it. To hide a brown van?

He drove on up the road to a spot where he could turn around, his heart in his throat. All his instincts told him that Maggie was in that building. Maggie and Jenna? And Clark Terwilliger? Or was he in Gilt Edge collecting the fifty-thousand-dollar ransom?

"Maggie?" Jenna whispered through the vent. "I heard a vehicle but it wasn't him coming back again."

She quickly lay down on the bed beside the old heat vent. "I'm here." It gave her comfort, the sound of Jenna's voice through the vent and knowing she wasn't alone.

Clark had come back earlier with a burger and fries for her. He'd allowed her to use the bathroom under the stairs. It was small and there was no window, no way to escape. But then, he'd known that, hadn't he?

"Daddy has something he has to do. I want you and Mommy to be very good while I'm gone," he'd said. "When I come back I might have another surprise for you."

Maggie had already decided that she didn't like his brand of surprises. "What kind of surprise?" she'd dared ask.

"We might be leaving here," he'd said, but had avoided her gaze.

She'd felt a tremor move through her. Had he already gotten tired of playing house with them? Surely he wasn't so crazy not to realize that she was a grown woman, not the child he'd lost. Or had this act been merely to torture Jenna?

After he'd left her alone, she'd gobbled down the burger and fries. Neither was from a fast-food restaurant, so she suspected, given that he hadn't been gone long the last time he'd left, that the burgers and fries had come from a café or bar close by.

At least it was a clue to where they were. Help might not

be that far away. Not that she had any idea where she was. She wasn't even sure she was still in Montana.

"Are you all right?" Jenna asked now through the vent.

"I've been better, but the food helped. Did he bring some for you?"

"I'm fine. I don't want you worrying about me."

But she was worried. "He said we might be leaving here."

There was no sound from Jenna. Apparently she too worried that the news wasn't good.

Now she lay listening to the sound of her heart. Clark had turned off the lights again, pitching them into blackness. She had no idea if it was day or night. It was disorienting if she let herself think about it. Instead she thought about her...parents. "Did you want to keep me?" The words were out before she could stop them.

"Oh yes. Even with the way it had happened, me getting pregnant, I wanted you. But I was fourteen and there was no way my parents were going to let that happen. I'm so sorry. Was your childhood...awful?"

"No. Just strange. I understand now why I would catch the woman I thought was my aunt watching me as if she thought I might grow two heads at any moment." But this wasn't what she wanted to talk about. "Jenna, you said you had a plan to get us out of here."

"It's dangerous."

Maggie almost laughed. "Compared to being here with Clark." She didn't know him, yet even she could tell that he was going to lose it at some point. Because of that, she could see only one way this would end and it wasn't with him moving them to somewhere nicer. "Tell me. I'll do whatever I have to to get out of here."

Flint parked down the road and quickly dressed in a warm coat, taking the weapons he'd brought but leaving behind the rifle. It would be too cumbersome. Also, if he ran into Clark Terwilliger on the property, it wouldn't be at a distance.

As the light began to fade, he walked back up the road and dropped down, trudging through the deep snow as he approached the back of the garage. His breath came out in icy white puffs as he busted through one drift after another. He'd thought about staying on the road longer, but he couldn't chance that he might be spotted.

Even with the whirling snow, he figured Terwilliger could be watching. If the man wasn't in Gilt Edge collecting the ransom, then he could be inside the old roadhouse. It was impossible to know until he reached the garage to see if his van was in there.

Even as he thought it, he reminded himself that this might be a wet and cold wild-goose chase that would only leave him exhausted and horribly disappointed. A rancher could be using the garage to store his tractor. And yet, when he thought of the tracks into the roadhouse, he felt that shiver of anticipation. Someone had come out several times in the last few days. Not a rancher checking his tractor.

The wind whirled snow into his face and for a moment he was blinded. He tucked his head down, stopping to let it pass, before he looked up again. He was almost to the garage. Just a few more yards.

He had the sudden impulse to run in his need to hurry, but it would be a waste of energy in the deep snow. He felt the day slipping away. But he could still see well because of the brightness of the white snow at his feet.

When he reached the back of the garage, he pulled out his flashlight to peer in through one of the broken windows. He'd hoped to find a brown van sitting in the freezing-cold garage. Instead he saw that it was empty. But it had been used. He could see the tracks in and out. And it had been driven into more than a few times.

With a burst of hope, he realized that if he was right, Terwilliger wasn't here now. If Maggie and Jenna were in the old roadhouse alone... Moving with even more purpose, he headed for the back of the building, following fresh tracks in the snow where someone had come and gone numerous times during the storm.

As he neared the back, he saw that someone had put a new padlock and latch on it. His heart raced. *Maggie is in there.*

Flint almost called out her name but it would have been quickly stolen by the wind. Instead, he took out his pocketknife and went to work on the new latch. He could feel time slipping through his fingers. Terwilliger could come back at any time. He could have sent someone else to pick up the ransom. Or maybe worse, had no plan to ever come back. Maggie and Jenna could have been left somewhere inside this building to die. Or already be dead.

The latch broke. He tossed the lock aside, reminding himself that if Terwilliger did come back, there would be no surprising him. He would see the tracks. He would see the broken latch. He would know he'd been found.

Flint opened the door and peered in, seeing nothing but cold darkness. He listened. Hearing nothing, he turned on his flashlight and stepped inside.

The undersheriff stared through his binoculars at the ransom drop spot, worrying it would soon be getting too dark for him to see. He'd tried to call Flint earlier only to find out that he'd left town. Again.

Where had he gone this time? The DCI had put him on paid leave. He wasn't supposed to be investigating even though it had become pretty clear who probably had Maggie—and why.

Still... Worse, this whole ransom demand seemed to be a bust. He lowered the binoculars long enough to glance at the time. The alleged kidnapper was late.

The drop site was in a city park that had a lot of pine trees. He assumed that was why the alleged kidnapper had chosen it. But it was a rookie move since getting out of the park would be a problem. Right now, there were people watching from houses on all sides. There was no way the person could get away with the money—unless he was somehow missed in the darkness.

Flint's brothers Hawk and Cyrus had shown up with the fifty thousand dollars. Mark hadn't wanted to use that much, but they'd argued.

"Let's not take any chances," Cyrus had said. "My brother is in love with Maggie. He's planning to ask her to marry him. If this money might save her..."

Giving up, Mark had taken it, thanked them and started to send them on their way.

"Look, we know you're short staffed," Hawk had said. "Let us help."

He'd started to explain that he couldn't do that, when Cyrus had said, "You need us. I know you go by the book just like my brother, but this is Maggie we're talking about."

Hawk had agreed. "You need to deputize us. Just for tonight."

Mark knew what he was saying made sense. "I'll tell you what. The drop site is such that I could use eyes and ears from one of the houses across the way. However, I can't have any heroic crap going down. I can deputize the two of you. But if you see something tonight at the drop site, you call me, understood? No playing heroes." They'd both agreed, maybe a little too readily.

But it had all been for nothing, Mark thought as he stared through his binoculars at the bag of money he'd left by the park bench as darkness descended. The alleged kidnapper wasn't going to show.

He was about to call it, when he saw movement. He focused in as a person dressed in dark clothing came out of the trees, grabbed the bag and ran.

Flint took two steps inside the old roadhouse, let the door close quietly behind him and stood listening. He heard nothing but his own racing heart thundering in his chest. He let the beam of his flashlight skitter over the worn linoleum floor and saw that he appeared to have entered the back side of the kitchen. Off to his right he could see what was left of an old commercial dishwasher. There were some plates and cups, most of them broken on the floor, and what looked like a menu stuck to the floor under layers of grime.

To the left was a hallway that led to the dining room. The place was huge, but he'd seen that from the outside. If Maggie was here, she could be anywhere. He moved down the hallway, telling himself he couldn't be sure that Terwilliger hadn't parked his van somewhere else. If he was in the building and heard him coming... Or Terwilliger could have gone to collect the ransom and left someone with Maggie and Jenna. Someone who had already heard Flint break the lock to get into the building.

Flint couldn't bear the thought of getting this close only to have Maggie and Jenna be killed now. He slowed his footsteps, noticing a women's bathroom, then a men's. Someone had left a chair by the women's bathroom door.

As he shone his flashlight beam toward the front of the building, he saw an even larger dining room with some random furniture.

Turning, he almost missed it. There was a third door. He had thought it was a storage room, but as his flashlight beam skittered over the worn floor, he noticed footprints in the dust. His—and someone else's. The second set of prints had come and gone numerous times. The prints stopped at the third door.

He tried the knob.

CHAPTER NINETEEN

"Shh," Jenna said suddenly. "I think I heard him." She frowned. "But I didn't hear his van this time."

Maggie held her breath, listening. Above her, she thought she heard a floorboard groan under the weight of a boot. Before that, Jenna had laid out her plan for their escape.

"Clark might leave the keys to his van in it. Or he might have them on him. You will need those. You'll have to check his pockets. Once he's down, no matter what happens, you have to get the keys if they are on him and make a run for it. Do you understand?"

"No, I can't leave you here with him, especially after you've struck him with something. You said yourself that you doubted you can hit him hard enough to knock him out, possibly not even knock him down."

"But if I distract him and you get the keys and run—"

"Jenna, no. There has to be another way. He'll...he'll kill you."

"I just have to make sure that you're safe. That's all I care about, Maggie. Please, in order for this to work, you have to get the keys and get away. I'm not sure how long I can hold him off."

"Maybe if we wait—"

"We can't. I know this man. He's getting tired of this, just like he would have gotten tired of having a wife and child. At some point, he isn't going to come back. He's going to leave us here to die. Or maybe worse."

Now as Maggie held her breath and listened, she picked up the sound of someone walking on the floor above them and knew Jenna was right. For some reason he was sneaking back here. This might be their last chance because next time might be the last time for both of them.

"Eyes peeled," Mark said into his radio. "Perp has bag and is on the run." He quickly texted Hawk, then started his patrol SUV and with lights flashing headed for the park below him.

He found himself hoping like hell that the man was Clark Terwilliger. If it was just some creep after money... He was almost to the park.

"Got him!" came a deputy over his radio. "Perp is down on the south side of the park."

Racing to that side of the park, he leaped out, seeing that there had been a struggle. One of his deputies was cuffing a man on the ground, but Hawk and Cyrus were both covered with snow and standing over the man. Both were grinning a little too broadly.

"Cowboys," he said under his breath with a shake of his head as he approached them.

He knew he shouldn't have been surprised. As he reached them, he said, "Let me guess. You chased him down."

Hawk laughed. "Surprised me that I can still run like that."

"But you wouldn't have been able to hang on to him if I hadn't helped you," Cyrus pointed out.

Mark shook his head, unable to not grin. The county

needed its force back and soon. With both Flint and Harp now out of commission... "Either of you know where your brother Flint is?" he asked as he picked up the bag the perp had dropped.

Both shook their heads, although he got the feeling that they knew more than they were willing to tell him. Where had Flint gone alone? It worried him. He'd worked with the man for years. He knew how determined he could be. With Maggie being the one missing...

"Come by my office tomorrow and I'll release your money," he said to the pair. "And tell Flint to call me when you hear from him."

As he turned away, the deputy making the bust lifted the alleged kidnapper to his feet and began reading him his rights. Mark got his first look at the man.

Flint stopped in front of the door and listened. Still, he couldn't hear anything over his own pounding heart. The hairs rose on the back of his neck. He turned, half expecting to see Terwilliger sneaking up on him.

But there was nothing in the hallway except for his snowy boot tracks in the dust. He turned the knob, telling himself that time was running out. If Terwilliger was behind the ransom demand, he could have an accomplice picking it up and could return at any moment.

The door swung open with a groan. He shone his flashlight down the steps into the basement, noticing the footprints in the dust. A terrible feeling filled him. What if they weren't here anymore? What if Terwilliger had moved them? That, he realized, would be better than finding them both down there dead.

He took a step, reminding himself that the man could be expecting him. This could be a trap. The wooden stair groaned under his weight. He took another. He was almost to the bottom before he could see any of the huge basement. He shone his flashlight around what appeared to be a maze of storage crates and boxes, old furniture and garbage bags filled with who knew what. Narrow paths cut through the catacomb.

As the beam of his flashlight shone to the left, he saw that part of the basement had been closed off with walls—and a door. He moved toward it and tried the knob. As the door swung open, he moved to the side and peered into what appeared to be a 1950s kitchen. Past it, he saw a short hallway and two more doors.

At some time, people had lived down here? Were still living here?

Gun drawn, he crossed the kitchen. It smelled of burgers and fries. He was about to try the first door when he heard the sound of a vehicle engine approaching.

Mark swore as he saw who their kidnapper was. He couldn't believe he was looking at Johnny Burrows, a former classmate of his. But at the same time he realized he shouldn't have been surprised. He'd watched Johnny's life go down the tubes over the past few years. First Johnny's father had been arrested for embezzlement from the construction company in which he'd been a partner. Of course, his father had dragged Johnny into the mess. And finally Johnny had gotten in trouble for withholding evidence in a murder case.

"I didn't kidnap anyone," Burrows said quickly as Mark approached him. "You know me."

Mark just shook his head.

"It was stupid, okay? But I thought..." He hung his head, looking like a man who had nothing to lose. "I just... I just needed money. I was desperate. I thought—"

"Desperate to get back at the Cahills?" Mark asked. Johnny's best friend since grade school was Trask Beaumont, who'd just married Lillie Cahill. The two had a falling-out about the time Johnny had been willing to let Trask go to prison for a murder he didn't commit.

"No, it wasn't like that," Johnny said. "It was only about the money. I need the money." The man broke down.

He realized he hadn't seen Burrows around for months. He'd just assumed he'd left town. "Load him into your patrol car," he told his deputy. He looked at Burrows. "We'll talk at the sheriff's office."

As he watched Burrows being taken away, Mark fought a wave of disappointment. He had been hoping that they would catch the person who'd taken Maggie Thompson. He'd wanted the person they caught tonight to be Clark Terwilliger. If it had been him, he would be on his way to a cell right now and maybe willing to make a deal to release Maggie and Jenna.

But in his heart, he had agreed with Flint that the ransom demand was probably some fool hoping to cash in on Maggie's disappearance. Still, he'd hoped it would help find her and bring her home.

Now that hope was gone. Burrows had just been after the money. While Mark would make sure that was all it had been, he figured Johnny's story would check out. Burrows didn't drive a brown van.

In fact, the last he'd heard, Burrows had sold his car, lost his fiancée, been forced to sell his new home for a lawyer for his father and hadn't had any luck getting a job locally. For years Johnny's father had pushed his son disgracefully to succeed at any cost—only for the two to go down in flames.

Mark couldn't help but think how ironic it was that Johnny Burrows, the boy voted most likely to be the CEO of a Fortune 500 company, would now be joining his father in prison.

"Flint?" Maggie cried. She couldn't believe what she was seeing in the ambient glow of the flashlight. Flint. He'd found

her? She'd thought she would never lay eyes on him again. He'd opened the door and she'd seen his handsome face and thought she must be dreaming.

Then she'd heard Flint call her name as he rushed to her.

She began to cry, but he quickly hushed her. "Who else is down here?"

"Just Jenna. She's in the next room."

He nodded. "Tell me how to get you out of there. We have to move fast. I just heard a vehicle."

She pointed him toward the mechanism out of her reach. He moved to it and sprang the latch, before lowering the gate and helping her out and into his arms. He held her so tightly that she couldn't breathe for a moment, but she never wanted him to let her go.

"Is Clark acting alone? Is there anyone else?"

She shook her head. "Just…him."

"We have to get you out of here. Now." That was when he noticed what she was wearing.

She looked down at the ridiculous dress. "Don't ask."

"Where are your clothes?" He shone his light around the room, stopping on the pile of clothing in the corner.

She grabbed them up from where Clark had tossed them and quickly pulled them on. "Don't wait for me. Get Jenna."

He had his cell phone out. "I just tried to call for backup." He swore. "No service down here. There might not be service for miles. Let's get Jenna and see if there is a way out of here."

She followed the path of Flint's flashlight beam as they stepped back into the hallway and to the adjacent room.

As the door opened, Maggie saw that Jenna was locked in a metal cell much like her own. The difference was that her room was bare. One side open to the rest of the basement, which she saw was filled to overflowing with what looked like secondhand furniture as if the place had been a junk shop at one time.

"Sheriff?" Jenna cried as she saw him in the ambient light of the flashlight beam. "You have to hurry. I heard Clark. He's coming back."

Maggie listened. She realized she couldn't hear the sound of the van engine anymore. "I think he's already here." Her voice broke. Once the van engine shut off, it was only a matter of minutes before she would hear his heavy step overhead.

She could see that Flint was having more trouble opening this cell than he had hers. Maggie could tell he was hurrying as fast as he could. Finally the latch gave and he helped Jenna out.

"Is there another way out of here besides the stairs?" Flint asked.

Jenna shook her head. "Not that I know of." She fell silent at the sound of a door opening overhead. "It's too late. He's in the building."

CHAPTER TWENTY

Vicki turned the ring on her finger so she could see the diamond. She hadn't gotten it sized and she knew why she'd kept putting it off. The ring didn't fit because marrying Harp didn't fit. Not when the only reason he was marrying her was a lie.

At the sound of his footfalls on the stairs, she stood and waited for him to unlock the door and come in with the groceries. There'd been so many days when she'd stood in this very spot, telling herself that today was the day. She'd told herself that she couldn't live with a lie—and yet she had. Each time when she'd seen his handsome face, she'd chickened out. But none of the excuses kept the guilt at bay.

Harp looked up as he came in the door and seemed to hesitate. "Vicki?"

She hadn't realized she was standing there, turning her engagement ring in nervous circles. She stopped herself, sliding it off as she stepped forward and laying it on the coffee table.

"What's going on?" he asked as he took the few more steps into the tiny apartment and put down the sack of groceries. He looked down at the ring, then up at her.

"I lost the baby."

Harp had never been much of a poker player, she'd heard. She could understand why. She watched one emotion after another cross his face. Shock. Regret. And ultimately relief.

"When?"

"It's been a while. That's why when you asked me to marry you..." She didn't need to finish.

He swallowed, looking from her to the rest of the apartment as if saying goodbye. "I don't know what to say."

Say you love me anyway and still want to marry me. But she didn't voice the words. She'd seen everything she needed to see in his expression.

He picked up the engagement ring from the coffee table with his uncast hand and stared at it for a long moment. "I need some time," he said and, pocketing it, turned back toward the door.

Vicki had promised herself she'd be strong. Mostly, that she wouldn't cry. But the moment the door closed, she dropped to the couch in tears of relief for telling the truth and heartbreak at Harp's reaction. She told herself she didn't want to marry a man who didn't love her, but still it hurt so badly because she loved him. Flaws and all.

The last thing Flint wanted to do was leave Maggie. He'd been to the point where he'd believed that he would never see her again. Now that he had, he just wanted to hold her in his arms and not let her out of his sight.

But if he hoped to get them out of this basement, he had to hide them until it was safe to go up the stairs. He'd read enough of Clark Terwilliger's rap sheet to know what he was dealing with—a career criminal with nothing to lose. They were the most dangerous kind.

He was also pretty sure that the vehicle they'd heard was Terwilliger's van returning. "I need you two to stay here for a minute," Flint whispered before turning back toward the door. He had to find a way to get them out of there.

Maggie grabbed his hand. "Please be careful. Clark is... crazy."

He nodded, leaned in to kiss her, and then, weapon drawn, he eased out into the hall. He had to find another way out of here. Flint moved to the bottom of the stairs to listen. There was no sound above him. Terwilliger had opened the outside door. That meant that he'd seen the broken latch. He would know someone had found his hiding place.

Would he run? Flint could only hope.

Or would he start a fire and try to burn them out? He wouldn't put anything past the man and, given all the old furniture down here, this basement would go up like a tinderbox.

But there was a third option, he realized. Terwilliger might be determined to get the women back. In that case...

Flint moved through the maze of old furniture and auto parts and crates. He recalled seeing a loading dock. It was the only way all of these things could have been brought in.

But when he reached it, he saw that there was only the large garage door out. Laying down his flashlight, he tried to open the ancient-looking door. The metal was thin and had holes in it in places. He could feel cold air coming in one of them. But it wouldn't budge.

From overhead, he heard a door slam and quickly picked up the flashlight and headed back through the maze to what must have been an apartment down there. Jenna was right. There was only one way out and it was the stairs.

He could hear footsteps overhead. Clark wasn't sure where he was. Otherwise, the man would already be heading down the stairs. He swore under his breath and rushed back to where he'd left Maggie and Jenna. He had to get the two of them out of here. But with the window wells filled with dirt after years, they were trapped.

On his way back, he looked for a place to hide them as he improvised a plan. He hadn't come this far to lose either of them.

Opening the door to the room where he'd left Jenna and Maggie, he whispered, "Come on," and led them back through the kitchen and out in the honeycomb of partitions. The stairs had walls on each side all the way down until the last few steps. On this side, there was a tiny bathroom under them large enough for the two women to hide. There was no lock on the door.

"Stay in there," Flint whispered as he pointed the flashlight beam into the space. "Once he comes down, I'll try to stop him. If that fails, I'll distract him. I want you to go up the stairs as fast as you can and out of the building to his van." He handed Maggie his cell phone. "I couldn't get coverage, but in case he left his keys in the van, drive until you can. Call for backup."

Wide-eyed with fear, Maggie nodded, but he could tell she didn't want to leave him.

"You'll see that she gets out of here?" he said to Jenna, who nodded.

"What if he has the keys on him?" Jenna asked.

"Then take mine. My patrol SUV is parked up the road to the north. You'll find my tracks behind the garage." He handed over his keys.

The floor overhead groaned under the weight of a careful step. Terwilliger hadn't opted to run, Flint thought with a silent curse. That meant they were in for a fight.

"What does he have for weapons?" he asked Jenna.

She shook her head. "I know he has a gun. A pistol. That's the only one I saw. But he had a lot of ammunition."

He nodded and motioned for them to go and hide as overhead he heard another footfall, then another, each coming closer to the door to the basement stairs. He had to assume

Terwilliger was armed and looking for him. Otherwise why not run? Or just trap them down there?

Because hard-core criminals like Terwilliger thought they could win. Why else would he have just opened the base-ment-stairs door? He was coming down.

"Don't move until I tell you to." With one last look at Maggie, he stepped to the side of the stairs, extinguished his flashlight, pitching them into blackness.

Flint knew his best chance of taking Terwilliger down was as he came off the last few steps into the basement. If the man got past that, he could disappear into the rows of junk. Many of them were piled almost to the ceiling.

To his surprise, he heard the door at the top of the stairs close and Terwilliger's footfalls retreat. Maybe he was leav-ing, making a run for it. Flint thought about going after him, but realized that might be exactly what the man was hoping for. He wouldn't be able to get up the stairs quickly without the man hearing him. He'd be a sitting duck. It was a chance he couldn't take.

Right now, his only thought had to be about getting Jenna and Maggie out of there and to safety. As much as he wanted to take down Terwilliger himself and see him behind bars for good this time, he couldn't do it. He waited for the sound of the man's van engine, praying Terwilliger would make a run for it. Once he had Maggie and Jenna out of there—

But what he heard sounded more like a small generator starting up. A moment later, the lights came on and he heard Terwilliger's footfalls again at the top of the stairs.

While the kitchen and the bedrooms had light coming out of them, there were only a few bulbs still working in the larger part of the basement, so that area was pitched in darkness. If he let Terwilliger make it down the stairs and into the dark and junk, he would be hell to find, let alone stop.

One of the stairs creaked under the man's weight. Flint

looked around for something he could throw. In the corner was a pile of old books. He picked up one and moved into position.

His plan was simple. Terwilliger seemed determined to come back down here. With walls on both sides of the stairs—except for the last four steps—he was shielded. But once he reached those bottom steps, Flint would have a clear shot.

Terwilliger would know that, so he'd be moving fast. Flint would get only that one chance before the man disappeared into the stacks of junk.

He hefted the book in his hand and bided his time, listening to the creak of one stair, then another, gauging what the man would do and when.

In order to pull this off, though, Flint wouldn't have much cover. All his instincts told him that Terwilliger would come down the last few steps fast—and probably blazing.

Another stair creaked.

"Whoever you are," Terwilliger called down, "you need to show yourself. You have no business down here with my wife and daughter."

His wife and daughter.

Flint said nothing. The man was trying to find out where he was so he knew where to fire once he hit the last few steps.

"You're trespassing, but I don't want any trouble, so just come on out and leave. I'll overlook you breaking in the way you did."

That was big of him.

Another stair creaked. Flint got ready. He hurled the book into the junk on the other side of the stairs and raised his gun.

Terwilliger came down at a run and firing—just as Flint had expected. The sound of gunfire exploded in the basement. The trick had worked. The noise of the book hitting on the opposite side of the stairs had fooled Terwilliger. He'd come down firing in the wrong direction.

Flint had a brief few seconds where the man's broad

hunched back was facing him before the man dived into one of the narrow paths through the junk. He heard the kidnapper let out a groan and knew that he'd taken at least one of Flint's bullets. The man had stumbled, but he hadn't gone down. And then he was gone, disappearing into the darkness and the maze filling the other side of the large basement.

Unfortunately, Flint couldn't be sure that Terwilliger had gone deep enough in the junk that he wouldn't have a shot at Maggie and Jenna when they made their run up the stairs. He was going to have to go in after him. He moved away from the light coming out of the kitchen and quickly ducked behind a huge crate as Terwilliger fired—giving away his position.

Out of the darkness somewhere deep in the junk came a laugh, then Terwilliger's voice. "In case you're interested, you winged me. I'm bleeding like a stuck pig, but it isn't going to stop me. You can't have them. I'd rather see them both dead. Is that what you want?"

Flint fired through a space between a stack of stained mattresses and an old commercial refrigerator, but Terwilliger was already moving.

Maggie peered out of the bathroom door under the stairs. Flint had closed the kitchen door, cutting off most of the light, but some still bled out to where they were hidden.

"With the lights on, he'll be able to see us," she whispered to Jenna. "If we make a run for it…" Before Jenna could stop her, Maggie sprang from her hiding place and rushed to the door of the kitchen. She heard gunfire, but couldn't be sure if it had been aimed at her. She thought she heard Flint swear.

She ducked into the kitchen and closed the door. Now Clark knew where she was. All he had to do was circle around to where Jenna had been kept and come through that way. She knew she had to move fast. She quickly looked around for something she could use. An old broom sagged against the far wall. Picking it up, she swung it, breaking the light bulb overhead and pitching the kitchen into darkness.

She hurriedly moved to the bedrooms, before making her way back in the dark toward the kitchen door. She waited, knowing that Clark would expect her to make a run for the stairs. She remembered what Flint had done to fool Clark. Feeling around on the table, she found the cup she'd seen there.

As she carefully opened the door, she saw that the bottom of the stairs was now pitched in darkness. Jenna came out of the bathroom under the stairs and stood with her back against the wall in the semidarkness, out of sight from the rest of the basement.

Unfortunately, there was enough ambient light coming from the other bulbs in the larger part of the basement. If she ran now, he would see her.

She got ready to throw the cup toward the other side of the basement, doubting Clark would fall for it a second time, but figuring it might give Flint the opportunity he needed.

Chucking the cup, she waited until it hit and ran as gunfire boomed and Flint yelled, "Run!"

Jenna grabbed her hand and pulled her toward the stairs. Maggie couldn't bear leaving Flint down here with that madman, but she had no choice. Even if Jenna let go of her hand, Maggie knew she had to do what Flint had asked her to. It might be their only hope. They had to get him help.

She felt deaf from the gunfire. Now more gunfire echoed through the basement. Jenna tightened her grip on Maggie's hand as they stormed up the stairs. Those were the longest steps Maggie had ever taken. She expected to feel a bullet slam into her back at any moment. She stumbled in the darkness once, but Jenna's grip kept her upright and then they were at the top of the stairs and the open doorway and the light.

They burst through and around the corner. Maggie was breathing hard. So was Jenna. "This way."

With Jenna still clutching her hand, they burst out of the
building. Maggie blinked, surprised to realize it was twilight.
How many days had she been here? Jenna let go of her hand
and ran toward a brown van parked in front of what appeared
to be an old two-car garage.

At the sound of more gunfire, Maggie hesitated, but for
only a moment. *Get help.* But leaving Flint down there was
the hardest thing she'd ever done in her life, even knowing
that she couldn't save him.

She ran after Jenna, her shoes quickly filling with the deep
snow. She shivered from the cold and the fear. Jenna had
opened the driver's-side door of the van. "He didn't put it in
the garage. Maybe…" She let out a cry.

Maggie couldn't tell if it was one of disappointment or excitement until she heard the jingle of a key ring.

Flint leaned against a stack of old cabinets and reloaded
his weapon. He hadn't heard Terwilliger for a few minutes,
but wasn't about to give away his location by moving. He'd
thought he'd wounded the man again. But Terwilliger had
veered at the last minute, disappearing behind a pile of boxes.

Now Flint listened for both the madman in the basement
with him and the sound of a vehicle engine turning over. He
just hoped the keys had been in the van. That Maggie and
Jenna would go for help. Not that he was counting on help
reaching him anytime soon.

Town was miles away. Getting Maggie and Jenna out of
this basement had been about making sure they were safe—
not actually getting help. He couldn't count on them getting
cell phone service for miles. By the time they reached town,
notified the sheriff's department… Well, it would be too late.

Flint knew he wouldn't have that long. He and Terwilliger could only play this cat-and-mouse game so long before
one of them ended it. He checked his ammunition. He had
only one clip left.

★ ★ ★

"Hop in," Jenna said, and Maggie ran around to the passenger side and slid in as Jenna cranked over the engine. The motor roared to life and Jenna let her foot off the clutch. As the van leaped forward, Maggie looked toward the building where she'd been kept prisoner, shocked to realize it was out in the middle of nowhere.

She saw no other houses, only rolling hillside and a narrow stretch of snow-covered pavement. And now she was leaving Flint down there in that basement alone.

Glancing in the back of the van, she saw shopping bags. Some of the items had spilled out on the rough road into the roadhouse apparently. So that was where he'd gone, into town to buy supplies.

There were several rolls of duct tape, a large roll of plastic sheeting, several box cutters, a twelve-pack of Scotch towels and a shovel.

Clark had said he was going to move them. Her heart pounded at the sight as she realized what he'd really been planning to do with them.

As Jenna started to pull away from the roadhouse, Maggie knew she couldn't leave Flint—no matter how this ended.

"I can't go," she said and started to open her door.

"You can't help him!" Jenna cried, hitting the brakes as Maggie began to jump out.

"Here's his phone. Call for help as soon as you can, but I'm not leaving."

"Maggie, no. He's a sheriff. He knows what he's doing."

"He doesn't know Clark like we do."

"Listen, there's nothing you can do to help," Jenna pleaded. "Please."

"It only takes one of us to get help." She stepped out of the van and started to close the door. Then she said, "Hurry."

"At least take this," Jenna said and tossed her a large army coat that had been flung over the seat.

Slamming the van door, she shrugged on the coat, trying to ignore the smell of Clark on the fabric. As she walked back toward the old building, Jenna took off in the van. She knew this was crazy, but she couldn't leave Flint. In her heart, she feared that he needed her. She couldn't think of anything worse than not being there for him.

At the sound of the van's engine revving as it pulled away, Flint felt a wave of relief. Maggie and Jenna were safe. Now all he had to do was find Terwilliger and end this. Or if he got the chance, get to the stairs. He could block the basement door until an army of deputies arrived. It was the smartest idea he had.

Unfortunately, he knew that the madman down there with him probably had the same idea. With the paths through the junk all facing the stairway, neither of them could make a run for it without being seen—and shot. Without someone covering him, he was stuck in the basement until one of them killed the other.

If he could last until help arrived, it would still be hard for anyone to get to them. Terwilliger would have heard his van leaving. He would be expecting the law and a shoot-out. Whoever came down those stairs would be shot unless Flint was close enough to the madman to keep him from firing.

"Maggie and Jenna have gone for help," he called and quickly moved as gunfire pelted the stack of boxes he'd been hiding behind. "Pretty soon, this whole place will be filled with cops." He moved again, backtracking. He didn't want to stay far from the stairs. He had a feeling Terwilliger was doing the same thing. Only one of them would be leaving there.

He reloaded with his last clip, telling himself he had to conserve or he'd be out of bullets and then it definitely would be over. As he started to move, he froze at a sound upstairs. Someone had just opened and closed the back door.

Terwilliger must have heard it too, because he let out a laugh deep in the junk. "Well, I wonder who that is?" he called before moving. There was a shuffling sound, then nothing.

Flint felt his heart drop. He didn't think the man had an accomplice. At least not one that Maggie and Jenna had known about or they would have told him. But no matter who it was up there, this would change things. "It's probably a lawman who saw my patrol SUV pulled off up the road," he called and hurriedly moved as gunfire followed him. "Give yourself up."

Gunfire came in answer. The man had to be running out of ammunition, didn't he? Maybe not. Jenna had said he had a lot of it. Apparently he'd planned for something just like this.

Flint realized that he didn't know exactly where the gunfire had come from but that Terwilliger was closer than he'd thought. The realization came a few seconds too late. He'd been hiding behind a column of wooden crates stacked almost to the ceiling.

He heard something falling and realized Terwilliger had overturned one of the stacks of junk. It fell, slamming into the crates where he now stood. He started to move to the side, but he was too slow. The crates tilted at him and began coming down.

Flint tried to get away from them, but Terwilliger opened fire at the side where he'd been headed. The crates fell. They were much heavier than he'd thought. One hit him and knocked the weapon out of his hand. As he watched his gun skitter across the floor, one of the crates knocked him to the concrete. He tried to push it off, but there were too many of them and they were heavier than they had looked. He managed to get most of his body out, but one leg was caught, the crate crushing down on it.

Flint frantically tried to reach his weapon, but it was a good foot too far from his fingertips. He could hear Terwilliger making his way around to him. It would be just a matter of time before he reached him and finished this.

He looked for something he could use to pry the crate off his leg and spotted a table leg. Hurriedly, he began to unscrew the leg closest to him from the table.

Overhead, he heard the basement door open.

CHAPTER TWENTY-ONE

Standing in the freezing cold of the dark building, Maggie had had no idea what to do next. She'd heard more gunfire from downstairs, then what sounded like something large crashing to the floor. Now she heard nothing. She didn't know what was going on down there or who she might be coming face-to-face with as she opened the basement door.

A musty smell rose up from the blackness at the bottom of the stairs. Beyond, she could see only a little light. She stepped to the side to listen and heard a disquieting silence. Was Flint still alive? If he was, he would have said something. And if Clark was the only one alive down there...

She looked around, an idea coming to her. Someone had left a chair just down the hallway by the ladies' room. She moved away from the door, walking as quietly as she could, and picked up the chair. The plastic seat cover had been torn open, most of the stuffing gone. Its metal legs were icy cold to the touch.

At the basement door, she carefully peered around the edge, ready with the chair if she needed to hold Clark off. But there

was no one on the dark stairs that she could see. She didn't
know any other way to get a response from the basement.

She raised the chair, ready to hurl it downward.

Flint heard Terwilliger approaching him cautiously. The
man wouldn't know that Flint couldn't reach his weapon.
Nor did Flint suspect Terwilliger knew who was upstairs.
He gripped the table leg and, grimacing in pain, tried to pry
the crate off his leg.

His first attempt failed. When the crate dropped back on
his leg, it was so painful that he almost blacked out. But while
his vision blurred, he knew he had no time. He tried again,
knowing it might be his last chance before the man put a
bullet in him. If whoever was upstairs was an accomplice of
Terwilliger…

Suddenly the basement filled with the clatter of a large
object cartwheeling down the steps. In the path just on the
other side of him, Flint heard Terwilliger turn and fire toward the steps.

With his last gasp of strength, he levered the crate off just
as the gunfire subsided. He crawled over to his weapon and
pulled himself up in a sitting position. He had no idea what
had just come crashing down the stairs. Whatever it had
been, it had bought him time. Also, it had answered one of
his questions.

Whoever was up there, it wasn't Terwilliger's accomplice,
and now they both knew it. But he had a bad feeling he knew
who it was. More than ever, he had to end this and soon.

But he was still a sitting duck. All Terwilliger had to do
was peer around the end of this pathway and he'd see him. He
had to try to get to his feet, but he feared his ankle might be
broken. Which meant he wouldn't be walking out of there.

Harp needed a drink. He started to get into his patrol
SUV, but then realized it would be better if he walked. The

last thing he needed was to get picked up for drinking and driving. He headed down the street toward the closest bar.

He felt poleaxed. Vicki wasn't pregnant. She hadn't been pregnant for who knew how long. She'd let him believe she was. She'd let him buy her a ring, ask her to marry him, break his damned hand trying to bust down a door.

Feeling like a fool, he pushed open the door to the bar. The first beer went down like water. He ordered another and silently cursed the cowboy who kept playing sad love songs on the jukebox.

"You all right?" the bartender asked when he ordered a third beer.

"My girlfriend...actually, my former fiancée...just gave me back my ring." He pulled it out of his pocket and laid it on the slick surface of the bar.

"Sorry. Maybe it's for the best," the bartender said and placed another draft beer in front of him.

"Yeah, you're right, I guess." He picked up the ring and spun it like a top on the bar. The diamond caught the light as it circled. He thought of the day he'd bought the ring, how excited and happy he'd been. The tug on his heartstrings surprised him. "We were going to have a baby. She lost it."

"Tough break," the bartender said distractedly.

"Yeah. It isn't like I was in love with her," he said, but the bartender had already walked away.

Harp finished his third beer, feeling the rush of the alcohol and suddenly needing some fresh air. He stepped outside, but didn't know where to go. Actually, he had nowhere *to* go. He'd given up his apartment when he'd moved in with Vicki.

He turned toward the center of town, walking aimlessly. He'd never felt so lost. This time of night, there wasn't much going on. He used to joke that they rolled up the sidewalks in this tiny burg at eight o'clock.

There was little traffic since all the stores were closed. Only the few bars were open still, but the night was cold. The winter storm had left behind a good two feet of snow that was now plowed up into piles until the city could get it all hauled away. The winter scene had a sad, desolate feel to it.

"It isn't like I was in love with her," he said to himself again. But the words seemed cold and brittle on his tongue. He felt that pull on his heart again and stopped walking. "I do love her." His voice broke.

Turning back, he started for the apartment. He had to tell Vicki how he felt. He fished in his pocket, afraid he'd left the ring on the bar. But there it was. He gripped it in his palm. He couldn't wait to put it back on her finger.

He hadn't gone far when he heard footfalls behind him. He turned in time to see the man holding the tire iron before he took the first blow.

Now what? Maggie asked herself as she leaned against the wall out of the hail of bullets. The basement grew quiet again, but in the distance she heard the sound of a vehicle coming up the road.

She frowned. Jenna couldn't have gotten to town this quickly. But she'd thought there was a café or bar close by. Or maybe she'd been able to get cell phone coverage and had called for help. Was that why she was coming back?

Maggie swallowed, reminding herself that Jenna was her mother. Like her, she couldn't leave someone she loved with Clark Terwilliger.

Going to the back door, she looked out as Jenna pulled up, put down the passenger-side window and shouted, "Come on! I called for help, but in the meantime, I have a plan."

Maggie hesitated, but for only a moment. At least Jenna had a plan. It was more than she had. Terrified that Flint was already dead in the basement, she ran through the snow to the van.

"What's your plan?" she asked as she slammed her door and

Jenna threw the van into Reverse. "I'm so scared that Flint is trapped down there."

Jenna nodded. "I thought that might happen. Clark won't stop until one of them is dead. On my way back from making the call to the cops, I saw something in the van's headlights. It appears there is a road that descends down to the basement level. There is a loading dock, but next to it there is an old garage door at ground level. It has to be the way they got all that junk into that basement. I thought if I could get this van going fast enough, I could break down the door and into the basement." She looked over at Maggie. "What I'm proposing is dangerous. We could wait for help from town—"

"No. I'm scared there isn't time."

"What's been happening while I was gone?" Jenna asked.

"Lots of shooting." She shook her head. "I don't know what's happening down there. I just have this awful feeling that Flint is in terrible trouble."

"He's still alive. Otherwise, Clark would have come out. I'm glad I got back when I did. I was so worried about you." She gave Maggie a smile and reached over to touch her arm before shifting the van into gear. "I'm going to drive down the road to what appears to be a loading dock," she said as the headlights of the van shone on the side of the old building. "You're going to get out. Then I'll back up and try to bust down the door. If this old van can do the job."

Maggie started to argue but Jenna stopped her. "Your part is even more dangerous. Have you ever fired a weapon?" Jenna reached down to pull out a pistol. "I found this in the van's glove box. It's loaded and ready to go. All you have to do is point and shoot. Be ready. If I manage to break through the door... If you see Clark..."

Maggie nodded and took the pistol. "Just point and shoot?"

"That's it," Jenna said. "I'm thankful that Anvil taught me to shoot." She sounded sad. "He is a good man."

Jenna turned down onto a lower road, busting through the snow until she reached an area where the wind had blown off, leaving open ground. She stopped the van. "Ready?"

Flint heard the sound of a vehicle headed in his direction. It was too soon for the law even if whoever had left earlier had reached the sheriff in Sheridan. Which meant whoever was driving was coming back.

He groaned inwardly, terrified how badly this could all end. At least with Maggie and Jenna safe, he could face whatever was about to go down there. But if they were both back...

Gritting his teeth, Flint grabbed hold of one of the crates still in the tall stack with his free hand and used it to pull himself up on his good leg. Tentatively he tried to put pressure on his injured leg and grimaced in pain. It wasn't broken, but it was injured bad enough that, while he might be able to stand, maybe even walk a little, he wasn't going far.

"Sounds like my van," Terwilliger said, his voice way too close on the other side of the closest stack. The man let out a laugh. "Women never listen."

Flint worked his way, holding on as he shuffled away from the fallen crates to a spot where junk was piled high. He found a space where he could push his body into an indentation in a stack of furniture and waited.

Terwilliger would have heard him moving, but there was nothing he could do about it. Either the man was out of ammunition or he was saving what he had just as Flint was doing.

He waited, wondering how long it would take for the local law to get there. Too long. Terwilliger was no fool. He would know time wasn't on his side. The sound of the van's engine revved outside. Earlier he'd heard the back door open and close. Did that mean whoever had been upstairs had now gone?

He told himself he couldn't worry about that now. He had

to tune in to Terwilliger and his next move. He had only a few shots left. He had to make them count.

He heard the van engine die away. Good—they were leaving again, although that didn't make a lot of sense. Had at least one of them contacted the local sheriff? He could only hope. What else would they be doing?

That was when he heard the van coming back. Only this time, it was from a different direction. This time the engine was revved up so loud it sounded as if it was headed right for them. What in the—

Maggie held the pistol to her chest. The evening was cold and clear and surprisingly bright because of the snow. She'd moved to the side of the building and now stood waiting. Jenna was right. The door into the basement looked like it had seen better days. But the snowdrift in front of the door was high. What if she hit the door and nothing happened except she got hurt behind the wheel?

It wasn't a great plan, but it was the only one they had, as Jenna had pointed out. "You love this man, don't you?"

Maggie had nodded, her throat too tight to speak as tears had burned her eyes.

"Then we have to try to save him."

Maggie had stared at the woman, telling herself, *This is your mother. Your birth mother. The woman who tried to protect you for years and still is. She is willing to lose her own life to save yours—and Flint's.*

Now she shivered as she heard the van engine rev and watched as Jenna roared down the road. Snow flew up over the windshield as she busted through one snowdrift after another. She was going too fast, Maggie thought as her heart lodged in her throat. She realized with a cry of anguish that she might have found her mother only to lose her.

The van hit the snowdrift in front of the large old loading-dock garage door and seemed to disappear into a huge cloud of snow crystals before the sound of screaming metal filled the air. The initial impact was like a cannon going off.

Maggie rushed around the edge of the building to find the van halfway into the basement, the engine still running. Steadying the gun in both hands, she stepped over the debris and worked her way along the side of the van and into the basement. She couldn't see Jenna behind the wheel. She couldn't see anyone.

Flint realized what was happening just moments before the van crashed through the old loading-dock garage door. The bumper that had torn through the thin metal crashed into the first pile of junk. He heard what was coming and tried to move as quickly as possible.

Like a line of dominoes, the rows of junk began to topple. In the light from the van's headlights, he could see years of dust rising like smoke into the air. Over the clamor, he couldn't hear Terwilliger, but he had a pretty good idea where he was headed. Either out the stairs or the open doorway before he was crushed under the weight of the debris now coming down.

Flint shuffled toward the stairs, his leg causing him so much pain that he had to fight passing out. But he was almost to the end of one of the rows. Once he could see the stairs…

The sound of the gunshot made him flinch. He looked over, half expecting to see Terwilliger through a space between a stack of furniture. But with a jolt, he realized that the shot hadn't been fired at him. Another gunshot filled the air, this one ending in an explosion of glass.

Terwilliger was firing at whoever had crashed the van through the door.

Maggie flinched at the sharp gunfire. She'd moved only a few yards inside the basement, when the stacks of secondhand goods had begun to fall. In the dust that rose, she didn't see anything for a few moments.

Her gaze had shifted to the van, hoping to see Jenna. But there appeared to be no one behind the wheel. Had she climbed out? Or was she lying in there injured?

She realized there was nothing she could do for her mother right now. Clark had fired at the van and shattered the windshield. She thought she heard a groan come from inside the cab. But it was another sound that made her quickly step behind a large armoire that was still standing against the wall.

For a moment, she couldn't tell where the approaching footfalls had come from. Then she saw him. Clark was heading toward her, his gun dangling from his right hand. She saw his bloodstained shirt and the odd way he was moving. For a moment, she forgot about the gun in her own hand.

But seeing the way he moved toward her, she knew there would be only one way to stop him. Hurriedly, she raised the gun and fired. The shot went wild. She tried to steady the weapon in her hands, her heart a thunder in her chest, her breath coming out in rasps.

"Don't," she called to him. "Don't. I'll shoot you."

He raised his gun. An instant later a bullet whizzed past her head, making her jerk back as it lodged itself in the wall behind her. "You fire again and next time—"

His words were lost as out of the corner of her eye Maggie saw Jenna sit up behind the wheel of the van again. She didn't look good. There appeared to be blood running down the side of her face. The engine was still running although the van had rolled back a little, leaving just enough space between its destroyed front end and the fallen junk that Terwilliger was making his way toward Maggie through that open pathway.

Clark didn't seem to notice Jenna. He was too intent on closing the distance between himself and Maggie. It wasn't until Jenna ground the gears that he stopped directly in front of the van to turn his head in her direction.

The van engine roared as Jenna tromped on the gas. The heavy vehicle lurched forward. Maggie screamed as Clark raised his gun and fired. The bullet shattered the rest of the windshield. But the van didn't stop until the wall of junk brought it to a jarring halt. The motor died.

Maggie looked toward the now-missing windshield. There was no sign of Jenna. Nor a sign of Clark. All she could assume was that he was crushed under the van and the debris. She looked into the huge basement now in a jumble of fallen treasures.

"Flint!" she called. *"Flint?"*

There was no answer, but in the distance she could hear the sound of sirens headed their way.

Flint was edging along the wall near the stairs when he heard Maggie call his name. Before that he'd heard more gunfire followed by the roar of the van engine before it crashed again into the piles of junk. More had tumbled, some of it hitting the walls of the apartment and breaking through the Sheetrock.

"Maggie?" he called back. "Where is Terwilliger?"

"I think he's under the van."

"And Jenna?"

He heard a sob in her voice when she answered. "I can't see her."

"But you can see Terwilliger?"

Silence. Then the words he feared most. "He's not—" Maggie let out a cry, and even before Flint cleared the first downed pile of junk, he knew. All his fears came in a rush. Standing next to the van with a headlock on Maggie and a gun to her temple was Terwilliger.

CHAPTER TWENTY-TWO

Flint could see that Terwilliger was bleeding from a head wound near his temple. The man had to have lost a lot of blood from his earlier wound and now this one. But he appeared to be strong enough to either choke the life out of Maggie or pull the trigger and shoot her in the head.

Flint worked his way closer, trying hard not to show how difficult it was to walk on his injured leg. The last thing he wanted was to look vulnerable in any way. A man like Terwilliger would feed on that.

"You're a monster, Terwilliger, but not even you would kill your own daughter," Flint said.

"You sure about that, Sheriff? She tried to shoot me."

"Because you're scaring her—just like you are now. Let her go. This is between you and me."

The man shook his head. "Not until you drop your gun."

"That doesn't seem fair unless you drop yours, as well."

Terwilliger laughed. "Looks to me like you aren't getting around all that well, Sheriff. Did you hurt yourself?"

"I'm okay. How about you?"

"I'm fine," the man lied. Flint could see that he was in pain and bleeding badly. He figured only meanness was keeping the man on his feet. Backed into a corner, though, Terwilliger could kill Maggie just out of spite, Flint knew. It didn't matter that she was his blood. Finding her and abducting her hadn't been about love. It had been about control, and right now he had all the control.

"I said put down your gun," Terwilliger repeated and tightened his grip on Maggie.

Flint looked into her eyes. He saw her pleading look. Like him, she knew that the moment he put down his weapon, Terwilliger would kill him.

The law was on its way. He could hear sirens growing closer and could see how this was going to end. Terwilliger had probably told himself, like a lot of ex-cons, that he'd rather die than go back to prison.

Most of them changed their minds when the time came, but he didn't think this man was one of them. Terwilliger would never see daylight outside of prison again and he had to know that.

"Now!" the man barked. The hold he had on Maggie was cutting off her air. Flint saw her struggling. Even if Terwilliger didn't shoot her, he would strangle her to death if Flint didn't do something.

"I'm putting down my weapon." He kept it pointed in the man's direction as he slowly began to lower it to the floor. Flint told himself it was too dangerous to take a shot. Terwilliger was using Maggie as a shield. Flint's only chance at a shot was at the man's head. And if Flint actually managed to hit him, Terwilliger might pull the trigger before he hit the floor and kill Maggie.

But if Flint didn't take the shot...

"If you don't drop your gun..." Terwilliger had lifted Maggie off the floor in the headlock. Flint could see her clutching at his arm with her fingers, fighting for breath. The gun was still at her temple.

"Drop the gun!" the man yelled.

It was now or never. The sirens were close now. Terwilliger was shifting on his feet nervously and glancing toward the open doorway next to the van. If he made a run for it, he might be able to get away. If he didn't... In a few minutes this place would be crawling with cops.

His hand was only inches from the floor and yet the thought of chancing such a shot... He suddenly looked past Terwilliger. Jenna. She was barely able to stand but she'd picked up the gun that Maggie had dropped.

Flint saw Terwilliger's eyes widen in alarm because none of them had seen Jenna since he'd fired into the van. The man hadn't turned to see who was behind him, but Flint could see him filling in the blanks. If Jenna was alive and had picked up the gun that Maggie had dropped...

Terwilliger started to turn. Flint had no choice; he had to take the shot. He could see that Jenna was having trouble lifting the gun in her hand. He raised his weapon and fired.

The bullet caught the man in the side of the head. Blood and gore filled the air for a moment. It seemed to all happen in slow motion. Flint saw Maggie go limp in the man's arms. Then both of them dropped to the floor. Past them, Jenna dropped the gun and slumped to the floor as well as the sirens grew louder and louder.

Flint tried to run to Maggie, but his bad leg gave out. He fell and had to crawl the last few yards as the winter night filled with flashing red and blue lights. Pulling himself to her, he touched her face, terrified that Terwilliger had managed to get off a shot. If they'd both fired at the same time...

Her face was splattered with blood, so he couldn't tell if it was hers or Terwilliger's. Her eyes were closed, but they fluttered open at his touch. He'd never seen such beautiful brown eyes. She began to cough as she gasped for air, and he realized that it hadn't been a gunshot that had dropped her. It had been a lack of oxygen.

"Maggie?"

Tears filled her eyes as he took her in his arms. She cried against his shoulder as armed men began to spill in through the open doorway.

"Jenna?" she asked as one of the officers knelt down to check Jenna for a pulse.

"This one's still alive," the officer said and checked Terwilliger. He got on his radio, calling for an ambulance—and, looking at Terwilliger, a coroner.

"Maggie," Flint said, reaching into his pocket. "I can't wait any longer. Marry me?"

CHAPTER TWENTY-THREE

Earlier Mark had gotten a call from the Sheridan, Wyoming, sheriff's department. He'd been waiting to hear from Flint, waiting and worrying. There was no doubt in his mind that Flint had gone off to look for Maggie, so the call hadn't come as a complete surprise.

"We heard from a woman named Jenna Holloway," the Wyoming sheriff had told him. "She said she and another woman, Maggie Thompson, had been held captive by a man named Clark Terwilliger at an old roadhouse just across the Montana border. Sheriff Flint Cahill rescued them, but he is still with the abductor in the building. We're on our way out there now."

Mark had quickly filled the sheriff in on what he knew. "You'll call me as soon as you know something?"

The sheriff had promised he would.

Mark now waited, too anxious to do anything but sit and stare at the phone. Flint had found them. He let out a laugh, not surprised given his boss's determination. Still, it had to be like looking for a needle in a haystack. Mark had never believed in psychic connections, but he couldn't help but wonder if love hadn't played a part in it.

He laughed again, telling himself he needed sleep if he was thinking such things. When his phone finally rang, he practically jumped out of his skin.

Praying that the law had gotten there in time, he picked up the phone. "Ramirez."

Frank and Nettie were still in North Dakota when they got the call the next day.

"Flint found Maggie and Jenna," Frank told his wife. "Jenna was shot and is in the hospital, but she's stable. Maggie is fine." He filled her in on everything that Flint had told him happened.

"Before we leave town, I'd like to stop by Edna Burns's and let her know the good news," Nettie said.

They left the motel and drove the few blocks to Edna's house. Frank was relieved that the news had been good. He'd heard the happiness in Flint's voice. This could have gone so badly...

He parked and they walked up to the door to knock. Opening the door, Edna looked surprised to see them, then worried. "Are Jenna and Margaret—"

"They were found. They're both safe."

Edna's eyes filled with tears as she ushered them in. "I was so worried."

"We thought you'd want to know," Nettie said after they were all seated in the living room. "Maybe now you can tell us the rest of the story?"

Edna nodded slowly.

"When did Jenna call you and ask about her daughter?"

"A few years ago," the woman admitted. "She'd found her. She wanted to know the truth. She knew that I'd lied to her.

It broke my heart but I was just doing what her parents had asked me to do."

"They put you in an unbearable position," Nettie said.

Edna wiped her eyes with a lace-edged hankie from her pocket. "Last March, Jenna called to say that Clark was out again and he'd found her. I was terrified for her and begged her to tell her husband but she refused. She asked me to watch out for Margaret if something should happen to her."

"But you'd already watched out for Margaret, I'm guessing," Nettie said.

The elderly woman raised her head and locked eyes. "Jenna had called. She'd seen Margaret in Billings, seen a bruise on her wrist and thought she might be in a situation where she needed help."

"So you helped her. But it wasn't the first time, was it."

Edna smiled sadly. "My friend who was raising Margaret died when the girl was seventeen. I paid for Margaret to go to beauty school. I didn't have enough for college, but when my husband died, I was able to help a little more."

"I figure you gave the loan to Maggie for the salon she opened in Gilt Edge," Frank said.

Edna nodded. "If her parents ever found out what I did…" She shivered. "My sister had warned me not to go against her husband's wishes. If Les ever found out…"

"Why does your sister stay with him?" Nettie asked.

"I wish I knew. I've told her she can come live with me. I'll never understand what she sees in that man. I think there are just some women who can't live without a man."

"Why didn't Jenna tell Maggie that she was her mother?" Frank asked.

"She'd been made to feel shame for the pregnancy. She never wanted Margaret to know how she'd been conceived. She never wanted her to know about Clark." Edna smiled. "But she had her hair done there when she could afford it, she told me, just so she could see her. She'd married some older farmer who was tight with money." She tsked. "Just like her mother."

"I'm assuming that Jenna married Anvil Holloway to get away from her father," Frank said.

"And her mother. I'm not sure my sister was any better with her after…after what happened with Clark. They were so filled with shame and blamed that girl." Edna shook her head. "It wasn't her fault any more than this latest mess is her fault. It was that man."

"Clark Terwilliger is dead."

Edna closed her eyes and crossed herself. "I know it's wrong to be glad, but I am. He was just plain…evil. I'm not sorry he's dead. You said Jenna is going to pull through?"

"She is," Nettie said.

"And Margaret?"

"She's strong and she has a good man to help her through this," Nettie said. "A sheriff. They just got engaged."

Edna smiled. "I would love a happy ending for that child. She hasn't had it easy. I'm afraid my friend spent much of Margaret's life looking for the father in her. Whenever Margaret did something wrong, my friend was convinced it was his bad genes coming out. I have to admit, I worried too. Silly, I'm sure, but still, I think Margaret knew something was wrong and I feel bad about that."

"You did your best to save her," Nettie said and took the woman's frail hand. "Thank you for telling us the truth."

"I should have the first time," Edna said. "Funny how lying becomes so easy after a while. Maybe if I'd told the truth years ago… How nice it would be not to live a life of regrets."

"Yes," Nettie said and looked over at her husband. Years ago he'd asked her to marry him, but her mother had talked her into marrying a different man because his family owned a country store. At that time, Frank was just a good-looking cowboy who could ride a horse or a motorcycle like he was born to it. Too often Nettie thought about how different her life would have been if she had married Frank all those years ago. Maybe they would have had children of their own.

"I have my own regrets," Nettie said to the woman as she got to her feet. "But sometimes things turn out for the best. Sometimes you get a second chance. Jenna has that chance and so does Maggie."

"You say Margaret's engaged to a sheriff?" Edna asked, perking up a little.

"Flint Cahill is a good man," Frank said. "You don't have to worry about her anymore."

"I can't believe you asked her to marry you at a crime scene," Cyrus said the next day when Flint and Maggie walked into the Stagecoach Saloon to cheers and congratulations. It had been thirty-six hours since being rescued from the roadhouse. Flint was moving slowly but much better since getting the walking cast. Nothing was broken, but it would take time for the tendons to heal.

"Such a romantic," Hawk agreed good-naturedly.

"The timing probably could have been better," Flint admitted as his family rushed over for hugs—even Cyrus and Hawk.

"The timing was *perfect*," Maggie said as Lillie threw her arms around her.

"Welcome to the family," Lillie said and began to cry. "It's the hormones," she said, wiping at her tears. "And we were all so worried about you. I'm so glad you're all right."

"Flint, you did have us worried," Hawk said. "I know you always have to be the hero, but…" He shook his head, and Maggie saw real worry in his expression.

Her future father-in-law, Ely, pushed his way through to shake Flint's hand and hug him. "Took you long enough to ask her to the post," his father chastised.

Flint only laughed as he met Maggie's gaze and pulled her over next to him. "I agree." He looked at his father. "But I thought you were headed back to the mountains." For a man who spent most of his time as a recluse, it surprised Maggie too that he was still here.

"Couldn't leave until I was sure my son was going to be all right. This calls for champagne," Ely announced and moved to the bar where Darby began to pour. He poured himself water and they all toasted.

Maggie could tell that Flint was touched by his father's concern. She felt overwhelmed by this boisterous family, but also grateful to be included. She listened to the good-natured ribbing Flint took and saw how much love was in this room. Before that moment, she supposed she hadn't realized that she wasn't just marrying Flint. She was marrying his family. She found herself smiling for the first time in days.

"Now, what about the rest of you?" Ely demanded as he put down his glass, his gaze turning to Hawk and Cyrus.

"Another wedding!" Lillie cried and turned to Hawk and Cyrus. "Wouldn't it be great if it was a triple wedding?"

Her bachelor brothers both held up their hands as if to ward off even the thought.

Flint laughed and pulled Maggie closer. She could tell that he'd hated having her out of his sight even to answer questions about the abduction. But once everything was cleared up with Terwilliger's death and his leg healed, Flint would be return-ing to work. He couldn't watch her 24/7 even though she suspected it would be a while before he felt he didn't need to.

Maggie planned to take some time off, as well. She still felt jumpy even two days later. This morning, she'd told Flint everything about Gary Long and her relationship with him. She'd told Flint that Gary had contacted her saying he had to talk to her and that if she didn't meet him he was going to cause trouble. Foolishly, she'd met him in Billings when she'd gone down for the salon event. She'd thought she'd made her feelings clear.

"When I saw him standing in your house… I thought we'd settled everything in Billings," she'd said. "If I'd thought he'd come to Gilt Edge… I should have told."

"I should have asked," he'd said.

"I just didn't want my past coming between us."

He'd chuckled at that. "Unlike my past. I was so sure Celeste had taken you," he'd said.

It would have been Maggie's first thought if she'd been Flint. He'd told her that he'd tried to choke the truth out of Celeste. She was just sorry that she'd missed that.

After their talk, she'd felt closer to Flint. He'd risked his life to save her. She'd never forget that and said as much.

"And you risked yours," he'd said with a shake of his head. "I couldn't believe you'd come back to the roadhouse. But if you hadn't…" He'd pulled her to him and held her tightly. "That's all behind us now."

"Can't have a triple wedding if these two cowboys don't even have brides," Ely was saying.

"Must be time for us to go chase some cattle," Hawk said.

"You're not getting off that easy," Lillie said. "Surely there's someone in your life other than Cyrus."

"Hey, you're going to hurt my feelings," Cyrus joked. "But Hawk's right. The cows need to be fed and watered and there's that tractor to be fixed," he said as he backed toward the door. On his way out, he patted Flint on the back.

"I suppose this means you're back in your own house," Hawk said. "I'd say we were going to miss you, but we hardly saw you."

"Thanks for everything," Flint said, his voice cracking with emotion.

"Don't you want to stay and talk about their wedding plans?" Lillie called after her two brothers as they scurried out. "We have to invite Hawk's old girlfriend Drea," she said with a laugh. "I think there are some unresolved feelings between them." There was a twinkle in her eye that made them all groan before she turned to Maggie. "So tell us everything."

"We would love to give you a blow by blow," Flint said, taking his fiancée's hand. "But we need to stop by the sheriff's office and then the hospital."

"How is Jenna?" Darby asked.

"That's right—she's your mother," Lillie said, wide-eyed. "All these years you were told that your mother was dead?"

Maggie nodded. "It definitely came as a shock. She and Flint saved my life."

"Jenna is in stable condition and expected to recover," Flint interrupted. "Maggie will tell you all about it at some later date." He shot his sister a warning look. "She's been through a lot. Okay?"

"We'll talk," Maggie said, touching Lillie's hand as Flint got her out of there.

"I'm sorry. My family…" He shrugged.

"They're delightful," Maggie said, making him laugh.

"Now, that is a word I have never heard used about the Cahills."

"Watch it. I'm going to be a Cahill," she joked.

He smiled over at her. "Yes, you are, just as soon as I can get you to the altar." He squeezed her hand, worried about her. She was putting on a good act, but he could tell it would be a while before she got over the trauma of everything that had happened—maybe especially learning about her mother… and her father.

"I got a text from Mark at the office. He asked me to swing by," Flint said as they drove away from the saloon. "Is that okay with you?"

"Sure," Maggie said, looking out at the mountains. "I called the hospital this morning." They'd stayed at her house, though neither had gotten much sleep. Flint said he thought his house might have too many bad memories. "Jenna hasn't regained consciousness."

Vicki took Harp's hand and raised it to her lips. His fingers felt warm but so lifeless. Sitting in the chair next to his bed, she fought tears as she kissed his palm and laid it back down on the white sheet.

The doctor said Harp could come out of the coma at any time. Or never. The thought scared her so badly. He had to be all right. She needed him more than ever.

She'd been so shocked when she'd gotten the call. Harp had been attacked on the street by an assailant? She worried about him being a deputy, but two nights ago he hadn't been working.

"Why would someone do this to him?" she had demanded of the undersheriff.

"It appears he was mugged. His wallet was open on the ground and whatever money he'd had was gone. But he'd managed to hang on to your engagement ring."

She'd listened to how Harp had had the ring clutched in his one good fist. Mark had speculated that it might be why it appeared he hadn't fought back. Or maybe he didn't get a chance.

"Either way, the mugger didn't get your engagement ring," Mark had said. "Clearly the ring meant something to him."

That news had made her cry. If only she'd told Harp when she'd first lost the baby, but she'd been so afraid he would have walked out on her. Just as he'd walked out two nights ago.

But it appeared he'd been headed back toward the apartment, the undersheriff had said, when he'd been jumped. Harp had been coming back to her.

"You're going to be all right," she whispered as she smoothed the sheet. "You have to be because I need you. I love you, Harp. We can have another baby." She began to cry. "Oh, Harp, all I ever wanted was to give you a family."

Maggie said she would wait in the reception area while Flint visited with the undersheriff. "I'll be fine."

He studied her beautiful face. "Yes, you will."

Down the hall, he stepped into Mark's office. "Harp is in the hospital in a coma. They don't know if he is going to make it," the undersheriff said.

His first thought was another domestic dispute. "What happened?"

"Apparently, he'd walked uptown and someone jumped him. Beat him up bad with a tire iron. We weren't able to get any prints off the weapon because of all the blood."

Flint winced. "Someone he pissed off?"

"That would have been my first guess. But his wallet was empty of cash and on the ground next to him, and Harp had a diamond ring gripped in his hand when he was found."

"A ring?"

"The engagement ring he had given to his girlfriend. Apparently she'd given it back." Mark shrugged as if to say "who knows?"

"He was conscious when he was found?"

"He was, but lapsed into a coma before we could find out what happened. From his injuries, though, it appears he was hit from behind and didn't even get a chance to put up a fight."

Flint shook his head. "Has his girlfriend been notified?"

"I called her myself. She took it hard. I was worried, with the baby and all, but she told me that she'd lost the baby. She said they broke up before Harp left the house."

"Think she had anything to do with his being attacked?"

"I don't think so," Mark said. "She's been by his side at the hospital since I called her."

Flint felt bad for her and Harp. "Might be hard to find his attacker given his past reputation around town."

"I found the bar where he had a few beers," Mark said. "The bartender remembers the ring and Harp's sad-luck story. If he comes out of the coma, he might know who attacked him. If he doesn't…" The undersheriff shook his head.

"I wanted to get rid of Harp enough times," Flint admitted. "But not like this. I'll stop in and see how he's doing since Maggie and I are on our way to the hospital."

"I've read your report on what happened," Mark said. "Good work. It will be nice to have you back."

Maggie was relieved when they walked into the hospital and were told that Jenna had regained consciousness.

"Go see her," Flint said. "I'll check on Harp and catch up with you."

As she entered the room, she stopped to study the woman lying in the hospital bed. Her mother. She still couldn't believe it.

Maggie no longer saw the almost-invisible woman who used to come into her beauty shop. *This* Jenna was strong and courageous. It was as if she'd finally faced her demons and had now come into her own.

Jenna must have sensed her in the doorway because she turned from where she'd been looking out the window to smile at Maggie. She held out her hand to her and Maggie moved to the side of the bed.

"I'm so sorry," Jenna said, squeezing her hand.

"All that matters is that you're okay," Maggie said, surprised to find herself close to tears.

"I should have told you years ago," Jenna said. "My aunt thought she was doing what was best for you. She couldn't bear to see you go into foster care, so she talked her friend into raising you with her financial help. She had to keep it from her sister, my mother."

"My grandmother."

Jenna looked full of regret. "None of this is your fault."

"Or yours. Did they really believe I'd died?" Maggie had to ask.

"Apparently it was something they wanted to believe, but I think my mother knew the truth all along. Well, they know now. The scandal they thought they'd nipped in the bud will be in all the news."

"Will they—"

"Contact you?" Jenna shook her head. "I'm afraid they wrote us both off years ago. But if you want to meet them—"

"No," Maggie said. "I don't need to."

"Their loss." Her mother smiled at her. "I am so proud of you. You have accomplished so much."

"With your help. Flint told me all that you did for me."

"It was mostly my aunt's doing because I didn't have any money."

"But you talked her into it," Maggie said.

"She was happy to help as much as she could. She loved you."

Maggie smiled. "I loved her too. I'm sure she told you that I used to go down to her house all the time. She taught me to bake and sew..." Tears filled her eyes. "We used to fix each other's hair. I guess it's no wonder I felt closer to her than the woman who raised me."

"We might have helped you, but you're the one who turned your life around."

"What will you do now?" Maggie had to ask. "Does your husband know?"

"No. It wouldn't make any difference. I hurt him too badly. He could never forgive me and I don't blame him. When I left him, I cut all ties. I thought it would be easier for him.

I think all I did was hurt him worse." She shook her head. "He's a good man. He deserved better, but I was so afraid that Clark would kill him if I didn't leave."

"We don't have to worry about Clark anymore."

Jenna met her gaze. "He's really dead?"

Maggie nodded.

"I'm so sorry you had to go through what you did because of me."

"It wasn't your fault. You were the real victim. But now you're free. There is nothing holding you back with Clark gone."

Jenna nodded, but there was a haunted look in her eyes. Maybe in time, she would forget what the man had done to her.

"You won't leave Gilt Edge, will you?" Maggie hadn't realized how much her answer mattered. She didn't want to lose her mother again.

"No. I'm staying." She squeezed Maggie's hand again. "That is, if you want me to."

"I do." Maggie bent down to carefully hug her. "Mom." The word sounded so strange on her lips since it was one she'd never used before.

Jenna held her tightly. "Then I'm not going anywhere."

After stopping in to check on Harp, Flint went to find Maggie. Just as Mark had said, Harp's girlfriend, Vicki, had been beside the man's bed. She was such a tiny, frail woman and clearly so in love with Harp. He gave a silent prayer that Harp would recover. Maybe there would be a chance for the two of them.

His sister, Lillie, would have said he was becoming a romantic. Maybe he was. He found Maggie as she was leaving Jenna's room.

"She's conscious. I would imagine you'll want to question her."

"I'll leave that to Mark, but I will go in and see her. Wait for me?"

As Flint tapped at Jenna's hospital-room door, he realized Jenna was now his soon-to-be mother-in-law. He owed her his life and so much more. She'd given birth to Maggie. It didn't matter under what circumstances, as far as he was concerned. He was just thankful to her. She'd saved his life and Maggie's.

"Come in," Jenna called, and he stepped inside.

Moving to her bed, he said, "Glad to see you're better."

"I'm sorry I put you all through that."

"That was Clark Terwilliger's doing, not yours. Jenna, you aren't to blame for any of this. You were a child when this all began. I just appreciate what you did for Maggie. You saved both of our lives."

"If you hadn't shown up at that old roadhouse when you did…"

"You're safe now. Maybe you can find some peace."

She smiled, but he could see it was going to take time. "I was going to come see you after I got out of here. I did some things before I left town that I feel terrible about. I shoplifted makeup and stole other things. Maybe I wanted to get arrested and locked up. Anywhere that Clark couldn't get to me."

"You were in a bad place," Flint said. "But don't worry about any of that. Anvil returned the items you took and paid a fine."

"He took the blame for me?" She sounded surprised, but then nodded as if she could see him doing such a thing.

"Have you talked to him?" Flint asked.

"No. I'm sure he doesn't want to see me and I don't blame him. I'll get a job and pay him back the money I owe him."

"I doubt he'll take it."

"Doesn't matter. I have to try," she said. "I suppose you know why I began writing to men in prison."

"You were looking for help."

She chuckled at that. "I thought it would take a hardened criminal to stop one. But I even failed at that. Kurt wasn't..." She shook her head. "He was a nice guy who tried to help me but ultimately Clark would have killed him."

"I think I've pieced things together with the help of two private investigators I hired to find you. But I have to know how Clark found you in Wyoming."

Jenna nodded. "I called my friend Dana, Clark's sister. I knew he was out of prison. Somehow he'd found out that I'd had his child. He was determined to find her. Dana told me that he'd called her and said that he'd found her. I didn't believe it at first. But Clark wasn't anything if not smart. Apparently he'd seen me coming out of the beauty shop the last time. He'd seen me crying in my car and knew it wasn't over my latest haircut. Seeing Maggie and yet not being able to... It broke my heart. I think he took one look at Maggie and knew."

"So you got his cell number from Dana and called him."

"I told myself that I was the one he wanted and that he would leave Maggie alone. I had the money Kurt had set aside. I actually thought I could buy Clark off. Or at least make some kind of deal with him. The next thing I knew, Maggie and I were both prisoners in that old roadhouse."

"Well, that's all behind you now, and as far as the law is concerned, you have nothing to worry about. Will you stay in Gilt Edge?"

"Maggie wants me to." He heard the pleasure in her voice.

"I'm glad. Once you're better, there's going to be a wedding." As he left, he knew what he had to do.

CHAPTER TWENTY-FOUR

Sitting at the gas station, Frank watched two crows having what looked like a romantic date on the telephone line. Crows were such intelligent birds and so much like people that he'd always loved watching them. He remembered one of his and Nettie's first dates had involved crow watching and smiled.

Of course, Nettie had told him that a real date didn't involve bird-watching, so he'd kissed her and said *That more like it?*

"What are you smiling about?" Nettie asked now as she climbed into their SUV. She put down the bag of road-trip treats she'd picked up inside the convenience store while he'd been filling up the tank with gas.

"Just remembering our first date."

She laughed. "Let me guess. Those two crows reminded you of it." She nodded toward the courting going on over on the telephone line.

"You weren't all that impressed by my vast knowledge of crows, as I recall," he said and started the engine.

"True, but I did like the kiss."

He grinned. "That right?"

"Those crows have nothing on us. I still like your kisses."

"Get everything you needed for the trip home?" he asked, anxious now to get back to their small ranch near Beartooth, Montana—not to mention their investigative business.

"I got some of your favorites, of course," she said, reaching in the bag. "We did good, huh."

He laughed. "I think we did. Flint texted me a minute ago to say that Jenna was conscious and expected to have a full recovery."

"And Maggie?"

"They announced their engagement."

"Is that safe?" Nettie asked, wide-eyed. "What about Celeste?"

"Guess we'll have to see how she takes the news."

"So we might get called for another job up this way?"

"You never know," he said and put out his hand for one of the candy bars. They had a lot of miles to cover.

Flint dropped Maggie at her house. He had one more thing to do before he went home to her. As he drove out to the Holloway farm, he thought about what he would tell Anvil. By now, the farmer would have heard that Jenna was back in town after an ordeal involving her daughter, Maggie Thompson.

But Flint had realized that the man needed to hear the truth. Like Jenna, he doubted it would change anything, but he couldn't let the man go on believing the worst about her.

As he was leaving her hospital room earlier, he'd stopped in the doorway, realizing there was something he needed to know. "Did you love him?"

Jenna had looked up in surprise. "Anvil? Oh yes. I could have been happy with him as long as I got to see my daughter once in a while. But then Clark showed up." She hadn't needed to say any more.

Parking in the front yard at the Holloway farm, Flint got out of his patrol SUV and limped toward the house. He wouldn't have been surprised to have Anvil throw him off his property. He thought of all the other times he'd come out there, accusing the man of murder.

Anvil came to the door, looking happier to see him than Flint had expected.

"You heard that Jenna was found and that she is going to be all right?"

Anvil nodded.

"I thought you might want to hear the whole story."

The farmer seemed to hesitate, but for only a moment before he opened the door wider and invited him inside.

Harp opened his eyes. The first thing he saw was Vicki asleep in the chair next to his bed. He smiled when he saw the engagement ring on her finger. How long had he been out? She'd had it sized and it now fit perfectly.

Her eyes fluttered and widened when she saw him looking at her. "Harp!" She leaped from the chair and practically fell into his arms.

"Easy," he said, realizing more than his aching head was injured.

"I was so worried about you," Vicki cried. "I knew you would wake up. I knew it."

He couldn't help but smile at her. His father had told him that a woman could change him, but he'd never believed that until now.

"I see you found the ring," Harp said.

She drew back to stare down at it. "I hope it was okay. I had it sized. The jeweler came up here and took it to have it done so I didn't have to leave your bedside. But if you—" She started to pull it off, but he stopped her.

"It's right where it belongs." He met her gaze. She hadn't

left his bedside? He couldn't help but smile. "I want to marry you, Vicki. I don't care if you're pregnant or not. The baby wasn't the only reason I was going to marry you."

She burst into tears and hugged him a little too hard again. He grimaced, but said nothing as he held her to him.

"I need to call the sheriff," she said, pulling back to take out her cell phone. "I promised I'd call the minute you opened your eyes. We were all so worried. Your father was by earlier."

He wondered if that was true, but at least Vicki had been concerned about him. For now, that was enough. He listened to her tell the undersheriff that he'd come out of his coma and realized he'd been hit a lot harder than he'd thought.

"How long have I been out?" he asked after she'd hung up and told him Mark was on his way.

"Two days."

Days. That surprised him. He listened as Vicki filled him in on everything that had been happening since he'd been out.

"Wait," he said, his head aching, but it felt so good to be alive that he wasn't about to complain. "Maggie Thompson and Jenna Holloway?"

"Jenna is Maggie's mother."

How about that? he thought.

"Anyway, the sheriff saved them. The man who took them had raped Jenna when she was thirteen. Pregnant, her parents forced her to give up the baby. Maggie never knew."

Vicki came up for breath and he had to laugh before he asked, "How did you find all this out?"

"Gail, at the sheriff's office. She's been by to visit you a few times. She was worried that you were going to die too."

They both turned as the undersheriff stuck his head in the door. "Mind if I have a few words with Harp alone?" Mark asked Vicki.

She rushed out, stopping only long enough to smile back at him and promise she would just be out in the hallway.

Mark pulled up a chair next to his bed and took out his notebook and pen. "I need to ask you what happened."

Harp shrugged. "The last thing I remember, I was headed back to the apartment to see Vicki when someone jumped me."

"You recognize your attacker?"

Harp thought about that for a moment. Thought about Larry Wagner and his wife, Shirley, and their oldest son, who was the spitting image of Harp.

"You see his face?" Mark prodded.

Harp shook his head even though it hurt to do so. "Didn't get a good look." That much, at least, was true.

"Well, if you remember anything else," Mark said, putting away his notebook and pen as he rose to his feet.

Harp saw his questioning look as if the undersheriff thought he was covering for someone. Larry hadn't killed him even though he suspected the man had wanted to—and could have. Harp felt like they were even. He hoped Larry did too.

"Hope you're well soon," the undersheriff said.

"Mark," he said before the man could leave. "I know I have a lot of making up for lost time, but I hope you'll give me a chance."

Mark met his gaze.

"Maybe it was almost dying a couple of times, but I think it changes a man," Harp said.

"Only time will tell," the undersheriff said with a chuckle. "Just get well. And should you remember who jumped you…"

"Don't think I will." He shrugged. "I've put a lot of the past behind me. I don't see it coming back."

Maggie had never been more excited about Christmas in the days that passed. She'd gone shopping for Flint and found him a first edition of a book he loved. Flint had wanted to cut their own Christmas tree, but with the walking cast, he'd told her that Hawk and Cyrus had offered. They'd come back with a beautiful fir tree.

I hope you don't mind, but I told them to put it up at the saloon, Flint had said. *I don't want to have Christmas at my house, and your house doesn't seem the right place, either. Do you mind if we have Christmas with my family this year?*

She'd been surprised, thinking this year he would want them to have their own Christmas at home. Nor had he mentioned her moving in with him again. Instead, he spent almost every night with her at her house.

When she found him waiting for her at her house, she said, "What's this, Flint?" He had some brochures spread out on the coffee table in the living room.

"I should have said something before this." He led her over to the couch.

"I'm going to sell my house," he said. "I was wrong to ask you to live there. That was the house that Celeste and I shared. Sometimes I'm such a fool. I should have thought of that before."

"But you love that house."

He shook his head. "I love you, Maggie. I'd live anywhere with you, but this is a new beginning. We deserve our own house with no bad memories."

She leaned toward him to give him a quick kiss. "I'd live anywhere with you. I love you, Flint, but are you sure?"

"I've never been more sure of anything in my life. Please understand, my being gun-shy had nothing to do with you. First, it was just a case of being scared. I'd failed badly already. I was terrified I'd mess this up and did, numerous times. I should have listened to you about Celeste."

"She wasn't the one who abducted me."

"No, but she could have. As it was, she withheld information in the investigation. We might have found you sooner if she had cooperated and told us what she knew."

"But you *did* find me." Tears welled in her eyes. She thought about her drowning dream and the fear that no one could save her. But she'd been wrong. Flint had saved her from something worse than drowning. She'd never forget seeing him standing in that doorway. "You saved my life."

"You saved mine. So I guess we're even." His smile made her heart beat even faster. "Now let's find a house that we can love together. Or we can build up on the ranch on the section that will be ours. You decide."

That night after dinner, Flint and Maggie sat down and talked about everything that had happened to them. Flint loved how close he felt to her. He'd been afraid before but that was past them. Secrets were Celeste's game, not Maggie's. He'd just been afraid to ask about her past. He realized it had kept them at arm's length, each of them keeping something from the other.

"There is so much we should have talked about. I never even asked you what brought you to Gilt Edge."

"I heard about a hair salon that was for sale, and when I was offered a loan to take it over… It was described to me as a young businesswoman organization loan. I know now that my mother had something to do with me coming to Gilt Edge. Apparently she talked to her aunt who had inherited some money."

"And maybe had a guilty conscience," Flint suggested.

She nodded. "Those were a different time when even a child out of wedlock was considered taboo, let alone one that was conceived the way I was. Also, it sounds like my grandparents are…quite strict."

"And unforgiving. Have you heard from them?"

"No," Maggie said. "And I don't plan to. Jenna said they will never change."

"Probably not, from what I've heard about them. Their

loss." He smiled at her and touched her face. "There is so much I want to know and so much I want to tell you," he said. "After you disappeared and I was looking for you, I was going crazy. Why hadn't we talked about the past? Why didn't I know important things about you that could have helped me find you sooner?"

"But you did find me."

"Finally, but I don't want us to have secrets from each other."

"Me either."

It seemed that they'd just met as they talked for hours.

"Still, I don't understand how Jenna found you. Had you met her before you moved here?" he asked.

"It's funny, but when I moved here, I thought she looked… familiar. Now I'm pretty sure I saw her once down in Billings at the salon where I worked." Maggie chuckled. "She could even have been the person who mentioned the shop for sale in Gilt Edge. Maybe she'd seen that I was looking for a way out of a bad relationship with Gary…"

"How are things with your mother?"

"The doctor says she's going to recover nicely. I just worry what she will do now. You don't think she'll go back to Anvil?"

"Probably not," he said. "But she's still young. Maybe there's something she'd like to do with her life now that she doesn't have to worry about her past."

"Will charges be filed against her for disappearing the way she did?"

Flint shook his head. "She feared for her life. Any judge would understand under the circumstances. And she saved our lives."

Maggie nodded. "I've never been so afraid in my life. My…" She couldn't say the word *father*. "Clark was insane."

"I know."

"Yes, I guess you do. When I think about him and how I

was conceived… I always knew there was something wrong with the story I was told about my mother and father. I would catch people whispering and I knew it was about me."

"I'm sorry that happened. As you said, thirty-three years ago things were much different than they are today, fortunately," Flint said. "You are an amazing woman."

He looked down at the diamond he'd put on her finger at the crime scene. His family was right. He didn't know one darned thing about romance. "I had planned a romantic dinner to ask you to marry me." His gaze came up to meet hers. "I'd been carrying this ring around in my pocket for months. So in that basement after everything had happened, I… I just couldn't wait a moment longer."

She gave him that smile that had stolen his heart. "I'm so glad you didn't."

"Now I can't wait to make you my wife. So tell me, what kind of house do you want?"

She looked away for a moment as if thinking. "A house with a big backyard. One with a tree swing for the kids."

"Kids?"

She met his gaze. "I want children, Flint. I want a half dozen of them."

He laughed. "Then we'd better get started right away."

"You'd be all right with that?"

"*All right?* Maggie, I once dreamed of the kind of backyard you're talking about—and the children who'd play there. I was afraid to dream it again, but there is nothing I would love more than having a half-dozen babies with you."

"Well, maybe not a half dozen, but at least three?"

He leaned down to kiss her. "At least three. But what about your salon?"

"I might have to hire another stylist," she said. "Maybe sooner than later since business is really good. With the wedding and everything—"

"And us hoping to get pregnant right away." He smiled at the thought of Maggie pregnant. He couldn't wait. "I should warn you, though. Lillie is so excited about the thought of helping plan another wedding."

"Thank goodness since I know nothing about wedding planning. I could use all the help I can get."

"You do know how bossy my sister is, right?"

Maggie laughed. "I've met her. She can plan the whole thing. I'm fine with it. All I care about is becoming your wife."

"You aren't still worried about Celeste, are you?" he asked.

"Not anymore. Look what we've been through. It makes Celeste seem almost harmless."

He smiled as he cupped her face in his hands and kissed her. "I love you so much."

The engagement announcement hit the papers the day before Christmas. Flint was so happy that he wanted everyone to know—maybe especially Celeste. He'd already heard that she was out of jail. So he wasn't that surprised to find her waiting outside the flower shop as he limped out. His leg was better, but he still had to wear the walking cast.

One look at Celeste, and he could tell that she'd heard about his engagement to Maggie. She looked at the bouquet of daisies and tiny white roses, Maggie's favorites, and then at him with resignation.

It was the first time he'd seen her since that incident at the sheriff's office where he'd tried to choke the truth out of her.

"I'm glad you found Maggie," she said quickly, as if sensing he was in no mood to talk to her. He noticed right away that she wasn't dressed up like she usually was. But even her idea of dressing down was expensive jeans, a sweater and calf-high leather boots.

"No thanks to you," he said. "You got out of jail."

"I got community service."

No surprise there. Money and a good lawyer usurped the law every time.

"I don't expect you to believe this, but I'm happy for you."

"I'd like to believe it, but under the circumstances..." He started to step away, but she grabbed his arm. He looked down at her hand and she quickly removed it. He couldn't help the anger he still felt toward her. A lot of that anger, admittedly, was at himself for letting her come between him and Maggie.

"I'm sorry." Tears welled in her eyes. "I won't be bothering you or Maggie anymore. I'm leaving town. The judge was kind enough to let me do my community service elsewhere."

"Another spa?"

"No." She smiled at his sarcasm. "Wayne and I are divorcing. I'm going to California. I have a friend down there. She's been trying to get me to move for some time now. I need a new start, as well. I won't be back."

He hoped everything she was saying was the truth, but he'd learned a long time ago not to believe this woman. For so long she'd been the monster he had to fear. Looking at her now, he saw that she didn't look scary at all. In fact, she looked a lot like the woman he'd fallen in love with.

For so many years, he'd blamed Celeste for everything. But now he could admit that he'd started to pull away from her in the marriage and that had only made her try to hang on harder. He hadn't realized how needy she was back then. Wayne had filled that need. For a while.

His next words surprised even him. "I'm sorry about you losing your baby."

Her eyes widened for a moment. She nodded and dipped her head as if to deny the sharp pain. One tear broke loose. She quickly brushed it away.

"Good luck, Celeste. I hope you find, if not happiness, at least peace." With that, he walked away and knew he would never look back.

★ ★ ★

Lillie splayed her hand over her swollen belly and smiled as she felt a kick. Across the room she saw her sister-in-law Mariah doing the same thing. They caught each other's eye and smiled as Christmas music played.

Darby had insisted on having Christmas as a family at the saloon. "I think everyone will be comfortable there." Everyone had pitched in to decorate, including Maggie and her mother, Jenna.

Lillie now looked around the beautifully decorated saloon and couldn't help but smile. They'd done an amazing job—without much of Lillie's or Mariah's help with the decorations that required a ladder.

It had driven her crazy, watching from the sidelines. Her brother was right. She couldn't stand not being in control. But Trask kept telling her that once the baby was born, she would have no control over her life, so she'd better get used to it.

She smiled as her baby gave her a swift kick as if he agreed with Trask.

"Isn't this amazing?" Mariah asked as she joined her.

Lillie didn't know if she meant all the gifts under the beautiful tree, that they were both pregnant and happy, or that they were as close as sisters. "Amazing."

"Maggie and Flint," Mariah said as if to clarify. "They look so happy together. I'm glad we're all together for Christmas."

"You saw her, Maggie, when she was missing, didn't you?" Lillie asked.

"I suppose I did." Mariah looked embarrassed. "I don't want to have...the gift. But if I helped Flint find Maggie..."

Lillie hugged her. "You did." Past Mariah, she watched Flint nuzzle Maggie's neck, making her laugh. "I never thought I'd see the day. It's like a Christmas miracle. Now, for Hawk and Cyrus to find love."

"What about your other brother?" Mariah asked.

"Tucker?" Lillie shook her head. "We haven't seen or heard from him since he left right after high school. We don't even know if he is still alive."

"That's awful. Why would he leave like that?"

"We have no idea."

"Maybe he'll come back someday."

"Maybe," Lillie said, thinking of the oldest of them and how handsome he was. "Maybe."

"Time to start opening all these presents!" Ely announced from near the Christmas tree.

Lillie felt tears flood her eyes. She loved her family. They were often annoying. Look how often she and Flint had been at odds, especially over their father. But she couldn't have loved him more than she did at this moment. Flint in love was a beautiful thing to see, she thought as she and Mariah headed for the tree to the sound of Christmas music and the sweet fall scent of hot apple cider.

Flint had his arm around Maggie as they watched Ely open one of the last presents. Lillie and Mariah were busy picking up all the used wrapping paper and throwing it into the stone fireplace.

"How was your Christmas?" her fiancé whispered next to her ear.

She smiled, so full of love and joy that she never wanted the holidays to end. Her mother had joined them and was now visiting with Darby. Flint had loved his first-edition book and she'd loved the rocker he'd given her for their home— and hopefully soon for the nursery.

Maggie looked up to see Anvil Holloway standing just inside the door from the saloon kitchen. He held his hat in his hand and looked embarrassed to be intruding. She quickly stepped to her mother and motioned to the doorway.

Jenna seemed to hesitate, but then got up and walked toward him. Maggie couldn't help but notice that Anvil was wearing a clean pressed shirt and a pair of new jeans. He looked shy, his face flushed.

Maggie watched the two of them, feeling her heart near bursting. She knew Jenna felt guilty about the way she'd treated her husband. They spoke for a few moments, and then Anvil touched her arm and her mother stood on tiptoe to kiss the man on the cheek. Anvil smiled, even more flushed, put his hat back on his head and seemed to apologize for interrupting the party before he left the way he'd come in.

"Is everything all right?" Maggie asked her as she stepped to her mother.

Jenna nodded, tears in her eyes as she smiled. "He brought me a Christmas present." Her voice broke. "Forgiveness. He'd like me to come home."

"Will you?"

"I don't know. Maybe. We'll see."

Maggie hugged her mother, seeing how pleased she was with Anvil's gift.

It was cold and snowy the day Flint took Maggie up the mountain to the site where their home would be built. After looking for a house for months, they'd finally decided they would have to build to get what they wanted.

Flint walked her out to the edge of a rise. Below them, the town of Gilt Edge gleamed. Past it, the mountains rose to surround them.

"There's something I want you to see," he said and reached for her hand.

There'd been a time not all that long ago that she hadn't really believed it could happen. A time even before she'd been abducted by Clark Terwilliger. She still couldn't think of him as her father. Back then, she'd believed it was true that she wasn't good enough for Flint.

His love had changed that.

"Check out that view," he said, pulling her close. She could hear the pride in his voice. He was as excited about their home as she was. "We could put a bay window right here."

"It's breathtaking," she said, her words coming out on frosty white puffs.

"You're breathtaking." He pulled her close and kissed her. "Come on—one more thing I want you to see." He took her hand and led her around the mountainside. "This is your backyard."

The land ran to the pines and the creek. Closer was a large old cottonwood with a tire swing hanging from one of its lower limbs. "Oh, Flint, it's perfect."

"The crew will start construction in the spring, as soon as the ground is thawed enough to start digging. But in the meantime, there's something we need to do first."

CHAPTER TWENTY-FIVE

"I now pronounce you husband and wife. You may kiss your bride."

Flint met Maggie's gaze and felt himself smiling like a fool. He couldn't remember a day when he'd felt more alive or more deliriously happy.

She smiled back at him and he remembered how that smile had made him fall in love with her even before he'd ever met her.

But now that he knew her, he couldn't wait to spend the rest of his life with her. Reaching for her, he pulled her into his arms and kissed her.

Over the pounding of his heart, he could hear his family and friends cheering.

The pastor introduced them as husband and wife, and they began the walk down the long aisle decorated with daisies and tiny white roses. He caught a whiff of the roses and knew he would never smell them again without thinking of this moment.

He tightened his hold on Maggie's hand as he looked over

at her and saw that she was smiling at him, her brown eyes shining bright. They had a secret that was all their own. Not that they would be able to keep it from his sister. Lillie was already asking how soon they planned to have children.

As they burst outside into the warm spring sunshine, they were surrounded by well-wishers. It felt as if the whole town had turned out.

Across the street, he saw Harp leaning against his patrol SUV. The deputy gave him a thumbs-up. It had been Harp's idea to stand guard over the wedding so nothing went wrong.

"I'll make sure no one interrupts your day," Harp had said.

"Celeste is gone."

The deputy had nodded. "Just the same. It's my day off, but I'd be honored to see that your wedding day is perfect."

Flint had been touched. Maybe it wasn't too late for some people to change. "Thank you, Harp."

In a shower of birdseed, he and Maggie ran toward the waiting SUV and jumped in the back. Harp climbed behind the wheel and turned on the sirens as they roared away from the church.

In the back seat, Flint could only shake his head. Harp had changed but he still had trouble with regulations. But the sheriff was willing to let it go this time, he thought as he looked over at his wife. His *wife*.

He drew Maggie to him and kissed her as they sped away. Their lives were just beginning. Flint couldn't wait.

★ ★ ★ ★ ★